Caverns of the Deep

other books and stories by Jeanette O'Hagan

Heart of the Mountain: a short novella
Blood Crystal: a novella
Stone of the Sea: a novella
Shadow Crystals
Akrad's Children
The Herbalist's Daughter: a short story
Lakwi's Lament: a short story
Treasure in the Snow a short story
Ruhanna's Flight and other stories

stories in these antholgies

Tied in Pink
Let the Sea Roar
Another Time Another Place
Glimpses of Light
Like a Girl
Mixed Blessings: Genre-lly Speaking
Crossroads
Futurevision
Tales From the Underground
Mixed Blessings: As Time Goes By
The Quatum Soul
Like a Woman
Gods of Clay
Challenge Accepted
Tales of Magic and Destiny
From the Edge

Caverns of the Deep

Jeanette O'Hagan

Story 5 Under the Mountain Series

By the Light Books

Caverns of the Deep
By Jeanette O'Hagan
Story 5 in the Under the Mountain series

Cover design: Jeanette O'Hagan ©2019 ©2021
Typesetting and Layout: Jeanette O'Hagan
Copyright Jeanette O'Hagan ©2019 ©2021 http://jeanetteohagan.
com

 NLA Cataloguing-in-Publication entry at National Library of
Australia:

A catalogue record for this
book is available from the
National Library of Australia

ISBN-13: 978-0-6481640-7-4

Published through By the Light Books
By the Light Books PO Box 2520, Brookside Centre, Qld 4053
Email: Bythelightbooks@gmail.com

Note: This book follows Australian style conventions for spelling,
punctuation and grammar.

Subscribe to Jeanette O'Hagan's Newsletter for the latest on new
releases, giveaways and other news– http://eepurl.com/bbLJKT

To Elsie who shared our adventures
in Mt Isa and Zambia.

Zara walked towards the tall ebony gate, the first of seven leading outside. The hair prickled on the back of her neck. She didn't need to turn around to sense the many eyes of her former captors watching her. She took a steadying breath and placed one foot in front of the other.

The first gate some fifty tanis distant beyond the control panel stood firmly shut despite all Nebam's efforts. Long strands of cobwebs waved in the downdraft of a nearby ventilation shaft. Glimmerlight shimmered on thick layers of dust and grunge. Though many footprints led to the panel, few led beyond. Zara averted her eyes from a mound of rags jammed in a crevice some way off the pathway.

A shadow passed over her. She caught her breath at the huge bat circling near the roof of the vaulted cavern. The silver streaks identified the creature as shapeshifter and Kinleader, Telsima, keeping watch on her.

The fate of the realm rested on her slender shoulders. Her baba, the deposed Overseer, had always said the outside was a place of untold evil and danger. The Sea Dragon King's sole purpose was to destroy them. This was why her da-baba had sealed the mountain off from outsiders. Perhaps it had been true. Maybe it still was true, though Head Watcher Gilarth and the new Overseer Havilah said otherwise. Zara no longer knew who to believe.

Yet with only one Glimmer Heart still working and the farm caverns devastated, food would soon run out.

'Why not trigger the trap, take cover until the barrage is over and then move toward the gate?' Retza asked.

'Because there is not enough time to do anything useful before the mechanism resets,' Nebam growled. 'Now, stop asking stupid questions.'

Zara flipped her blonde hair over her shoulder. Retza had a point. 'I could easily walk to the ebony gate in ten minutes.'

'Take one step beyond the pedestal, and the trap will trigger. You'd be skewered before you get halfway. Two and three-quarter minutes, Zara.'

Terrific. This was a very bad idea. A horrible idea. A spine-tingling, you-are-going-to-die idea.

She rubbed the grimy glass with her sleeve and peered at the lettering beneath.

INS*RT *EA* *O PR**EED

Her brow wrinkled as she puzzled out the missing letters. 'Insert seal to proceed.'

She didn't have the seal, didn't know what it looked like. She only had to touch the Glimmer Heart and it responded to her, so maybe this would be as simple. She slid her hands over the panel, looking for clues.

The humming grew louder, more insistent. A blue light started flashing. Letters flickered on the panel. 'Warning, warning. Insert the Overseer's Seal of authority to proceed.' Ghost fingers whispered down her arms.

'Two minutes left,' Nebam called out. 'You need to hurry, girl.'

Think, Zara, think!

Apart from the flashing display, the sloped top of the control panel seemed smooth. Except for the trace of a handprint that would fit Gilarth's huge paws. She peered closer. Not a print, a shaped indentation.

She placed her hand in the depression before she could change her mind. A tickling sensation ran along her

They were all slowly starving. Getting help from outside was now a matter of survival. Which meant someone had to open the Gate.

'Remember, Lady Zara, the opening mechanism should be in the control panel,' Secondwun Nebam called from the safety of the archway behind her.

'As you've said.' She stared at the waist high bronze panel now a few paces away, willing it to give up its secrets. Its design was similar to the Glimmer Heart's control panel that powered the realm.

'When the mechanism triggers, you'll have mere moments to get away.'

'Yes, Secondwun,' she snapped. He'd already repeated the instructions and warnings a thousand times. What mad impulse had made her agree to this? Just because the glimmer crystals were now attuned to her, didn't mean whatever wards and traps her grandfather had placed on the Gate would spare her. But she had to try, if only to prove herself to these prickly toolwuns that she did care about the fate of the realm. But mostly for her brother Jesson ... and maybe Retza.

Zara ran her moist hands down her skirt. Another step and she drew level with the bronze panel. She took a deep breath and gagged at the foul air. In a few places the layers of dust coating the control panel were thinner, as though scraped away by curious hands. Shadowy and mysterious carvings were etched across its surface.

Her skirt brushed against the panel and it emitted a sudden soft hum. Her skin tingled at the static in the air. A moment later a pale blue light winked on beneath a glass-sealed display on the sloped surface of the pedestal.

'Once the light activates you have three minutes before the first trap is triggered and arrows shoot out of the walls and from the roof.' Nebam's gruff instructions echoed from behind her, palm and fingertips. A soft whir and a small hidden tray slid open, revealing a round slot and a button. No doubt the place to insert the seal.

'What next?' she called back to the spectators standing at a safe distance near the archway.

'First time we've got this far,' Nebam responded.

A good sign then. She could do this. The mad tap of her pulse settled into a steadier rhythm. A cylindrical, round hole. She poked the tip of her index finger into the hole. A tight fit. What next? She pressed the knob. A discordant click, a tiny stinging prick on her finger pad, and the pulsing light settled into a steady purplish beam. Was that it?

'Good, good. Now see if the gate opens.' Nebam's voice took on an upbeat note.

'Be careful, Zara,' Head Watcher Gilarth added.

Zara firmed her shoulders and stepped towards the tall ebony gate. Something brittle crunched beneath her boot. She didn't want to look down, didn't want to know what she'd stepped on, didn't want to imagine its likely origin.

She had deactivated the traps, hadn't she? She took another step forward, her legs like slurry.

A broken arrow shaft caught the muted glimmerlight. It stuck out of a pile of dirty rags and ... She shuddered and looked away. The smell of old death clung all around her. This wasn't a littlewun's game. She could die here, just like that poor toolwun. Her breath came in gasps and her legs locked.

'Blasted girl, don't stop now!'

Bootsteps with a limping step ran toward her. 'Slow and steady, Lady Zara.' Retza's gruff voice came from behind her.

'Retza!' She twisted around, her brow furrowing. 'What are you doing here?'

'In case you need our help,' Retza said. He gripped a rectangular metal sheet as tall as he was.

Her cheeks warmed. 'Well, don't get in my way. I don't want to die because of ... of your gammy knee.' But she did feel stronger with the young watcher beside her.

A wry grin crept across Retza's face. 'Don't mind me.' He waved her on.

Zara clamped down hard on her mounting terror and counted off the paces. One, two, three, four ... On ten, the control panel emitted a soft pinging sound. Was it supposed to do that? On twenty, the light reflecting off the gleaming ebony gates deepened to blood red and started flashing.

Not good. Not good. Not good.

'What now?'

'Get back here!' Nebam screamed. 'The trap's activated.'

'Hurry,' Havilah shouted over the escalating alarm.

A clunk, clunk, clunk came from the walls and roof, followed by a whirring creak. Zara's heart rammed against her breastbone, a trapped cave bat desperate to escape.

Unlike the Crystal Heart, the gate hadn't responded to her touch or heartbeat. At least Jesson was safe with the old Scrybe Barekia. Whatever happened, the rebels would care for him. She touched the crystal pendant lying on her breast. No one else had survived the death about to shower down on them.

'No time.' Retza pushed her to the floor and pulled the metal sheet over them.

Retza pulled the sheet over them not a moment too soon. Arrows rained down, pinging off the makeshift shield and clattering on the stone floor like stones tumbling against the sides of a barrel grinder. Ping, ping,

ping, pingety, ping. The barrage continued for several minutes, but at last silence settled in the cavern.

Retza's limbs went limp with relief and he licked dry lips. The shield had worked. He pushed it to one side. Arrows lay in great drifts on the floor and heaped up around them in small piles.

'Are you injured?' Gilarth called out.

'No, no, we're fine,' Zara said, her sapphire-blue eyes dark in her chalk-white face.

Retza stood and offered her a shaky hand to help her stand. Her sweet caramel scent took some of the foulness out of the air. Was that it?

Zara stepped back and stared toward the ebony gate just five paces away. 'We can reach it before the trap resets.'

'Not enough time. Get back here!' Nebam said, voice shrill.

Zara's back and shoulders stiffened. 'We'll lose what progress we've made.'

Ever since the second cave-in, the Secondwun seemed to have misplaced his emotional ballast. But he'd been working on this problem longer than any of them, he would know how long things took.

'Come, Lady Zara, best do as he says.' Retza waved his arm for her to go first.

After a short hesitation, she lifted her chin and picked her way toward the archway. The arrows made the floor treacherous, rolling and sliding beneath their feet.

At ten strides, a soft rumble came from beneath them. Retza could feel it trembling under his boots and the air seemed to sizzle around them. His arm hairs bristled. Was the trap resetting already? He grabbed Zara's hand. 'Hurry.'

Zara slipped on an arrow shaft and stumbled, 'Ow, my ankle.' She put weight on it and fell back down. 'I ... I can't walk.'

Retza crouched and lifted Zara up in his arms, ignoring the sudden stabbing pain in his injured knee. He staggered towards the others.

Gilarth burst into action, striding toward them.

With a sudden sizzle, lightning zapped down from the cavern roof. The big watcher fell, sending arrows clattering and skittering across the floor. He sat up, a dazed look in his iron-grey eyes.

Retza took a couple of steps and another bolt zapped down so close it tingled through his boots. He swallowed hard. Not just one ward, of course, but many. The Gate had shut the realm from the outside for over two hundred years. There was no way he could make it to safety carrying Zara.

As though hearing his thoughts, she wriggled from his hold and stood on one foot. They huddled together, stranded halfway between the panel and the first gate. The rumble grew louder.

'What now, Secondwun?' Retza called. 'Should we wait?'

'You can't stop there. Run and hope to blazes you don't get hit.'

The silver-streaked bat swooped over them. 'I can see a pattern in the pavers,' Telsima said. 'I'll show you the path.'

Retza nodded. 'Go on.'

'Go left, now three steps straight, now one to the right.'

They followed Telsima's directions, Zara leaning on him and he on her. Sweat slid down his forehead and his limbs trembled with the strain and missed meals. His knee burned. The long rosters of decreased rations and the time trapped in the cave-in were taking their toll on his strength.

'Straight another two squares.'

The floor shook under Retza's boots. What other joys did the long dead Overseer Hezikah have for them? Rows of square flagstones began to tilt down toward each other. Retza's boots slipped and Zara's grip tightened on his arm.

'Almost there. A pace to the left and four in front.' Telsima hovered above them.

'Hurry.' Gilarth stood and brushed away a couple of arrows hanging off his breeches. He jumped over the blue stone, balancing against the increased tilt of the floor. As they stepped closer, he grabbed their arms and dragged them with him past the bronze panel. Other hands stretched out from the archway and helped them across the threshold.

A screeching, grinding noise accompanied the slithering clatter.

Retza twisted round, his eyes wide. The scattered arrows slipped and fell down the widening gaps between the stones.

'What's it doing?' Zara asked.

'Resetting, rearming.' Nebam pulled at his scrappy ginger beard, grey eyes anguished. 'We think it reloads the arrows.'

With a thud that echoed through the tunnel, the flagstones tilted back together again.

Retza chewed his lip with frustration. They'd been so close to succeeding. The control panel had responded to Zara's touch, but it was clear more was needed. The Overseer's seal.

'This is too dangerous.' Gilarth winced as he pulled arrows from his clothing, some tipped in blood. 'Without Retza's shield Lady Zara would have died.'

Nebam thrust out his chin. 'We have ten days before the food from Tamra arrives outside the Gate. If it's not open by then, our options are grim.'

'Danel and Delvina should return from the Lonely Isles with answers,' Retza said.

'After so long and no messages ...' Nebam's voice faded.

Retza's chest felt hollow. His sister—his twin and best friend and all the family he had left—had to return.

Havilah clapped her hands. 'Let's focus on what we can do. Zara did give you more time, Nebam. And Retza's idea of using shields worked. Use it. Once we reach the ebony gate, force it open.'

Gilarth folded his arms. 'Let me send teams out to look for Temple's Rest and the seal.'

The great bat swooped down towards them, seemingly on a collision course with the archway. At the last minute, its shape wavered and changed, legs lengthening and wings becoming arms, shifting into the slender figure of Kinleader Telsima. 'Josenif can help you search.'

'Right,' Havilah said. 'Nebam and Zara work on the Gate. But Nebam, don't put Zara's life at risk, especially given her connection to the Crystal Heart. Gilarth, find Temple's Rest and Uzza. Hopefully, Thirdwun Danel and the delegation will return from the Lonely Isles with the answers, but we'd be unwise to rely on any one solution.'

Surely, Danel, Delvina and the others would be back soon, though there was still no news since the party left Redhaven for the Lonely Isles twenty-four days ago. Bad enough to be without protection of solid stone above one's head, but to replace the stone beneath one's boots with fickle water seemed like madness. Retza's stomach squirmed. He only hoped his twin and their friend Zadeki were safe.

'No, absolutely not!' The Mariner Habbiah's neck veins stood out like ropes as he stared down his daughter.

Delvina hoped he never looked at her like that. She pulled her borrowed Tamrin cloak closer to shield her from the drizzle of rain and icy wind.

The White Rose rocked on choppy waves and above them, storm clouds raced across the sky, partially obscuring the pale crescent of Argenti in the east. Across the bay, the saltbush was still smoking from their encounter with Avardin's forces. Perhaps she should join Zadeki and Danel lounging against the railings several paces away, or better yet, go below decks and leave father and daughter to spar in private. Though surely everyone aboard ship could hear them.

'Baba, please listen. I need to do this.' Ariel's honey-brown hair whipped about her slivery-white face and slim shoulders.

'We have to leave with the tide. Princess Avardin's forces will resend her rabble against us soon enough. It's not safe to stay on the island.'

More to the point, time was running out for the people of the Glittering Realms. Delvina and Danel needed to get back to the mainland. She bit down on exasperated words already repeated, and edged along the railing.

'I know, Baba.' Ariel twisted her hands in her billowing skirt. 'But we can't let Avardin win.'

Habbiah folded his arms, his legs spread wide to counter the constant roll of the ship. 'How do you intend to stop her? She is now the Regent with both the watchers and the rebel ebed under her command.'

'Not all the ebed, not all the watchers either. And she intends to kill the prince.'

'You don't know that.'

Ariel thrust out her dainty chin. 'It's a good guess. She murdered the Grand Technician, then blamed the Forest Folk and killed Gentle Bikan. It's obvious now. Princess Avardin seized power unlawfully by isolating each group and setting them against each other. Isn't that so, Delvina?'

Delvina's cheeks flamed. 'Um ... yes. She's a

treacherous snake.' Avardin had enticed her with lies, pretending to be her friend while all the time plotting to kill her true friends, the Forest Folk. And she had almost succumbed. She gave a guilty glance at Zadeki, who returned it with a sad smile.

'It's true,' Danel stepped across the deck, his voice tired and his head half-swathed in soot-smudged bandages. 'I would stay behind to help.' He shrugged. 'But we have to get back. Our people's situation is dire.'

'The daughter of deceit seizes power and bends the rules to her benefit.' Zadeki leapt off the railing, towering over Danel.

Mariner Habbiah waved his hands as though shooing away an annoying fly. 'I don't doubt it. There were rumours that the Sea Dragon King chose his old friend Iulien as regent because he mistrusted his niece's motives. Think on this. Samwin and the other ebed can blend in on my cousin's estate and hope for the best, but Avardin has named and banned us. To stay is a death sentence.'

'Only if she takes us.' Ariel stood her ground. 'And once she has repaired the White Ships, don't you think she'll come after us? Redhaven won't be safe for long, Father, unless we stop her here.'

Zadeki nodded. 'She plans to take the wide land from my Kin and the Tamrin, overturning her grandfather's treaty with us.'

Mariner Habbiah swung around to face Zadeki, arms akimbo. 'And will you stay and fight, young shapeshifter?'

Delvina stopped moving. Would Zadeki stay with Ariel? He'd said he wasn't interested in the Vaane lass, and she believed him. Still, could the shapeshifter resist a new adventure?

'We gave a promise to help and protect the mountain dwellers. Besides, such a decision is up to the Kinleader and the Elders.'

'I thought as much.' Habbiah turned back to his daughter. 'Come to Redhaven with me Ariel. I will speak to the Warden Ealam and come back with watchers to join the fight.'

'Baba, now is the time to strike, while Avardin's still establishing her power. Samwin can persuade his fellow ebed, but will the highborn and gentles follow him? We need to unite against her. I can make a difference. Baba, I promise you, I won't take unnecessary risks.'

A shadow fell across Delvina's face. High above, a great albatross circled and dipped on the wind. 'Are you ready to go?' Korak, Zadeki's father, screeched. 'Tide's full and will drop soon. You'll not get through the Grinder if you wait much longer.'

Delvina's heart contracted. If they missed this tide it would be another half-day before the ship could leave. Time for Avardin to send more troops to attack and delay them.

Ariel threw her slender arms around her father's sturdy frame. 'Baba, I love you, but I have to do this. Let's not part at odds with each other.'

'When did you get so troublesome, child? I could order Second Jonan to restrain you.'

'But you won't.'

Mariner Habbiah's shoulders slumped. 'Cousin Teva is right to say I spoil you. You go to Redhaven, I'll stay and fight.'

'Baba, only you can steer the White Rose through the Grinder. I'll be fine.'

'You have an answer for everything.'

Ariel laughed. She pecked his smooth, unbearded cheek and wasted no time in climbing down the rope ladder to the small boat still secured against the side of the ship below.

'You two, go with her and keep her safe,' the Mariner

roared. 'The rest of you, raise the anchor, set the sails, we're leaving the Lonely Isles.'

Delvina let out a long-held breath. She admired Ariel's bravery, but felt a little lighter at the young Vaane woman's leaving. Best of all, they were heading home. They hadn't found all the answers they sought here. Hopefully, Havilah, Retza and the others were more successful.

The Grand Cavern was strangely empty, the glimmer lights dimmed. Glow-worms, rarely seen in this often-crowded space, shone in dotted ropes and swirls across the high natural cavern roof. Memories like eerie whispers swirled around Retza—Putarn adorning Delvina and Zadeki for sacrifices in this space, the clamour and desperation of the Old Guard attacks, returning from the Great Forest to find darkness and paranoia, the confusion following the first cave-in of the tunnel. Retza jumped as a heavy hand fell on his shoulder.

'Are you sure you want to come, Retza? Give that injured knee of yours a rest.' Head Watcher Gilarth's face looked gaunter, almost skull-like in the dim light, and his clothes hung off his big frame. Rations had been reduced yet again.

A group of watchers stood nearby with thumbs hooked into their belts and packs over their shoulder or at their feet. A small team in a desperate attempt to find Uzza and the seal to the Gate. At the other end of the cavern, a large jaguar prowled, tail twitching at its black tip. Zadeki's older brother, Josenif, by the markings.

Was it madness searching long-abandoned caverns on the slim chance of discovering the old Overseer? Havilah had suggested Retza work with Nebam and Zara on the control panel. But he wasn't a techwun and he wanted to keep his distance from the Overseer's comely daughter. She stirred feelings which he wasn't keen to encourage and he was sure would never be returned. No, better to be doing something far away from trouble.

'What about you, old man? Shouldn't you be in your duty room, attending to those arrow wounds?' Retza hoisted his pack over his shoulders.

'Hey, watch it,' Gilarth mock-shook his fist and gave a sheepish grin. 'Just a few shallow puncture wounds. Nothing serious. And Secondwun Timon knows what needs to be done here.'

Josenif bounded up to them. 'Did you bring some possessions of Hezikah's son that he alone would handle?'

Gilarth pulled out the felt-wrapped bundle of artefacts purloined from the old Overseer's abandoned rooms—a gem encrusted stylus, a beard curler of carved bone, an embroidered jerkin—and placed them on the stone floor worn smooth by generations of boots.

The jaguar crouched low, belly to floor, and rolled them over with his great paws, sniffing each object with care. He was a formidable presence, over two tanis tall of muscled bulk and raw power. His curved canines gleamed in the soft glimmerlight.

Retza turned away and refocused his gaze on the massive double door across the cavern that led to the northern precinct or node. Most of the Old Guard attacks had come from that direction, though the last had been several rosters ago.

'Didn't you search that way already?'

Gilarth rubbed his thigh and grimaced. 'There are so many connecting tunnels between the different zones, we may have missed one or two, especially on the lower levels. This time we'll focus on the Temple areas. As good a place as any to find Zara's Temple's Rest. I've sent another team to search the southern temple.'

Josenif sat back on his haunches. 'And Uzza's daughter says this is where you can find her father?'

Retza rubbed his mouth. 'She thinks that's what he said. To meet him at Temple's Rest.'

'Then let's go.' The jaguar bounded towards the doorway to the northern tunnels.

The two watchers flanking the door wobbled but stood their ground.

Gilarth beckoned the small party of watchers to join them. 'Open the gate.'

One of the guards pulled the leaver. The doors shuddered and swung open, admitting the smell of mildew and stale air. The tunnel could fit five abreast and pale glimmer lights ran along each side of the roughhewn walls. Grates in the ceiling above guarded the murder holes where rocks and other objects could be dropped on unwelcome guests.

Josenif stopped between the open doors, his rounded furry ears upright, his tail balanced. 'Are you coming?'

Gilarth barked a laugh. 'Let's go.'

Ignoring the squirming in his gut, Retza marched forward. It couldn't be worse than wading seven lek, chest deep in water in the dark, could it?

Several lek on, Retza shifted the weight of his pack and scrambled over the rubble that spilled across half the tunnel in front of the group. On the other side, the line of glimmer lights along both the walls trailed into nothing.

'Two abreast. Keep alert and watch for trip hazards.' Gilarth snapped on his glimmer torch, the dense darkness swallowing the narrow beam of white-blue light.

They trudged on in the near-darkness. Josenif prowled ahead of the group, Retza and Manoah bringing up the rear. The moments dripped by and weariness settled into Retza's limbs. No one spoke. The only noises were their own breathing, scrape of boots on stone, the faint clinking of tools, and the occasional drip, drip, drip of water in some distant tunnel. On occasion, Gilarth's torch lit up carved panels or even statues of highwuns flanking the tunnel, but most of the time it was the same rough-hewn stone coated in lichens and moulds and stretching endlessly into the distance.

'You'd think they'd put some glimmer tracks along here,' Manoah grumbled, his voiced echoing along the tunnel in whispers.

'There were tracks that connected the Farm, loading and storage levels between our precinct and the other two precincts, but we collapsed them to protect the inhabited areas against Old Guard attacks.' Gilarth rubbed the sweat off his face. 'Time for a break. Manoah and Levim, keep watch.'

Retza let out a long sigh. Lowering his pack, he sank to the floor, close to the other watchers, and took a sip of tepid water from his flask.

'Ration your water,' Gilarth said, settling down opposite Retza. 'Don't know when we'll be able to refill.'

Retza recapped the flask and rested his head against the tunnel wall. 'How far to the other precinct?'

'Another twelve lek.'

Retza closed eyes, and seemingly minutes later, startled out of a doze. The jaguar padded out of the darkness, cobweb strands tangled in his whiskers. The sight sent a brief frisson of fear through Retza.

Gilarth sat up straighter. 'Hey, Josenif, find anything.'

'He's been this way, though your earlier search and collapse parties have left the more recent trail. All of it at least an Alume old.'

'Alume?' one of the other watchers asked.

'Cycle of the golden moon. Three ten-days.'

'Oh, okay, one and a half rosters.'

Josenif leaned back on his haunches and stretched his

forelimbs. 'So do the north and south nodes have gates to the outside you could use?'

Gilarth shifted his seat on the stone floor. 'The only way out is through the central precinct. The glimmer tracks four levels down transported produce, ore and other goods between the nodes to be taken in and out through the main Gate.'

'This place seems more like a prison than a place to live.'

Gilarth raised bushy eyebrows. 'My old da-baba said the overlords weren't so happy when Hezekiah's baba expanded the farm caverns. As long as we needed supplies from outside, we had to do what the Sea Dragon King wanted.'

Manoah leaned forward, his face half-hidden in shadows. 'Seems the old Overseers were right to break off with the King.'

'They got some things right and some things wrong.' Gilarth's voice was sharp. He pushed himself to his feet. 'Let's keep going.'

Retza smothered a groan. It seemed they'd just sat down. He levered himself up and settled the pack on his shoulders. They wouldn't find anything sitting around in the dark.

Who knew what perils prowled in the deserted dark mines ahead? Even worse would be to find nothing at all. He couldn't help wishing Delvina was tramping beside him no matter what dangers they faced.

Danel gripped the railing, bracing against the rolling motion of the White Rose. His blistered hands stung and his injured eye throbbed beneath the bandages.

A steady wind filled the white sails and the ship's prow dipped and rose, cutting through inky-blue water and sending spray flying across the deck. He shaded his one good eye against the bright sunlight. The white-capped ocean stretched to the horizon in every direction.

Delvina stood beside Danel, her attention for once not drawn like a magnet to Zadeki's wild cheerful presence. The wind blew her pale blonde hair across her freckled face. She squinted at the sun, then glanced back behind them to where the Lonely Isles, with its strife and betrayal and columns of smoke, dwindled to a dark smudge on the horizon. Despite Silantis' astonishing architecture, Danel was eager to leave the Vaane city far behind.

Delvina glanced at the sun again. 'Shouldn't we be going away from the sun, not towards it?'

Danel shrugged. At home he knew the tunnels like the creases on his own palm, but the outside was still a mystery to him. 'The sun moves about the sky, sometimes on this horizon, sometimes on the other. It doesn't make a lot of sense to me.' But if they were headed in the wrong direction ... 'The Forest Folk might know.'

The two remaining shapeshifters slept several paces away, wrapped in their cloaks and resting after their ordeals in the Hole, the rigours of their escape from Silantis, and the strain of guiding the White Rose through the Grinder into open sea. It would be wrong to wake them.

Danel recognised one of the ebed rushing by. 'Hey, Second Jonan. We're sailing east to Redhaven, right?'

The sailor slowed his pace. 'Aye, true enough.'

'But we're not going east.' Delvina's full lips settled into determined lines. She pointed to the left. 'Redhaven's that way.'

Jonan dipped his head. 'Aye, that's true too. But we can't sail direct into the wind. Best course this time of year is to head south-west until we can pick up the winds going the other way.'

'That makes no sense.' Danel's neck and shoulder tensed. 'We need to get to the mainland as quickly as possible. Our people have food only for another fifteen days at most.'

'Can't change the pattern of the winds,' Jonan pointed his beardless chin toward Korak and Zadeki's sleeping forms. 'Maybe one of those two can transform into that fire-breathing beastie and take you faster. Though rather you than me.'

'They can't,' Delvina said. 'There's only so many shifts they can do before needing to restore their strength.'

They'd talked about this. It was why they chose to stay on the White Rose. Plus, Korak would need a high point to jump off and there were none on the heaving ship and endless ocean. 'So how long does this sailing in circles take?'

'A loop, not a circle. It depends on the wind and currents, but a ten-day or thereabouts. Got to go. Mariner's glaring at me.' Jonan strode off with a sailor's rolling gait.

Danel's mood plummeted from relieved to fuming. A ten-day. How many more days to get across the plains and hills to the high mountains? Their people might all be dead by the time he reached the caverns.

He slammed his hand down on the railing. 'We don't have the time for this foolery.'

Delvina's calloused fingers brushed his arm. 'By the Maker's favour, we will find our way back to them in time.'

The heaviness crushing Danel's spirits lifted a little at the hope in her voice.

Danel tugged at his bandages. 'In the meantime, we wait.' They didn't have any other choice.

'My favourite pastime.' Delvina gave a wry grin.

'Yeah,' he grinned back, remembering how frustrated she'd been waiting in Tarka and Silantis. 'Well maybe this Maker could change the winds for us.'

He turned from her sweet face and stared at the line of clouds merging into the dark blue of ocean. Silver Argenti's lonely crescent climbed in the sky. Delvina was the one good thing about this trip. Overseer Havilah may have appointed him as Speaker, but he couldn't find the words he really wanted to say. Especially when he knew another charmed her heart.

The constant warning hum of the control panel set Zara's teeth on edge. She folded her arms and watched Nebam run his thick fingers where the panels had slid out to reveal the slot for the seal.

Nearby, toolwuns erected bronze panels, riveted together to form four sides in a slowly growing rectangular tunnel pointed at the ebony gate. Others lined the inside of the structure with thick layers of felt, gluing it to the inner surface. Three minutes before she needed to open the tray and, once she touched the indentation, another ten minutes working time before the wards activated, and twenty for the floor to reset. And this was just the first gate.

'Why don't we destroy the arrows?' she asked.

'The lightning. Some arrows do break or are lost each time, or a component of the reloading machines could fail, but most likely long after we starve. Overseer Hezikah may have been mad, but he was cunning enough.'

Zara's cheeks flushed. 'That's my da-baba you're talking about.'

Nebam spun round and glared at her. 'Yeah, I'm painfully aware of that Lady Zara. I find it hard to forget.'

Zara took a step back at the intensity of his gaze. He was very like his older brother, despite a narrower build and grey eyes rather than Putarn's amethyst ones. He was developing the same wild look.

Zara dropped her gaze to the floor, criss-crossed with dusty footprints leading to and from the archway. Growing up in the Overseer's quarters, she'd always thought her baba was loved by the people, that he did what was right. Now, after all that had happened, she didn't know what to believe. Was it her da-baba and baba's fault that they were in this desperate predicament, or the fault of the rebel toolwuns and their leader Havilah? Either way, if she didn't help them open the Gate, she and Jesson would starve along with the rebels. She only hoped it didn't trigger the Dark Ones' anger. And with any luck, Baba would soon return. Whatever they said, she knew he was alive.

Nebam grunted and turned back to the panel. 'So, you put your hand in this indentation.'

'Yes.'

He plonked his hand in the depression. But instead of displaying the blue light, it went straight to red and the warning flickered on the screen. An ominous clunk, clunk, clunk sounded from the walls and roof, then a whirring sound as slots in the upper walls slid open.

'Take cover! Now!' Nebam dived for the tunnel shield.

Zara scrambled after him, her heart hammering to wake the shadows. The toolwuns piled in from the other end, except for the closest one, who dashed for the archway.

'Get in the tunnel, you fool,' Nebam screamed.

Arrows arced out of the walls and fell in swarms, landing with spurts of dust and pinging off the control panel and the shield walls.

One pierced the runner's calf. He fell forward, clutching his leg and yelping. Nebam grabbed a mobile shield, raising it with one hand and pulling the man in by the arm.

The salty tang of blood and terror sent chill bumps up

and down Zara's arms. She huddled against the felt, eyes wide, fingers brushing her crystal pendant

'We need to stop the bleeding,' Nebam broke off the shaft and cradled the injured toolwun. 'Zara, your dress.'

Nebam was right. She looked away from the pooling blood and tore a long strip off her skirt. She bound the wound as the torrent of death ricocheted off the shield tunnel.

Eventually, an eerie quiet settled over the cavern with an occasional sizzle of stray electricity. Then the floor rumbled, sliding and tilting below the layer of felt and metal. The construction shivered and rocked but remained bolted to the joists.

'Maybe you could jam the floor mechanism. Stop it collecting the arrows.' Zara pushed her words through stiff lips.

'Yeah, why don't you step out there and get fried by the lightning.' One of the other toolwuns, a woman, rolled her eyes.

Zara's shoulders drooped. She'd forgotten about that. Red seeped through the toolwun's rough bandages and his face grew chalky. She tore off another strip and wound it tighter than the first.

'Is ... is the toolwun going to be alright?'

Nebam stared at her a moment before answering. 'Should be.' He grimaced. 'So, now we know. The panel recognises you alone, Lady Zara.'

Was he actually smiling at her? 'It gives you extra time to work.'

But what they really needed was the seal.

Tall metal doors stood shut tight against them.

Retza rubbed the sweat from his face and eased the

straps of his pack. The other watchers looked as weary as he felt. Three shifts it'd taken to get here and with no gongs to mark the shifts, it was easy to lose track of time in the darkened tunnel.

'So, we're at the northern precinct?' he asked.

Gilarth stood in front of the doors, massaging his square beard. 'Aye, it is. This main entrance leads to the meeting hall. The doors weren't shut last time we came through.'

'Is it locked?' Manoah asked.

Gilarth gave the doors a shove. The two halves dipped in the middle before springing back. 'Maybe just stuck. Give us a hand here.'

Retza and a couple of the other watchers put their shoulders to the doors and pushed. The metal shuddered, then the leaves sprang open causing them to stumble forward into the dark cavern.

Foul air engulfed them. Retza's throat tightened and he supressed the urge to cough.

'Defensive positions,' Gilarth called.

They fanned out on both sides, using the door panels for cover. Josenif bounded past and disappeared into the darkness.

Nothing stirred. No movement, no sound, no indication of life except the soft pad of jaguar feet over the stone floor and their own choked breathing. Gilarth played his torch over the vast space, highlighting the jagged roof and the scattered debris on the floor—dented metal crates, rags, and other shapes hard to identify. Water seepage, green and orange lichen and slime coated the walls.

'Looks much like the last time we were here,' Manoah said, his voice returning in loud echoes.

Josenif reappeared in the glimmer torchlight.

'Find anything?' Gilarth asked, his voice gruff.

The jaguar lifted his blunt head and curled his upper lip, showing wickedly sharp curved teeth. 'Multiple scents, yours and theirs but nothing fresh for many days. No carrion odours either.'

Retza repressed a shudder. Though he'd no love for the Old Overseer with his mad demands of sacrifices, he wasn't keen to encounter the starved corpses of the Old Guard. A fate that might soon be their own.

'Is the layout similar to our home caverns?' Retza asked. This meeting hall is a lot smaller than the Great Hall. More a built than natural space too.

'According to the charts, it's virtually a mirror image,' Gilarth turned in a slow circle and waved toward the left wall. 'The entrance leading to the northern temple should be there.'

'There's an opening halfway along that wall,' Josenif confirmed. He pivoted and loped off.

The others trudged after him, their bootsteps echoing in the intense darkness surrounding the fragile bubble of light.

'Here,' Josenif called.

Gilarth directed his glimmer torch at a rusted rectangle in the furred and slimy stone. He pushed with his shoulder, the surface groaned and buckled.

'Locked?' Retza asked.

'Or rusted shut. Here, give me the mallet.'

A few well-aimed blows and the smaller door buckled and lurched slantways off its hinges. With some pushing and pulling, they were able to widen the gap enough for the party to squeeze through.

More darkness met them on the other side, though this time the air was fouler and the walls closed in around them.

Josenif snuffled the floor ahead of the main party, his rounded ears erect and tail held low.

'If we could find the glimmer light nodes, we could attach a power pack, get us some better light,' someone suggested.

'And signal our approach to whoever might be hiding here. Minimum noise and keep alert.' Gilarth waved them forward.

'If corpses can hide,' another guard mumbled.

'Let's not get complacent,' Gilarth said.

Retza's pulse fluttered and his muscles tensed. Above him the inky darkness seemed to swirl like a tangle of black snakes. The floor became slick underfoot, and a trickling sound raised the hairs on the back of Retza's neck. He took a deep breath of the putrid air. It wasn't uncommon to find water leaking against walls and floors in the tunnels. It didn't mean a wave of water would collapse the wall around them as it had in the cave-in.

Josenif stopped, a low growl in his throat and the nape of his neck ruffling.

Retza staggered against him. 'What is it?'

Josenif hooked an object with his paw and spun it into the torchlight.

Gilarth poked it with his truncheon. A tattered jerkin embroidered with the old Overseers' emblem.

Retza shivered. How long had it lain here? What secrets did it contain?

'It has the son of Hezikah's scent.' Josenif sat back on his haunches.

Manoah nudged the discarded clothing with his boot. 'This wasn't here when we came looking four rosters ago.'

'They probably hid in the deeper caverns, then doubled back once we left. A good sign, though.' Gilarth beckoned them to keep moving.

Retza crept on, senses alert and glad of the solid weight of the truncheon in his hand.

Further down, the tunnel butted into another tunnel.

A derelict lift stood to one side, the gates yawning open like hungry lips. More debris, grime and cobwebs blurred the railings and control panel. A thin sheet of water ran along the floor and dripped down the lift shaft.

'So, do we go right or left?' Levim demanded.

'If it is a mirror then left to the Temple,' Retza said, memories crowding in of heading for the Heart Room, guarding Barekia against attack, then rushing back along the tunnel to the temple to help Delvina and the others.

'Unless they holed up in the Heart Room,' Manoah said. 'We could split up. Cover the ground faster.'

'Uzza said to meet him at Temple's Rest, according to Zara.'

Gilarth rubbed his neck. 'Which way's the trail stronger, Josenif?'

'The water's doused what trail there was.'

'Then we stay together. About five hundred people fled with Uzza. We don't know how many remain, if any. Temple first, then Heart Room. Levim, Manoah, keep a lookout for attack from behind. Retza with me.' He dimmed his torch. 'We have to assume they're armed.'

Retza crept forward. Two days of travel-weariness washed away in the rush of energy. Every sound seemed magnified. His own heavy breathing, the soft splash of stealthy boots on the wet stone, the ever-present drip of water, the soft scuttling of creatures in the side room, cave rats or maybe roaches.

A faint glow came from up ahead. The door into the temple area stood propped half open. Retza tensed.

Josenif gave a low guttural growl that made Retza jump. The jaguar's fur bristled and the end of his tail flicked from side to side. 'I can smell other mountain dwellers.'

Gilarth stood flat against the wall and pushed the door wider. The screech of rusty hinges sent Retza's heart ramming up his throat. The echoes faded away.

'Empty.' Gilarth beckoned them forward.

The long rectangular room studded with blackened fire torches in tarnished brackets around the walls, about the same size and shape as their own Sunken Temple. The sickly-sweet odour of old incense and caked blood evoked memories of Uzza's attempt to sacrifice the youngwuns to the Dark Ones, including his twin, Delvina. The smells of smoke, fear and despair, the sight of youngwuns dressed in sacrificial finery and crammed before the altar, waiting their fate. This room was empty and covered in thick dust.

Retza stepped further into the room. A square altar stood at the other end, but without the central covered pit that acted as a conduit to the Dark Ones. Nor did the roof open up to a viewing area where the highwuns and the people, each at their stations, looked down on the ritual from above.

Josenif prowled around the room, restless and alert. Manoah and the others followed, searching in every corner, but there was really nowhere the Old Guard could hide.

Retza swallowed the sour taste of disappointment. He had been sure the answer would be here, in this room. Even finding the Old Overseer's body might help if he'd carried the seal on his person. What did Temple Rest mean, if not the temple areas? Maybe the Heart Room would yield a better outcome or the search team in the Southern node would be more successful.

It would take many days to search the other likely areas, the highwuns quarters', the watchers' rooms, the Great Hall, the supply outlets and cribs and creches and workshops and farms and recreation halls, not to mention the cesspools, farm caverns and maze of mining tunnels and ventilation shafts.

'What now?' Levim asked, his voice breaking the silence.

'This is as good a place as any to take a rest. Two on watch at all times.'

'At least the floor is dry.' Manoah pushed aside some debris and settled down. Retza joined him, chewing on small slithers of dried fish and algae from his ration pack. He took slow sips from his water flask. Maybe they should have filled up at the tunnel junction.

'What about the priests' preparation rooms and quarters?' another watcher, Wuben, asked.

Gilarth sighed. 'We'll check there next. If Josenif ...' he stood up. 'Where is the abovegrounder?'

Retza scanned the room but the shapeshifter was gone.

A cackling laugh started low and rose to a crescendo above their heads. A sharp chill stabbed down Retza's spine. He jumped up, eyes wide, heart pumping and spun around looking for the source of the eldritch sound.

With a deafening crash, the removable ceiling shattered. Rock splinters, dust and mortar showered over them. Grit stung Retza's eyes and choked his lungs.

A dark shape fell from above, landing on top of him. Retza's injured knee gave way and he fell, pinned down to the ground by a weight. All around him came yells, grunts and the sounds of struggle. They were under attack.

Delvina stared at the relentless rolling of the dark ocean stretching in all directions to a blurred horizon. Wind hummed through the rigging and the masts, with billowing white sails tilted against a black star-pricked sky. Alumi, the golden moon stood high in the sky, while the half-circle of Argenti hovered above the heaving horizon in the east. Five days and the land was still not in sight, might not be in sight for days to come. She felt like a cave moth spinning in sticky spider silk while danger stalked closer on eight legs, helpless to escape or prevent danger's advance. It didn't help that her heart was aching. As much as she and Zadeki had agreed to remain friends, she struggled to let go of what-might-have-beens. What still might be, a rebellious voice whispered.

'Couldn't you sleep either, daughter of the mountain?'

Delvina startled at the voice, so like Zadeki but more resonant with years. She ducked her head and scrubbed the tears off her cheeks, too choked up to answer.

Korak perched on the barrel beside her, his head tilted and his dark-green eyes reflecting starlight.

'Problems often look murkiest in the deep of the night.' He flashed her a sad smile. 'Or in the pit.'

Delvina bit her lip. Both Korak and Zadeki had lost someone close to them when the Grand Technician had shot down Highwun Bikan. She couldn't imagine what they endured dangling in the darkness in the days following her death. Even now Zadeki would be grieving.

She swallowed her tears. 'I'm sorry for Highwun Bikan's death. Do you now regret helping us?'

He didn't answer at once. The night returned only the swish of the ship moving through the foaming waves, the strumming of wind in the rigging, the crackle and creak of the sails. Had she offended Highwun Korak with her questions? 'I don't mean to intrude.'

'No, I appreciate your concern, daughter of the caverns. Ba-sestru's death is a bitter blow and Zadeki persists in blaming himself for it, though the blame rests with Iulien and Avardin. But no, we don't regret helping you. Your people's very lives hang on a thin thread. You need answers, solutions. I only wish we'd found out more on the island.'

'I feel as though we will never reach shore.'

'By the Maker's favour, it will be so. Take courage, the story is not over yet. Her death is not in vain.'

She picked at the end of a rope, not sure what to say next. The clouds from the east raced across the sky, obscuring the stars and moons.

Korak leaned forward, his fingers brushed her hand. 'Sometimes things are not meant to be. Even the sweetest flower withers out of season.'

Delvina's cheeks flamed in the dark. Was he referring to her and Zadeki? Anger sparked inside. 'You mean it would be unseemly for an ebed to marry a son of the Flame King.' A rock-rabbit matched with an eagle.

'That is not my meaning, Delvina, daughter of Holima. If you are both agreed then you would have our blessing. But consider this, our Kin are longer lived than most, so we take longer to reach maturity.'

She thrust her chin out, ready to counter any objections he might return to her. 'I can wait.'

'I do not doubt it. You are a determined young woman with a strong heart and great courage, a pathfinder for your people. Things are not always as they seem. Listen to the Maker's quiet voice and you will find your own true heart.'

Overhead the clouds parted and the full circle of Argenti painted a silver path across the dark waters. She had been so sure of her way on the journey here. Now her thoughts and emotions were as restless as the ocean.

Retza's arms were pinned down and the weight on his chest made it difficult to breathe. He gulped air and heaved against the wild thing gouging and snapping at him with wiry strength. All around him he could hear grunts and blows.

His opponent pinched Retza's arm. 'Nice and juicy.'

Or at least, that's what Retza thought he heard. Icy fingers squeezed his gut.

'You're mad.' He rammed his head into his opponent.

Whoever it was squealed and began to wail.

A sudden guttural roar and his squealing opponent was dragged off of him. Gasping for breath, Retza rolled over and pushed himself to his feet. Gilarth was fighting three men and the other watchers struggled with at least one other assailant. Many wore the emblem of the Old Overseer but none displayed Uzza's rotund figure.

Josenif, still in jaguar form, held the thin, long-haired madman in his mouth. He shook him before flinging him into a corner like a bundle of rags.

Retza pulled out his whip and lashed its tip around the wrist of a ragged figure slashing at Gilarth's back. A knife clattered to the floor.

One of the other assailants grappling the big watcher half-turned in his direction, his eyes big in a cadaverous face. He backed away as his gaze snagged on Josenif prowling toward him. Retza had thought everyone at the central caverns were thin, but not as skeletal as their attackers.

With two assailants disengaged, Gilarth sent the third one reeling with a heavy body blow and pulled out his whip. He backed to stand beside Retza, while Josenif charged at the two attacking Manoah. All around the room, the Old Guard were wheezing and trembling, as though they'd used up what little strength they possessed. Retza's companions were gaining the advantage, now that the first confusion of the surprise attack had worn off.

Gilarth wrapped his hand around the whip handle and pulled out his truncheon, his face set. Retza flanked him on one side and Josenif on the other. Together, they advanced.

'Surrender now, and you won't be hurt,' Gilarth called out.

The attackers faltered, some edging toward the door. The bundle in the corner sat up, his mad gaze darting around the closed space. His stringy, white hair flopped over his sunken face.

'To me, loyal fighters,' he wheezed.

The others disengaged and bunched around their leader. The man grabbed the nearest and pulled himself up. 'Would you steal this place too?' he snarled.

Gilarth lowered his truncheon. 'We mean you no harm, Elim.'

Recognition hit Retza like a mattock. His heart, which has begun to slow, sped up again. Elim, the old Speaker and Uzza's closest friend. Their chances of finding the seal had just increased.

Elim's upper lip curled. 'Then why are you here, traitor?'

Gilarth's lips tightened. 'We wish to speak to Uzza.'

'The rightful Overseer, you mean.' Elim spat the words as if ridding himself of a foul taste. 'What do you want from him?'

'I'm not arguing with you, man. Will you take me to him?' Gilarth took a step forward and Elim cowered back.

A craftly look stole over the former Speaker's face. 'You'll have to pay. Do you have food?'

'A little.'

'Good. You give me what you have, and I'll take you to the Overseer—you and the youngwun.'

'Half now ... half later.'

'It's a deal.' Elim's pale lips curved into a slow smile.

Uzza was alive. Retza relaxed a little more. He hadn't expected it to be this easy.

Josenif shook his blunt head and rumbled deep in his chest. 'He's lying.'

Gilarth lowered his voice. 'I don't doubt he has some trick tucked away under his belt, but it's a chance to speak to the Overseer.'

Josenif prowled forward until he stood teeth to chin

with the trembling Speaker, scattering the stick-thin Old Guard like terrified cave fish. 'He has no intention of taking you to the son of Hezikah.'

Elim's eyes widened. 'I'm not lying. I'm not. I'm not.' His big, bony hands shook and he grasped them to keep them still. 'He's ... he's upstairs in the living quarters. The man's voice quavered and his eyes flicked from side to side. 'Give me the food, and I'll take you to him.'

'Look at me, son of deceit.' Josenif stared unblinking into the quivering face.

One of Elim's companions, a woman on closer inspection, crept closer. Josenif curled his upper lip into a snarl and lashed his tail. She stopped and ran her hands down the grimy watcher jacket hanging loosely on her frame. 'Sir, the Overseer—

'She's lying, she's lying, she's lying, demon-beast,' Elim screeched, drowning out her words. He pointed a bony finger at Josenif.

The jaguar yawned, showing a red maw caged with sharp teeth. 'Be silent.'

Elim squeaked and backed against the wall.

Josenif swivelled his ears and turned back toward the woman. 'Now look at me, daughter of stone, and by the Maker's grace, tell me the truth.'

The woman took a shivering breath. 'The Overseer left over four rosters ago with his two oldest sons and a few close advisors. He said he would come back and save us, but he hasn't. Maybe he never intended to.'

Gilarth lowered his truncheon. 'Look, we won't hurt him. We have a request, and we can trade for it.' He glanced at Elim.

The woman gave a strained laugh. 'Don't you recognise me, cousin. It's Meriam. Believe me, the Overseer isn't here. He's abandoned us.'

'She's telling the truth,' Josenif said.

Gilarth rounded on him. 'How can you be so sure?' He frowned. 'Are you a far-speaker?'

'Not exactly, but you mountain-dwellers are not hard to read. Your thoughts are written on your faces.' His nose wrinkled. 'Besides, this one stinks of deceit. She doesn't.'

Retza wanted to believe Elim, but even a littlewun could see he wasn't to be trusted. 'So where did he go?'

'Temple's Rest,' the woman, Meriam, said. 'That's what I heard them say.'

Just as Zara said.

'And where is that?' Gilarth demanded.

Blank faces stared back at them.

'This is useless,' Manoah grunted. 'Clear as a glimmer crystal they don't know anything.'

'Yeah, let's get out of here,' Levim added.

'No, don't leave us.' Elim rushed forward and fell at Gilarth's feet. 'We have no food, no lights. There are so few of us left.' He licked his flaking lips. 'You can't leave us like this.'

Manoah snorted. 'Why not? We've got our own problems to deal with. We should go, boss.'

Josenif sat back on his haunches, his whiskers bristling. 'So, are you saying we should all only worry about our own problems then?'

Retza sighed. 'The abovegrounder is right. We should help, just as they have helped us.' More mouths meant the food stores would go quicker, but if they could get the Gate open in time it wouldn't be a problem. And if they didn't? Well, they'd all starve anyway.

Gilarth's iron-grey eyes met his cousin's and nodded. 'We're not leaving anyone behind.'

Elim's pale eyes narrowed to slits. 'No, just leave us food. We're not walking into a trap. Who knows what you plan to do with us?'

'It's not a choice, Elim.' Gilarth turned to Meriam.

'Are these couple of tens all that are left of you?'

'There are a few of us in the caves off the temple storage rooms. Maybe three-tens or more.'

Gilarth breathed in sharply. 'Fifty out of five hundred, no more? Very well, take us to the rest of the survivors.'

Retza shivered. All those lives lost to the darkness, and each day they edged towards the same fate as long as the Gate remained shut.

Zara slowly surfaced from the swirl of troubled dreams, a sense of danger clinging to her thoughts. The dreams frayed like old rope leaving only an impression of her father's voice calling from a deep pit. She clutched the covers and rolled over in a vain effort to catch more sleep.

The bell for the first shift echoed outside.

Giving up the fight, she threw off the blanket and pulled on her tunic and breeches. Not the most attractive wear but far more practical for avoiding the dangers at the Gate.

She'd heard the talk, when the toolwuns thought she wasn't listening. Rumours that rebels were searching the other nodes for survivors. She sluiced water over her face. How much could she trust the rebels? Would they tell her if they found Baba or the rest of her family? Some days she was convinced she could, other days not so much. She dragged a comb through her tangled hair. She had to stop thinking about the sturdy watcher, though dreaming about him was more pleasant than dreaming about dark shadows swirling in the mountain's dark throat. Somehow, she didn't think her father would be hiding in the old mining nodes.

She felt a tug on her jerkin. 'Can I come with you this time, Zara? I could help.' Jesson's blue-grey eyes widened in entreaty.

'It's too dangerous for youngwuns, Jesson. Besides, Scrybe Barekia appreciates your assistance.'

'Techwun Barekia, now.' His face crumpled, and his lower lip jutted out. 'Please, Zara, I won't get in the way. I'll do everything you tell me.'

Zara exhaled. She almost caved to his pleas, but then the image of the toolwun bleeding in the shield tunnel stopped her. The Gate was no place for a littlewun.

She knelt and placed her hands on Jesson's shoulders. 'Learn as much as you can from the oldwun, then one day you can help.'

Jesson scowled at her. 'Yeah, if any of us live that long.' Turning his back on her, he shoved the miniscule ration laid out for him into his mouth.

Her chest cracked open. She swallowed the tears, grabbed her jerkin and left the room. The assigned watcher escorted her through the tunnels to the staging post, where they took the glimmer trucks to the archway at the first gate.

'There you are.' Nebam smirked as though he was glad to see her.

'Good morning,' she said, not able to keep the sourness out of her voice. Had he been there all night? Did he ever sleep?

'Come, come. Let's get this show started.' He hustled her through the archway. She turned toward the panel, ready to place her palm every half hour, as required.

Nebam pulled her back. 'Don't worry about that yet. You've arrived just in time.'

Of course, last shift they'd extended the shield tunnel all the way to the Ebony Gate. Busy toolwuns now swarmed over the threshold.

'What are they doing?'

'Laying firepowder charges.'

'Is it safe?' Wasn't it firepower that caused the first cave-in?

'There's some risk, of course.' Nebam shrugged. 'But we have to get the Gate open.'

'Ready, leadwun,' one of the toolwuns called.

'Now, Zara,' Nebam pointed his beard at the panel.

Zara placed her hand in the indentation and the blue light shone steady. The toolwuns scrambled from the ebony gate, one laying down a long cord through the shield tunnel. Once everyone was on the other side, a woman toolwun Jazzia handed a black box to Nebam. 'Here you are, Secondwun.'

Nebam beamed. 'Take cover.' He pressed the button and the box emitted a spark. A small fire fizzed along the line until it reached the threshold. For a moment nothing happened. Then, clunk, clunk, clunk, creak. Arrows twanged down from the walls and roof, and then a moment later, baboom. A huge explosion engulfed the Gate and shook the cavern. Zara's ears rattled with the sound. Flaming arrows spewed everywhere, setting those next to them alight. Soon the cavern was a sea of leaping flame.

Nebam slapped his forehead. 'Why didn't we think of burning the blasted arrows?'

With a sizzle and boom, lightning sparked down in a frenzied show, set off by the burning arrows. Acrid smoke billowed over them.

'Out, out, out,' Nebam jumped up and waved. Zara needed no further urging. She breathed in a lungful of smoke and sprinted through the archway. Several tanis away, she bent over her knees, coughing and sucking in cleaner air, her eyes streaming.

'We need water and sand. Can't have fire spreading in the tunnels.' Nebam prodded the coughing toolwuns into action, his eyes wide in a face coated with grey ash.

After a while, the sounds of the floors sliding and resetting filled the space and then silence.

Cautiously, Nebam looked through the archway, then waved them through.

The ground warmed the soles of Zara's new workers' boots. Most of the smoke had cleared though the felt lining the shield tunnel still smoked and the panel was streaked with soot. Up ahead, the two tall leaves of the ebony gate gaped open in a tangled mess. Yes! It had worked.

Zara stepped out toward the blackened and heat-crazed floor. Nebam grabbed her arm and yanked her back.

She pulled away, her cheeks flaming, her hands curled in fists. 'The arrows are burnt.'

Nebam pulled his beard. 'Some, but we don't know how many stores there are. Stay put until I say so.' He turned away. 'Jazzia, douse down the felt. When things have cooled down enough, Zara will activate standby and we'll see if our firepower worked.

The moments ticked by, but at last Nebam was ready to proceed. 'Do the deed.'

Zara placed her hand in the panel a second time and followed Nebam through the still-warm shield tunnel.

Two toolwuns could fit through the gap between the two sides of the door. Zara squeezed in after Nebam and Jazzia. Glimmer lights winked on down both sides of another tunnel. In the far distance, the walls of the cavern curved round to meet a tall purple-black gateway. The amethyst gate and whatever dangers it would unleash.

Time to start all over again.

Retza hobbled along at the back of the rag-tag group shuffling through the tunnels, his knee on fire after the struggle with Elim. The pile of rubble and the pale line of the glimmer lights along the wall signalled that they were close to home. The way back to the central caverns seemed longer than their outward journey. Despite some prodding, the Old Guard survivors could only manage a slow walk with frequent stops.

'Should have left these slouches behind,' Manoah mumbled, his eyebrows angling down over narrowed eyes. 'Most of them are past saving.'

'You don't know that,' Retza snapped back. What was with Manoah lately? Though the constant gnaw of hunger made them all irritable.

A white-haired woman in front of them stumbled. Retza helped her up, shocked at the thinness of her arms.

'Sorry to be a burden,' she whispered.

'And what makes you loyal to the Overseer?' Manoah asked.

'I serve … served his wife, Lady Labine, since she was a lass.'

Zara's mother. 'So, she is not here?'

'No, she didn't survive nor—'

'Declare yourselves,' a voice boomed out from the murder holes in the ceiling above them. Retza's arm hairs stiffened, remembering the cascade of arrows, rocks and hot liquids they'd dropped through the holes during the Old Guard attacks. Perhaps the old Guard survivors remembered too. The group straggled to a stop.

'It's Gilarth and the northern search team,' the Head Watcher shouted from the front of the group.

'There's too many for that!'

'Blast it, Nate, don't pretend you don't recognise me. Get those gates open.'

A short hesitation, then. 'Yes, sir.'

Boots thumped down the stairs. One of the large doors swung open and stronger glimmerlight spilled out into the tunnel to reveal a group of watchers with truncheons and whips lined to greet them.

Watcher Natan stepped forward. His eyes flicked

toward Josenif, standing in his human form beside Gilarth, then to the bound prisoners—Elim and a few of the other highwuns. 'Gilarth, good to see you. You brought extras.'

'Glad you can count, Watcher. Secure these prisoners and take them to the cells.'

'What about the others?'

Gilarth pushed back his helmet on his forehead and sighed. 'See if they have family that will take them. Otherwise, break them into smaller groups to be distributed among the crews. Scrybe Barekia should check them out first.'

'Diamond South scrybe has taken over the medic duties. Barekia's focused on the Heart Room now.'

'Yes, of course.' Gilarth beckoned Retza and Manoah to join him. 'Any news from the southern search team?'

'They found nothing but dust and cobwebs.'

'And the Overseer. Is she in her ready room?'

Watcher Natan hesitated, then shook his head. 'Try the balcony. I can send a runner.'

'No, I'll go to her. Manoah, make sure the highwun prisoners are locked down securely. Retza, Josenif, you're with me.'

Retza's breath quickened. Tired as he was, he wanted to be part of this meeting.

They crossed the Great Hall and out into the forecourt, but instead of turning right to the Overseers' quarters, Gilarth led them to a set of winding stairs half-hidden by a recessed archway. The stairs were steep and Retza was panting for breath by the time they reached the top and walked out onto a narrow balcony hewn out of rock.

A hunched figure stood clutching the railing and staring at the scene far below.

Some distance beneath the balcony, the water burst out of a conduit in the middle of the black rock face and dropped with a thunderous roar into the ravine, running like a gash down the Great Causeway. The clothing and food outlets lined either side of the Great Causeway. The Commissary's Depot squatted near the balcony, with the ever-present line for rations snaking along the concourse. The figures like stick insects, strangely diminished when seen from above.

'Overseer.' Gilarth's voice was unusually gentle.

Havilah's shoulders rose and fell. She half-turned, the glimmerlight falling on her features in angular shadows.

'So, you brought me more bodies to look after, more bellies to half-fill, more tongues to wag and complain. But not Uzza.'

'No, not him or the seal.' Gilarth stood straighter. 'It didn't seem right to leave them to starve.' He gave a half-laugh. 'Might us well join us in the process. Elim and Uzza's leadwuns may know more than they're telling. We'll interrogate them.'

Havilah nodded, her hair glinting silver, more than there had been a few rosters ago. 'The other team also found nothing, just empty halls.'

'We can continue the search of other areas.'

'Hmm.'

'How about Zara?' Retza said, then bit his lip at speaking out.

Havilah raised her eyebrow. 'So, it's like that is it, Watcher Retza?'

Retza's cheeks warmed. 'No, no. I mean any progress in getting past the gates?'

Havilah clicked her tongue. 'Nebam has managed to bypass the booby traps outside the first gate following your idea with shields and bridges. He's blasting the ebony gate now to get through to the next section. What we find beyond it … we are not sure.'

'Six more gates and more traps most likely,' Josenif

said. He ran a hand through his hair, his silvery-white face gaunter than a few days before. 'Hezikah was nothing if not thorough.'

Gilarth raised shaggy eyebrows. 'You speak as though you knew him.'

'I saw him once, as a youngling.'

Retza blinked. That would make Josenif older than old Barekia, yet he looked not much older than Zadeki.

Josenif prowled restlessly in the small space. 'When Hezikah first sought freedom from the Vaane, he came to us for help. Later he seemed consumed with fears and shadows and he rejected the Kinleader's advice to negotiate with the Lonely Isles. He began to build defences beyond all reason, shutting himself inside the mountain.'

'And you did nothing?'

'Me? I am still young in my people's eyes. The Elders discussed the situation for many years, but decided that if Darian's people chose to shut themselves in their caverns, then it was not our place to interfere.'

'And Kinleader Telsima?'

'Da-matu wasn't happy. She wanted more action. She persuaded the Elders to send messengers, but all attempts were repulsed, and the ways barricaded against us. This is why the Elders were reluctant to get involved even now, except that Zadeki insisted we do something to help his new friends.'

'How can we blame you when we didn't act?' Havilah brushed her hair off her face. 'Our people trusted the Overseer. Then he killed the Techwuns, my parents as well as others, and the sacrifices of youngwuns began. Only a couple to start with. We were afraid to oppose him, until three brave youngwuns and Old Barekia demanded otherwise.' She nodded at Retza and he ducked his head at the praise. 'Sometimes the young see clearer than their elders.'

'To our shame.' Gilarth's voice was hard to hear.

Havilah glanced at the Head Watcher. 'I should have gone with you when you asked all those years ago, though ...' her voice faded and her face softened. 'Not everything was bad about that time.' A soft, sad smile softened her lips. 'Still, I should have listened to the Kinleader and evacuated the people once the food crops had failed. Some, perhaps, would have died on the trek across the mountains, but now, it is far, far worse.' Havilah's shoulders sagged. 'Every way we look at the tangle, we come to another knot, and all solutions take more time than we have.'

The balcony seemed to sway under Retza's boots. Havilah was a steady beacon that kept them on track. If she failed, who could stand? 'Your Honour, you cannot give up now.'

Josenif placed a hand over his breastbone, another on Havilah's. 'The son of Holima speaks true. We can only deal with the time we have now. Don't allow the fear and shadows to weaken you as they did your predecessors.'

Havilah looked from one face to another, finally resting on Retza's. 'I can hear Delvina in your words, Watcher. I know she would say the same if she were here.' Her voice gained strength. 'We need to give Zara and Nebam every help to get through the Gate. And whatever happens, we will seek to save lives and our realm to the very end.'

Danel tossed this way and that in the smothering darkness. A sense of encroaching danger twanged through him. Somewhere close by, a littlewun wailed with growing panic. Leaping flames surrounded him with a blistering heat, and he gagged on the pungent smell of smoke and burnt flesh. He reached for the child, clutching him to his chest and dodged a falling roofbeam. His eyes watered with the smoke and each breath burned his lungs.

'Danel, Danel, hurry.'

Figures called out from the doorway, arms stretched out and beckoning. Sheets of flame ran up the walls and along the ceiling. He ran, bending low. Almost there. Just a few more strides. The littlewun whimpered in his arms. An ominous creak and the roof cascaded down in a shower of sparks and burning debris. Searing pain, then darkness. A shudder ripped through him.

Danel sat up with a jolt and banged his head on the bunk above him. Where the blazes was he?

No fire here, no littlewuns, no danger. Just the recurring dream of the night Avardin's rebel forces burnt the house at Silantis. Maybe he should have asked Ariel if the littlewun had survived. She'd said he'd saved many lives, that he was a hero, but he didn't feel like one. He did what needed to be done, what anyone else would do. You don't leave your crewmates to die when the walls crumble around you.

He rubbed his smarting head. He wasn't in the Greenstone South's crib or anywhere under solid stone. Curved, wooden walls creaked and the floor rolled and tilted. The White Rose.

Seven days, and they were still at sea.

He grabbed his cloak, his bandaged hands fumbling the grip, and staggered out onto the deck. Sea spray cooled his heated face, and his hair caught in the wind. A line of light lit up one horizon, splitting the world in two. Alumi's golden half-circle looked down at him high in the sky.

A pungent smell mingled with the salt on the wind. Overhead an albatross circled the masts. It dipped and dived towards the ship. Just when Danel was certain it would collide with the deck, its outlines shimmered and stretched into Zadeki's long, lithe form, dark curls whipping about his silvery-white face. He hit the deck running and, in seeming defiance of the ever-moving ship, sprinted to the Second Jonan standing at the tiller.

Danel turned away and took a few unsteady steps. No wonder Delvina placed such faith in the young stranger with such amazing abilities. He offered the allure of mystery and adventure.

A hand clapped Danel's good shoulder from behind. 'Hey, Danel. You're up early.'

'Then so are you.'

Zadeki grinned, though his dark eyes held on to grief. 'Scouting for Mariner Habbiah. We're close to land by all the signs.' A fault line appeared between his dark eyebrows. 'Your skin is hot. Has anyone looked at your burns recently?'

Danel shrugged. Ariel has tended him in the night and day following the rioting that had destroyed half of Silantis. The wayfarers had applied another dressing before he and the others had escaped the island. To be honest, he'd forgotten about it.

'Aunt Bikan has healing knowle—' Zadeki broke off and squeezed his eyes shut. He took a deep shuddering breath. 'Maybe Baba could help,' he added in a clipped voice.

'Let me take a look.' Delvina emerged out of the shadows of the foredeck.

'Del ... er Messenger Delvina, what are you doing there?'

She offered a forlorn smile. 'It seems you're not the only one with troubled dreams, Speaker Danel. Come on.'

She led them below decks to one of the cabins and pulled out a medical kit. 'Sit here.'

Danel complied, and she carefully unwrapped the bindings on his hands. He gritted his teeth and jiggled his leg.

'Does that hurt?'

'A little,' he grunted.

'Here,' Zadeki dropped on his knees and put a hand on his shoulder. He sang in a low melodic tone. The words were of green living things, and water running beneath dappled sunlight, of life above ground and things Danel had no idea about, but the shapeshifter's song soothed the pain.

Delvina's hands trembled and she looked over Danel to the shapeshifter. 'It's my fault Highwun Bikan is dead.'

'No, it's mine.' Zadeki's voice wavered for a moment. 'We could have escaped if I'd followed her directions.'

'But you wouldn't have been in that situation if I hadn't told Avardin everything. I thought ... I thought she would help us.'

'You weren't to know,' Danel said.

Delvina barely glanced at him. 'Highwun Bikan warned me, you did too. I should have listened. I allowed my feelings to sway me.'

Zadeki looked away.

Danel coughed. Was he invisible here? 'Come on you two, enough of the guilt-fest. You both made mistakes. We all do. Thing is, you didn't stick with them.'

'That doesn't change the fact that Zadeki's aunt is dead or that you're badly burnt.' At last she looked at him, her round face full of misery.

'No, I guess not. But it's okay, Runner Delvina, at least from where I'm sitting.'

'I'm sorry I didn't think of this earlier,' Delvina said.

'Don't worry,' Danel said. 'Best just to get it over with.'

She pushed his hands out flat, uncurling his fingers. The palms were still blistered and angry in places, but he could see swathes of new skin, reddened and smooth. Some of his tension eased. Not as bad as he feared.

Delvina slathered Bikan's salve over the puss-filled bits. Only his left hand, the one he used the most, needed another dressing.

Delvina stood up. 'Better take off your tunic.'

He hesitated, his cheeks warming, and then pulled the garment off, the fastening catching a moment on the bulky bandage around his head. Her eyes lingered before she glanced away. She eased off the bandage scabbed onto his shoulder.

'This is healing well too.'

Which left the injury to the side of his face. What if he was blinded in that eye?

'Relax, Speaker.' Delvina unwound the long strips of cloth. 'Can you get me some fresh water, Zadeki?'

Danel closed his eye. He soaked in the sounds of her soft breaths, the groaning rasp of the ship's restless wooden planks, the screech of seabirds and a distant roar of the waves. The splash of water slopping in a bucket indicated Zadeki was back.

'Now for the pad.' Delvina lifted it slowly, the dressing pulling at his skin and eyebrows. Something wet swabbed his left eye, gentle fingers parted his eyelids. Light speared in. He blinked rapidly. The blur of shapes resolved into a glimmer lantern and two concerned faces.

A pale pinkish light trickled through the open door into the room.

'A bit blurry but I can see with both eyes.'

His wide grin faltered at tears brimming on Delvina's pale eyelashes.

'What is it?'

'Your face, it's …' She gulped and gave a trembling smile.

He felt the puckered skin across half his face, his creased eyelid, half-absent eyebrow, and marred ear. 'Guess I must look a sight.'

Zadeki glanced from one to the other, a puzzled frown

tenting his eyebrows. 'Aunt Bikan would say such scars are a mark of honour.'

Danel sat up straighter, pleased at the thought. He liked how the Forest Folk viewed things.

'Land ahoy!' A shout of excitement went up from outside.

Delvina's ice-grey eyes lit up. 'Did they say land?'

'Yeah, I said we were close,' Zadeki said. 'By the Maker's favour, the winds have been opportune.'

They looked at each other and all at once jumped up and scrambled out of the cabin and through the hatchway onto the swaying deck.

A long line of red cliffs edged with a heaving white frill of waves and foam swung in and out of sight beyond the bow.

Zara crouched-walked along the scorched felt of the shield tunnel, trailing behind Nebam and a bunch of toolwuns. The felt-muffled thud of their boots providing counterpoint to her lighter steps. Retza followed behind her carrying a metal sheet. Despite the limited height, the tunnel remained the safest way to cover the distance between the archway and ebony gate. Nebam had torched each volley of arrows until at last they ran out, but walking across the unshielded floor still activated the lightning strikes. The fire had removed the stench of decay from the cavern though now the smell of scorched metal and ash hung in the air.

Zara ducked her head, scrambling out of the shield tunnel, and stepped on the threshold. Gleaming black gates sagged open, like a discarded cave cray shell. She followed the others, squeezing through the first gateway. On the other side, the tunnel stretched out into the distance, a good twenty-minute tramp to the second control panel and the Amethyst Gate.

'We will need to extend the glimmer tracks to the second panel,' Nebam grumbled. 'It's at least six lek from the archway to the final Ruby Gate.'

Stone singer Peta chuckled. 'Yeah, but it's only one lek to the amethyst gate. You getting out of condition, Secundwun?'

Zara glanced at Retza walking close behind her, silent as a tomb. He hadn't lost his limp yet, though the grazes on his face from the cave-in were no longer noticeable at least in this dim light. She tingled at his closeness, his aura of strength and stability. He might be a lowwun, but she liked him, maybe more than liked him. She scuffed the dirt-encrusted stone beneath her boots. Not that he'd shown that sort of interest in her. Perhaps to him, she would always be the daughter of the hated Overseer Uzza. That was for the best, the sensible half of her said, but the other half moped and wished it could be otherwise.

'Any new thoughts about the seal or your father's whereabouts, Zara?'

She gave a guilty jerk at Nebam's question and shook her head. That's what she should be thinking about.

Retza perked up. 'The replenishing mechanisms must be powered from somewhere. Most likely from the Crystal Heart. If we cut the connections?'

Nebam folded his arms. 'We thought about that, Watcher. The Gate has its own shielded power source. According to the plans, it can only be accessed from the Citrine Gate.'

'Oh, that's awkward.' Retza lapsed into silence.

The purple-black gateway loomed in front of them, like a bruise on the grey rock. Three tanis closer, a bronze panel stood guard, a stack of bronze sheets and tools next to it, hauled there during the third shift.

Nebam held up his hand and they straggled to a stop.

'In the previous chamber, we faced arrows, lightning and a tilting movable floor. Here, the dangers may be different. The timing could be different or this panel may not recognise Zara's handprint. The dangers are real, but our task is vital to our realm's survival. Now please, Zara.' Nebam sounded a shade softer than in the past.

Zara hurried to the panel, pressing her palm against the indentation. Retza followed, dragging a bronze sheet as shield.

As at the ebony gate, the letters flickered into the warning and the tray slid out, revealing a small notch the same size as the first panel. She searched this panel for something different, something that would give some clue to the nature of the seal.

The toolwuns rushed forward to link the panels of a new shield tunnel and to bolt it to solid parts of the ground. The moments passed as slow as cold tar. Sweat trickled down her back and her neck prickled. Nine, ten minutes crept by. The warning light deepened to red.

'Time's up,' Nebam called. 'Fall back.'

'We might get longer,' a toolwun said, tightening a bolt.

Zara and Retza retreated several paces behind the panel and waited for the clunk, clunk, clunk of arrows loading. Nothing. And then, a soft hiss.

'Leave it, man! Get back, now!' The tardy toolwun dropped his wrench and scrambled after the others.

A gurgling sound came from the walls, mixed with a moaning scream. Zara clutched Retza's arm, resisting the urge to bolt back down the tunnel. Was that some kind of beast?

Jets of water shot from the walls and roof in a criss-cross pattern, filling the space with clouds of steam and a rattling roar as water struck metal. Scalding water splashed on Zara's face and arms. The toolwuns near the panel backed away further down the tunnel.

Nebam pulled his ginger hair. 'Fun. Instead of getting skewered, we can be broiled to death.'

Water ran in runnels into holes in the floor, no doubt to be stored and used again. White water vapour wisped into the cavern, carrying a comforting wet-earth smell.

'We might need a thicker felt layer for the shield tunnel,' Peta said.

At last the streams of water shut off, leaving a residual drip, drip, drip.

'All clear?' asked a toolwun.

Retza edged closer and threw a stone close to a blue paving stone. Lightning spiked from the roof.

'Give it another twenty.'

Zara collapsed on the dusty floor. Retza settled a pace away. No short cuts then. It took six days to build the shield-wall in the last section. Unless they found another faster way, it would be a roster or more before they opened the final ruby gate. She leant forward and traced words in the dust. Too late! If only she'd offered to help sooner, they might have had a chance. No, she would not see Jesson and the others starve. She scrubbed out the words with her fist and wrote above them. *Don't give up.*

The gold chain about her neck slipped forward and the crystal swung out, glimmering in the blue-white light.

Retza put down his water flask. 'Who gave you the crystal, Zara?'

Zara shrugged. 'Oh, I found it in a storage box in Da-Baba's old room.' Sadness welled up at the thought of her family, her matu and siblings. She caught the crystal and tucked it inside her shirt. It tingled under her fingers. It often felt warm when in the gate tunnels.

Her heart kicked against her chest. What if—

'Could it be the seal,' Retza said, his voice hoarse.

Zara's spine straightened, a bubbly feeling rising up inside her. Then as suddenly, the hopes crashed back down. 'It was just among a lot of junk. Da-Baba was something of a hoarder.' And more than a little bit mad in the end.

Retza rubbed the rim of the water flask. 'Still, don't you think we should try it? Even on an off chance.'

The Stone Singer jumped up from where she rested and walked over. She gave him a dazzling smile. 'Yes, watcher Retza.'

Zara's heart squeezed with an unfamiliar feeling and she glared at the pretty Stone Singer, not much older than she was. She pulled away from Retza, the stone swinging back against her chest.

Retza lifted an eyebrow, as if to say, 'What's wrong with you?' He tapped Peta's arm. 'What do you think of Zara's crystal, has it any power? You don't mind do you, Zara?'

'Too bad if I did,' Zara grumbled under her breath, but she allowed Peta to lift the stone. The Stone Singer held it in the palm of her hand, her eyes closed and head lifted. Her breathing slowed, then her mouth twitched and she snatched her hand away.

'It is a powerful stone.' She rubbed her hand. 'It has a strong soul-bond.'

Zara tilted her head to one side. Was the girl trying to impress Retza?

Peta met her eyes. 'Why did you choose it? It's pretty but not as flashy as the jewellery most highwuns wear. The setting is simple.'

Zara frowned. 'I don't know. It .... I don't know ... it felt like it was singing to me.'

Retza leaned forward. 'What if it's the seal? It can't hurt to try it.'

He was right. It would be the only way to know for sure.

Nebam threw a stone and then another. No electrical spikes struck the floor. 'Breaks over.'

The toolwuns dropped their things, jumped up and took their places, ready to fix together the next lot of panels.

Zara waited, her stomach fluttering like a flame in a tunnel wind.

'Now, Zara.' When everyone was settled, Nebam waved her forward.

She swallowed hard and stepped to the panel. Retza came behind. She placed her hand. The tray slid out as before. She stared at it, breathing hard.

'What are you waiting for?' Nebam demanded with a touch of his old sharpness.

She pulled out her crystal, newly aware of the prickling where her fingers brushed it. She could hear its song, not as deep or strong as that to the Glimmer Heart, but persistent and enticing. Was this the answer, at last?

She slipped the chain over her head and slotted the crystal in the hole. It fitted perfectly. The letters flickered and changed.

'Authorisation rejected.'

The sirens sounded and the pipes in the wall hummed and gurgled.

'Get back, get back, get back,' Retza yelled. Toolwuns dropped panels and tools and dove for cover.

The tray whirred and slid back. Zara snatched back her crystal a second before the tray snapped shut and scrambled out of range of the skin-flaying hot water.

Nebam kicked the stack of panels. 'Now we've lost working time.'

Hot tears stung Zara's eyes. Stupid, stupid, stupid. Stupid for getting hopes up. Her hand tightened on the crystal and she threw back her arm, ready to fling the offending rock into the inky shadows in the corners of the cavern.

Retza caught her arm. 'It's not the stone's fault.'

'But everything we try fails.'

'So, we keep trying.'

She leant back against him and allowed the anger to leach out of her. He was right. They just had to work harder.

Retza entered the watcher duty room at the change of second shift. He stretched his back and rubbed his sore knee. Two shifts back-to-back helping on the Gate had been long and hard and all he could think of was snuggling under the covers of his bunk.

A shout came from below. 'Hey Retza, want to help feed the vermin?' Manoah emerged from the stairs leading to the holding cells, carrying a couple of empty buckets.

'Nah, Noah, I'm off duty.' Retza pulled his token from the duty board.

'Not yet, you're not.' Manoah dropped the buckets and knocked the token from Retza's hand.

The blasted thing skidded along the floor and under a desk. Manoah bent over, his big frame shaking with a belly laugh.

Retza growled. He was too tired to put up with Manoah's stupid antics. 'By the Pit, that's not funny.'

'Come on, can't you take a joke?'

Retza didn't answer. He shoved a stone stool out of the way and crawled beneath the desk. The token was crammed right at the back.

'Hey, no hard feelings, right? Look, you've got to help me out. I'm running late and Jazzia agreed to meet me in the recreation hall. She's not going to wait forever, is she? I've done the clean-up, and some of the meals. Just got to finish half the block.'

Retza backed out, gripping the token, and pulled the cobwebs from his hair and chin hairs. Normally, he would help, but since coming back to the central caverns he hadn't stopped.

Manoah's eyes narrowed. 'I'll make it up to you. I'll give you a half-day of rations.'

Retza's stomach rumbled. He was so hungry he could eat a mountain or two. A little light work for feeling fuller for a few hours was worth the swap, though surely Manoah was just as hungry as he was.

'A sixth of an hour, that's all.' He pointed to the ancient timepiece on the wall.

Manoah grinned and clapped him hard on the shoulder. 'You're a goodwun. Here, I'll do the west wing, you do the northern cells.'

Retza hooked his token back on the board, grabbed the labelled bucket sitting against the wall and followed Manoah down the stairs to the holding cells that stretched out under the floor of the Grand Cavern. When Manoah turned left, he turned right and threw the labelled packets between the bars to the waiting prisoners.

Most were Old Guard survivors, former highwuns loyal to Uzza, often four to five in a cell. The old Speaker, Elim, had a cell to himself. Dressed in decent clothes and with hair and beard washed and trimmed, he looked less wild than he had in the northern precinct. Still, he snatched at the packet and devoured its contents in moments.

Retza turned to the final cell at the end of the corridor, this one with a locked door.

Elim's nasally voice stopped him. 'Who is in there, Watcher?'

'Former Secondwun Putarn and Watcher Javot,' Retza said, then kicked himself for responding to the command in the highwun's voice. 'Not that it is any of your business.'

'Interesting, Havilah's own son. She must be whipping out of control like broken lift cable.'

Retza ignored the mockery in the former Speaker's voice. He rapped on the metal door and yelled, 'On your bunks or no food.'

He peered through the viewer. Javot sat on his hands on the bunk, his pink eyes full of mockery. Putarn leaned against the far wall, staring at his hands, his face gaunt and drawn, huge bruises under his mauve eyes.

Satisfied, Retza unlocked the door and placed two small packets of provisions and a jug of water on the floor.

'Well lookie who we have here,' Javot said.

Putarn looked up with a jerk. 'Retza.' His face stretched into a rictus smile. 'Still in my esteemed matu's favour, I see. And what about that sister of yours?'

'You mean my twin sister you tried to kill? You were mistaken, you know. The Heart Crystals didn't need blood.' Retza swung the empty bucket and turned to go.

'I know, I'm sorry, I made a mistake.' Putarn's voice was raw with emotion. 'Not blood, but the crystals do crave a sacrifice.' He fingered something in his closed fist, too small to be a knife. 'It's the only way.'

'How would you know? You're mad, Putarn.'

'The crystals call to me, they speak in my dreams. Did you know the Overseer still lives?'

Retza's muscles seized up. He turned slowly. 'You can't know that. Besides, your matu, Havilah is Overseer.' He should ignore this rambling. But if the other Old Guard survived, then Uzza could have too.

'Not for long. Do you trust her? You shouldn't you know.'

'She is your matu. And, yes, I do trust her.'

Strong emotion distorted Putarn's face. 'My baba is dead because of her cowardice. Your matu and baba too.'

'My parents died in a cave-in. They were heroes.'

Putarn chuckled. 'Keep believing that.' He sobered in an instant. 'I was wrong about the sacrifice. There is no salvation, only anger and revenge. You'll see.'

Retza shook his head to dislodge the dark thoughts and strode out the cell.

'I feel sorry for you Retza, you don't know what's coming. Death, Darkness Destruction. You're in my dreams too. They're coming for us. They're coming.'

Retza slammed the door behind him, muffling Putarn's mad voice, but the predictions of doom tagged behind him. Nebam and Zara had reached the amethyst gate, but it was too little, too late. If only Delvina and Zadeki would return with a miracle.

Sea birds wheeled in the wind and long breakers ran towards the sharp edge of the cliffs in long orderly lines. It had taken several days to follow the wind back up the coast, but now they were nearing Redhaven and the White Rose sailed toward the long line of red cliffs on the horizon. Zadeki was buzzing at the thought of returning to the Wide Lands. How glorious it would be to stretch his wings, to keep flying over the plains and through the cool, clean air of the high mountains and the Great Forest beyond.

'We're going to collide with the cliff.' Danel gripped the railing, his half pale, half pink face screwed up with tension.

'I hope not.' Delvina flipped her plait over her shoulder. 'Nearly drowning is not something I wish to repeat.'

Zadeki jumped down from the rigging to join his friends and Baba. 'Maybe, I should teach you both to swim.' At least Delvina was looking him in the eyes again.

'Not me,' Danel held up his hand. 'Once we reach solid land, I'm not getting on a boat again.' A look of consternation slid over his face. 'I suppose we should take the river boat back up the river.'

'It would take too long. We've already lost nine days.' Zadeki paced along the deck, resisting the urge to take wing and fly straight there.

Baba rubbed his chin. 'Agreed, a journey upriver would delay us further.'

'Much as I prefer it, walking would take longer.' Danel rubbed his hand over the railing. 'Not that we bring many answers with us.'

'Yet even the little knowledge we acquired may be vital,' Baba said.

'You could fly us, Highwun,' Delvina said.

'The sea cliffs are too low here to launch with extra weight on my back, but I noticed they were higher further south. We can walk until we find a suitable place and then fly through the day and night, we should reach the mountains where precipices are plentiful.'

Up ahead, the top of Redhaven's farseeing tower was visible close to the break in the cliffs. The boat heeled over and Zadeki shifted his balance as the deck tilted. Delvina clung to the railing, knuckles taunt, and Danel slid a few tanis before Baba caught his arm.

Mariner Habbiah roared orders from the helm, and the sailors hurried to adjust the sails.

With a rush of foaming water, the White Rose slipped between the heads and into the calmer water of the harbour. The sun was above the horizon, its fresh golden light glinting off the mouth of the river. To the left the village of Akra, to the right the gleaming white buildings of Redhaven climbing up the hill.

It took a while longer and some masterful sailing, but Habbiah brought the ship alongside the wharf. Ebed rushed up and threw ropes to the waiting sailors. Nearby, seagulls screamed and mobbed a newly arrived fishing boat.

Redhaven seemed parochial, after the grandeur of Silantis. The simplicity of the Great Forest would be even better. But first the Warden and then the Caverns.

A rhythmic tramping sounded over the restless rumble of the waves. A squad of watchers armed with spears and led by Harbour Master Rebekka marched down the long avenue toward them.

Zadeki's shoulders drooped. He only hoped they didn't have to fight their way out of Redhaven as they had Silantis.

Danel rubbed his injured eye, watering from the glare of the sun climbing higher in a cobalt sky. He hitched his pack and followed Harbour Master Rebekka to the big domed building up the hill. Mariner Habbiah walked beside her, deep in conversation and from his gestures, perhaps informing her of the events on the island. Even so, the Redhaven watchers formed a cordon around their party with particular attention to the Highwun Korak and Zadeki. No doubt archers were stationed in strategic points, keeping their arrows trained on them like last time.

Despite all that had happened to them, the white columns and blue-tiled roofs of Redhaven's buildings looked just as sleepy as on their previous visit. Yet to Danel, it felt like years had passed.

Delvina's shoulders drooped as she stared at the few unhurried ebed going about their duties 'The Warden is unlikely to help us, given our last encounter.'

'Maybe Habbiah will persuade him to help us.' Danel looked sideways at the impassive faces of the watchers. 'Anyhow, it's faster to see what he wants, than fight our way out.'

'It might come to that anyhow.'

'True, Del,' Zadeki said, 'but this time we won't have our claws sheathed.' The young shapeshifter had a harder edge since the death of Highwun Bikan.

'Peace, son of the wind. We won't provoke an attack.' Highwun Korak spread out his hands. 'Besides, mountain's daughter, I'm curious to know whose side Ealam, son of Lotah, supports, Avardin's or the rebels.

Besides we should support Habbiah in return for his hospitality in Silantis and on the sea.'

Which all made sense. And they would need Korak's talents to shorten the journey. Even so, Danel itched to start for the mountains without more delays.

Halfway up the hill, they reached the Warden's House. Rebekka led them through the colonnades and high arched doors, across the atrium where she spoke to an ebed in elegant robes. He waved them through a short corridor and into an open courtyard similar to the one at Habbiah's house, with a central pool, statues, potted plants and screened-off rooms around the sides.

Ealam sat on a low couch, a range of dishes in front of him, most arranged with delicacies Danel didn't recognise. His own hasty meal of bread and cheese at first light seemed a long time ago.

A scowl deepened on Ealam's austere face. 'Why am I interrupted?'

Rebekka brought her hands to her chest and bowed her head. 'Warden Ealam. My apologies for disturbing you, but your orders were to bring at once any news of the Lonely Isles.'

Ealam sat up straighter, his eyes examining each of the party in turn. 'Well go on then.'

Mariner Habbiah bowed. 'I regret to inform you, your Honour, that the Grand Technician Iulien is dead.'

'How can this be?'

'Avardin killed him.' Zadeki said. 'As she killed da-sestru — Elder Bikan.'

Korak stepped closer, his hand gripping his son's shoulder.

'Is this true, Habbiah?' Ealam demanded.

'Yes, Warden. I'm afraid it is. Princess Avardin has seized her uncle's throne through deceit and the violent acts of rebels and traitors.'

'The Council wouldn't accept such a travesty,' Ealam spluttered. 'It was precisely because the Sea Dragon King doubted Avardin's motives that he appointed his friend as regent.'

Habbiah's lips thinned. 'She has Lord Hale's support and many of the council would fear to act against her. Avardin's thugs barricaded the harbour and damaged the White Ships. Silantis is in chaos, much of it is burning. I fear for the young prince. The situation is indeed dire.'

Ealam fell back on the couch, his hands clutching his chest. 'She will come here next. She'll have to.'

'Eventually, yes. But not before repairing the White Ships.' Habbiah glanced at Danel and the others. He gave a tiny shrug of his broad shoulders. 'She does not go wholly unopposed. A coalition—a group of Vaane highborns and ebed—plan to fight against her, including my daughter Ariel. I intend to return and help her.'

Ealam looked aghast. 'You cannot. It will be the death of you and ... and yours is the only ship we have left.' He swung around and glared at Korak and Zadeki. 'This must be your fault.'

'Unbelievable,' Delvina fumed.

Danel stepped forward doing his best to keep the ire out of his voice. 'Your Honour, this is not the Forest Folk's doing. The harbour was already barricaded when we arrived.'

'And without the Adelphi and Danel's brave actions, my daughter would have died.' Habbiah turned and held out his hands. 'I only wish they could help us further.'

'Pah!' The Warden pushed his plate away and stood up. 'We have no need of Flame-get aid. If the Council backs the Princess, then she has right of rule as regent. Tell me why I shouldn't arrest the lot of you?'

'Elder Bikan was right, you have no respect for your

word or honour.' Zadeki growled low in the chest and his hands curled like claws.

Danel tensed, ready for the onslaught. They were outnumbered three to one, yet the Forest Folk were powerful and he and Delvina would fight if need be. Highwun Korak was right. They may not have learned much, but they needed to take what they had learned to Overseer Havilah and help as best they could to save the realm.

Habbiah moved between the Warden and the Forest Folk. 'Ealam, would you side with Iulien's murderer? Avardin kills and destroys at will. I thought you had more backbone than this craven surrender to wrong.'

Ealam's jowls quivered. 'Remember whom you address. If you are so in love with of this riff-raff, you can join them and have your property confiscated for treason.'

Habbiah blinked then folded his arms. 'You wouldn't!'

Ealam sneered. 'Rebekka, secure these rebels and chain the shapeshifters. Report to me in my study when the deed is done.' He inclined his head. 'Now I have important matters to attend to.'

Danel moved closer to Delvina, wishing he had a hammer or liftbar to wield against the Vaane watchers. The two shapeshifters flanked them, a feeling of coiled menace emanating from their stance.

Rebekka stood as still as a stone column, her face impassive.

'You have your orders, Harbour Master.'

'Have you forgotten that the Grand Technician is ... was ... my uncle. That we all have kin and folk on the islands. Mariner Habbiah is right. Now is the time to strike against the usurper.' She pulled her bow from her back. 'You will have to put me in your prison also, if you persist with this madness.'

Ealam's mouth made a perfect circle. He swallowed

and recovered himself. 'Captain, you are now Harbour Master. Take all those who disobey my orders to prison.'

The captain gave a nervous glance at Rebekka and then at the two Forest Folk. 'Er, excuse me, your Honour, but Harbour Master Rebekka and Mariner Habbiah have the right of it.'

Fury suffused Ealam's face. 'Have you forgotten your oath to obey?'

The captain squared his shoulders. 'My oath is to Prince Selwin and all those who protect him.'

'Won't anyone do as I ordered?'

The watchers glanced at each other and, as a body, stepped back, falling in line behind Harbour Master Rebekka.

'I get your point.' Ealam held out his hands, a sulky look of a thwarted littlewun on his face. 'Avardin is the traitor—and we will support those who seek to restore the rightful rule.' He cast a sideways glance at Korak and Zadeki. 'Though I do not doubt this insubordination is your doing.'

Korak raised an eyebrow. 'You honour us too much, son of Lotah.' He looked around and caught Danel's eye. 'We'll accept your hospitality for a meal to sustain us before we leave.'

Harbour Master Rebekka gave a half-smile. 'The servants will see to your needs, and I will see to the replenishing of Mariner Habbiah's ship. I've a mind to avenge my uncle's death.'

'Quite,' Habbiah nodded. And then with a sudden movement, he pulled Danel into an embrace. 'It's been an honour to serve you, Speaker Danel, Messenger Delvina. We both have heavy tasks ahead of us. May the Maker give favour to your people and to mine.'

Danel wobbled a bit as Habbiah released him. 'Our thanks for your hospitality, Mariner Habbiah. We would return the favour if you ever visit our mountains.' He touched his hand to his chest and bowed as an equal. He turned to his companions. 'Let's do as Highwun Korak suggests—eat, replenish our provisions and go.'

The watchers parted to either side, providing a straight path to the door. Delvina and the Forest Folk fell in behind him.

A bubble rose inside Danel. Whatever they found when they returned to the mountain, at last they were heading home.

The glimmer truck came to a stop at the staging post on the second level. Retza rubbed his eyes and stifled a yawn. The area was quiet and the glimmer lights already dimmed for the start of the third shift. In front of him, Nebam scrambled out of the truck, his pale hair wild.

'I need to report on progress to the Overseer. Watcher Retza, escort Zara back to her quarters.'

Zara visibly bristled at Nebam's overbearing tone, but before she could respond, the Secundwun hurried away. Retza vaulted out of the truck and offered Zara his arm. Ignoring it, she climbed out and strode ahead on her own. Retza fell in behind her, all watcher efficiency. He followed her up the stairs and through the tunnels to the Great Causeway.

The supply outlets were shuttered tight as a lock. The area was dimmed and deserted, even more than usual for this time. High above them the pin-prick light of the glow-worms winked in the rock sky. The normal sounds of boots on stone, the mumble of conversations, the laughter of littlewuns were absent. Not even the soft scuffle of cave rats or the snoring of sleeping crewless in the commons disturbed the quiet. He'd never seen the Causeway so empty.

'Did you find my father among the Old Guard?' Retza jumped as Zara's voice echoed in the cavernous space. She'd hardly spoken to him all day. 'Gilarth, won't tell me.' Her voice quivered.

He stopped by the last bridge arching across the ravine and stared at the white ribbons of foaming water cascading down the sheer rock face. He drew comfort from the fine mist and deafening roar. It was close to this spot he'd last spoken to Delvina. Who knew when he'd see her again?

'I guess you won't say either.'

Why keep it a secret? 'We didn't find him, Zara.' He turned and caught her sceptical gaze. 'The old Speaker, Elim, was there and some of the other officials, but apparently your father took a group with him a couple of ten-days ago with the promise to return.'

She frowned and looked away, then back again. 'Where to?'

'Temple's Rest.'

'I thought … so it's not at the second precinct.'

'No. We don't know where that is.' Retza welcomed the damp feel of mist on his face.

'And the rest of my family? Or did they go with, Baba?'

Retza shook his head, remembering what both Elim and the woman had said. 'A couple of your brothers, but not the rest.'

'None of them were among the survivors. Gilarth said my matu …' she gulped and tears glistened on her cheeks.

It wasn't easy losing a parent or siblings. He wanted to put his arms around her, but instead brushed her shoulder. 'I'm sorry, Zara. Maybe your Baba took more with him. In the meantime, the best you can do for them is what you're doing. Overseer Havilah says yarmas with the food are only a day or two away.'

She scrubbed her cheeks with her fists. 'It's taken us almost a ten-day to get to the second gate. One gate conquered out of seven. How can we open them all in time?'

Retza's muscles tightened. He had no answers. The strongest among them might last days after the food ran out, but they'd already been on reduced rations for so long. It was easy to see the obstacles. Delvina would see the positives, if she was here. 'You'll get better at disabling the traps as you go.'

'Maybe.' She took a step closer and his heart sped up like a speeding glimmer truck at her soft scent of caramel and soap. 'We'd better keep going.'

She caught his hand, her eyes fixed on his face. 'Retza, thank you.'

'What? I'm following orders.'

'You treat me differently than the others. Maybe as a friend, like Delvina said.' Her lips parted.

He stopped breathing. Surely she didn't, couldn't mean that.

She lent in closer, her silky hair falling forward. Their noses collided.

'Oh,' she laughed. Then tilted her head and kissed him. Her lips were soft and her breath sweet. His pulse hammered in his ears. He'd not kissed a girl before, only chaste brotherly kisses on the cheek. He closed his eyes and kissed back. Her lips parted. For a moment, Retza was lost in a sweet oblivion. This had to be a dream. There was no way the Lady Zara, the Overseer's daughter, was kissing him.

They parted at the same time, both breathless. Retza searched her eyes, her face cast in shadows.

'Zara.'

She put a finger on his mouth. 'I think I'm half in love with you. Which is silly and not at all suitable.'

'Of course, a lowwun like me, a highwun like you.' He could feel his voice congealing.

Arrgh—Baaaaang, crash. A guttural yell followed by a sudden crash echoed through the cavern, lifting the hairs on Retza's arms.

Zara pulled back, her eyes like two moons. 'What was that?'

'Came from the commissary.' Retza loosened his truncheon and scanned the causeway. Nothing moved. 'Go get help, Lady Zara. That way.' He indicated the main stairs across the bridge that led to the Watcher quarters and the Grand Cavern. It was only a few hundred tanis. 'I should check this out.'

Pulling out his truncheon, he ran towards the source of the noise. As he neared the twin statues outside the commissary, he slowed his pace and peered into the long shadows. The store was shuttered, the door locked and unbroken. No sign of the watchers that should have been guarding it.

Running footsteps came from behind him. He spun around, swinging his truncheon at the intruder and then almost overbalancing in an effort to stop the blow landing on soft flesh.

'What the blazes, Zara! Go and find Gilarth or the duty watcher, like I asked,' he hissed.

Her face settled into stone. 'I'm staying with you.'

He stood undecided between the urgency of preventing a possible theft of their dwindling food supplies and his orders to escort Zara to her sleeping quarters. Where were the watchers?

The series of crashes and hurried scrapping sounds came from the back of the Commissary. Too loud for cave rats. The thought prodded him into action. 'Stay behind me, then, and keep out of trouble.'

Pulling out his glimmer torch, he crept along the

laneway running down one side of the Commissary. 'I've got a bad feeling about this,' he muttered.

Silence as though muffled by a mountain of felt blankets, disturbed only by his own heavy breathing, the thud of his heart, and the whisper of their stealthy footsteps. Perhaps it was only a stack of empty crates falling over. Pressing his back to the smooth-hewn stone of the wall, he peered around the corner into the large loading area at the back.

Empty, except for a jumble of empty metal crates and a pile of rubbish. Retza's stomach clenched. No watchers here either. Something was very wrong.

He stepped out, senses stretched to snapping point, and played his torch over the square space and the loading lift in the cavern's back wall. A flash of movement. The cables trembled and swayed. He ran forward and checked the lift's control plate. Warm from recent use.

'They came this way.' To escape or to access the store? Or both?

'Retza! Here!'

Letting out a frustrated breath, Retza spun round and raced toward Zara. The back door of the Commissary gaped open.

'Stay back.'

He edged into the corridor. The main storage room was a mess with disarrayed shelving, tipped over crates, torn packages scattered across the floor. Four humped figures in Watcher bat-leather lay sprawled in a tangled heap in the corner.

Zara ran and knelt beside them. 'They're alive. Just.'

Retza nodded grimly. Giving Zara orders was like spitting on a hot griddle. Useless. He searched the other rooms, but the miscreants were gone and most of the stores with them.

In the main room, Zara was tearing strips from her

shirt. 'They are in a bad way. I'll stay with them, you get help.'

'I've got a better idea.' He swung his truncheon, hammering it against a large empty barrel.

Dong. Dong. Dong. The sound echoed about them. Dong. Dong. Dong.

'You're going to raise the dead,' Zara shouted.

'That's the idea.' Retza stepped back. 'I'll see if I can find some water.'

A sneeze came from behind one of the crates in the corner.

Zara whipped around. 'What was that?'

'Not cave rats.' Giving her the torch to hold, Retza stepped over the crate and grabbed the small crouching figure by the arm. A littlewun, a girl, squirmed and kicked, twisting around in an effort to bite his arm.

'Got you.' But surely such a skinny scrap of a girl couldn't best four watchers and do all this damage.

Something slammed into his side. He stumbled and regained his balance in time to fend off a rain of blows.

'Get off her. Filthy watcher. Let her go.'

The youngwun looked up, his mushroom-grey eyes meeting Retza's, his thin face familiar. He'd been with the rabble that hassled the Forest people after the remembering ceremony all those days ago.

'Stealing food? That's rather low, even for a commons-rat like you, Darin. You're in big trouble now. Breaking into the Commissary, attacking Watchers.'

'Let her go!'

'No Daro, you go. Escape while you can.' The girl stopped struggling. 'We didn't do nothing, mister.'

'You're here, aren't you. Part of a gang, hey? They leave you behind to take the blame?'

'We saw the door open … Just getting a little food.'

Retza let out a frustrated breath. He knew what it was

like to fight for every scrap of food before being accepted as trywuns by the Greenstone South Crew. Yet, stealing food was a serious thing when there was so little to go around.

'Look, if you tell us who did this, maybe Gilarth won't drop you down a shaft as dirty rations thieves.'

Zara gasped. 'Retza, you wouldn't do that, would you? They're only youngwuns like Jesson.'

Another youngwun, with large holes in his breeches darted in the back door and threw a cracked paving stone at Retza. He ducked, losing his grip on the girl.

The sound of many boots on stone clattered down the causeway toward them. Someone hammered on the door at the front. 'Open up, in the name of the Overseer.'

'Run, Tosa, Ven.' Together the three imps made a dash for the back door.

Others came racing down the laneway. Moments later, a large figure blocked the doorway.

'What have we here?' Gilarth growled.

'Bat squirts.' Darin backed away and Retza grabbed him.

Gilarth hauled the other two youngwuns into the air. 'What's going on?' More watchers crowded behind him.

'These two watchers were robbing the Commissary. We were only trying to stop him,' Darin whined.

'And he was hurting us,' the girl Tosa added.

Gilarth's sudden laugh echoed in the storeroom. 'Right, Darin, and I believe you.' He shook his head. 'And you and your brother escaped from the creche again, Tosa? You should be ashamed stealing food. So what really happened here, Watcher Retza?'

'We heard a noise and investigated. We discovered the watchers on duty incapacitated and the stores ransacked.'

Gilarth's eyebrows rose. 'We?'

'Watcher Retza was escorting me to my quarters.' Zara moved from the shadows in the corner of the storeroom.

'These watchers here need help. I've unfastened their bonds, but I cannot wake them, and their breathing is strained.' Her blue eyes were dark against the chalky white of her face.

Retza rubbed the dab of blood from his arm. 'We found them like that. I think the thieves escaped down the supply lift.'

'We're on to it, Watcher Retza.' Gilarth strode across the room and studied the inert men. 'Someone, send for stretchers and a scrybe. We need to get these men to the infirmary. Wuben and Levim, take an inventory, see what's stolen. The rest of you, search the area for clues.'

'Can we go now?' Darin whined.

Gilarth glared at him. 'Tell us what you know, Darin. Who're you working for? Give me some names.'

'We don't know,' Tosa said. 'We heard a noise, thought we'd look. That's all.'

'Then why were you hiding?' Retza demanded.

'Didn't know who you were, did we. We were scared.' Darin waved his arms, but he wouldn't meet Retza's eyes.

Gilarth stroked his beard. 'I don't like the company you keep, Darin, and ration thieves even less.'

Darin's face turned grey. 'Please, sir, we didn't take anything.'

'Didn't have time, huh?' Gilarth's face hardened. 'Take them away.' He motioned his hand and the two watchers hauled them out the door.

Retza's gaze followed the youngwuns. 'You don't mean to drop them over a cliff? You know Havilah wouldn't approve.'

Gilarth gave a wan smile, the first Retza had seen on the big Watcher for a while. 'Sure. She's not like the old Overseer. But they know something. A fright might get them talking. Chasing up Darin's old mates would also be a good place to start.'

Retza chewed his lip. 'Gilarth, where are their parents?'

Gilarth sighed. 'Their baba was killed in the first attack by the old overseer and their Matu badly injured in Putarn's rebellion.'

Orphans and crewless, like he and Delvina had been. 'Greenstone South could do with some prentices.'

Gilarth shook his head. 'Can't see that working. This isn't the first time they've gotten themselves in strife. Minor ration thieves are an ongoing problem, but attacking watchers and robbing the commissary is worrisome. We need to track down the real thieves and stop the landslide before it gets started. He looked across at Zara. 'Lady Zara are you alright?'

Zara looked up and nodded.

'Good, Wuban here will watch over our injured.' Zara opened her mouth, no doubt to protest. Gilarth held up a large hand. 'Jesson may be getting worried about you. Watcher Retza will escort you back to your room.'

Zara bristled, then pushed the stray hair out of her eyes, weariness in every gesture. 'Very well.'

Gilarth stood to one side and she marched toward the front rooms and open door. Retza fell in behind her, fighting the urge to pull her into a comforting hug. The feel of her lips lingered on his own. Not that that seam was worth digging. Half-love or experimenting, either way she wasn't serious.

'And Retza, grab a few hours rest, then report back to me before first shift.' Gilarth's voice followed him out the door.

The day was all but spent in their search for a sea cliff high enough to satisfy Korak. The dull roar of waves and sharp tang of salt and seaweed were their constant companions. Delvina trailed behind Korak and Zadeki, while Danel tramped a couple of paces further back. Her calves ached from long hours of walking and her nose flaked in the blazing sunlight, despite the protection of her Tamrin shawl and Bikan's plant juice. Taciturn Bikan who was now buried among her ancestors and would never return to her Kin. Delvina rubbed the red dust from her eyes, overcome with sadness.

The sun sank behind the ocean in the west, painting the sky and waves carmine. Argenti's half-circle winked at them from high above. In the east, distant hills stood against the darkening sky and she could imagine the high, snow-topped mountains behind them. Her mountains, her caves and caverns, her people.

'How much further?' she groaned, sinking down on a nearby rock.

'We'll see, mountain's daughter.'

'This looks promising, Baba.' Zadeki loped toward the cliff line. With an apologetic shrug, Korak followed.

The two Forest Folk balanced on the edge, the wind tugging at their wraparound sarums. They showed no apparent fear of the sheer drop to the roaring ocean and rocks below. But then, why would they when they could change shape and fly away. There were times she wished she was a shapeshifter.

She took a long draught of the tepid water in her container, studying Zadeki's easy grace, his natural exuberance only slightly dented. Trying to tie him down was like mining the wind. Behind him, the light bled from the sky.

Danel stopped rummaging around in the packs and offered her food. A type of hard bread, a knob of cheese and a handful of dried fruit and nuts.

He bit into the bread and washed it down with water. 'Funny how this stuff fills you up without leaving you satisfied.'

'Right, Thirdwun. You're missing algae cakes?' She laughed, then sobered at the thought of the need for rations in the caverns.

'Ah, and mushrooms and snails and cavecrays and potato cakes.' He scuffed the dirt with his boot. 'The potato harvest should be half-grown by now.'

'And the Tamrin should be close to the Gate.' Her stomach dropped. Had Nebam dug past the collapsed tunnel and reached the outside yet? Had they managed to eke the food out to last? Her head buzzed and fizzed with questions and fears. At night she dreamed of finding the caverns empty and lifeless. Too late, too late, too late echoed over and over in her mind.

'If I know Aunt Havilah and Gilarth and your brother Retza, they won't have given up. They'll keep trying to the end. We'll be there soon enough.' Danel's fingers brushed her arm, his words solid and reassuring.

'If Korak finds a suitable cliff to launch from.'

The Forest Folk were now black silhouettes against the fire-ember glow of the sky, only their silvery-white skins giving off a starry light. Zadeki took a step forward into air and disappeared.

Delvina jumped up, her heart hammering and rushed forward.

Danel caught her arm a tanis from the edge. 'Careful.'

Her hands clenched. Silly. Of course, he was in no danger.

A few moments later, a large sea eagle swooped over the cliff edge, wheeling around Korak, dipping and rising before shifting back to human form and landing beside his father.

'Woohoo!' Zadeki ran a slender hand through his unruly curls and grinned at Delvina. Then his grin faltered and he looked away, uncertain.

Delvina chewed her lip. It was awkward. She still wanted his friendship, even if she needed to wait for more. Was she losing something valuable in holding on to the might-have-beens?

Korak clapped Zadeki on the back. 'This will work well. We can take advantage of the wind.'

Danel rubbed his hands together. 'So we wait until after the sun rises and heats up the air, Highwun?'

'You learn fast, son of courage, and see more than most. But in this case, we should go now while the sea breeze still blows.'

'You'll fly at night?'

'Yes, once I get high enough, I can use the upper winds, though not too high where the air becomes difficult to breath. But I can't stop until we reach the mountains. If we come down sooner, we have to walk or maybe ride or take a barge up the river.'

'We are thankful, sir. For all you have done, for ...' Danel's voice faltered, and he looked at Delvina in a mute plea.

Korak nodded. 'Da-Sestru's name will be woven into the songs of the Kin, her character and deeds not forgotten.'

A cool wind soughed over the ridge and ruffled Delvina's fringe and cloak. They quickly gathered their gear.

Delvina slung her pack over her shoulder. 'Will you head for the Gate or the Cauldron?'

'The Cauldron. It's further, but a landslide wrecked the only suitable launching point at the Gate. Enough talk, let's go.'

Korak threw himself forward, transforming into a great black koraktil; all snout, teeth, wings and tail. The magnificent beast blotted out half the night's stars and Argenti's half-circle. His size and fierce mien still unsettled Delvina, though she knew he was friend not foe. She and Danel fastened the rope harness over Korak's neck and shoulders before scrambling up with the packs.

'Ready?' Korak shook his head and roared. Galloping toward the cliff edge, he hurled himself out over the rocky beach and roaring waves below. Powerful wing strokes and the wind rising over the cliff lifted him into the air. He climbed in lazy spirals and at last headed toward the stars shining in the east against the purple-black sky.

Danel leaned closer, his breath tickling her neck. 'I might be getting used to this. Though it's easier in the dark. The distance to the ground doesn't seem so far.'

'Or the ocean.'

Danel's arms felt good around her waist. A reminder that she was not alone. She glanced at Zadeki's sea-eagle form soaring on the air currents without visible effort. Sadness touched her but it was threaded with joy. Cold wind rushed past, needling her face, and her heart lifted. At last she was going home.

Retza smothered a yawn. After the excitement of the night before, sleep had shied away like a reluctant visitor and came with dark gifts when it did agree to stay. Finding the raiders was priority as much for morale as for the loss of food. Once it became each for their own, they were lost.

Josenif in jaguar form completed a circuit of the loading area, snuffling over the confusion of bootprints in the dust. Havilah spoke in hushed tones to Nebam and Barekia, with Gilarth and Wuben standing behind them.

Retza ignored his throbbing knee and shins. That wild urchin Tosa hadn't held back her kicks. He should be mad, yet he remembered too well the deep, unquenchable ache in the days, rosters and solars following the death of their parents. Then Da-baba had died and it was only he and Delvina against the uncaring realm. Whatever else changed, they had each other

Nebam broke away from the leadwuns' huddle and strode toward Josenif. 'So, can you tell who the thieves are yet?'

The jaguar's tail flicked from side to side. He bounded past the Secundwun to Havilah and shifted into his lanky human form.

'It's the same as the storerooms. Hard to tell the difference between the thieves, the workers and the couple of tens of watchers that have traipsed all through here. If you'd called me in last night before you tramped over everything, I might have had some hope.'

Gilarth grimaced. 'Noted for next time.'

Nebam walked back toward them tugging at his scrappy beard. 'There better not be a next time. We need to make a severe example to deter others doing the same. The ones you caught—'

Retza's heartbeat quickened. 'They're youngwuns, orphaned from the strife.'

Gilarth agreed. 'The youngest hasn't lost all his milk teeth yet, misguided maybe—'

'They're all we've got in hand. Ration thieves are as bad as any murderer and should be dropped down a deep shaft.'

Gilarth's frame seemed to expand. 'Meanwhile the leaders of the rebellion sit in the holding cells being fed—'

'My brother, you mean? Yeah, well maybe you're right, but what about you? You worked for the old Overseer ... or those Old Guard survivors—.'

'Nebam! Gilarth! Calm down.' Havilah gripped Nebam's shoulder and glared at Gilarth. 'Have these youngwuns said anything yet?'

Gilarth looked away for a moment. 'My apologies, your Honour. They claim they didn't see the raiders, but Darin is hiding something.'

'How much food was taken?'

'We're still tallying it up.'

Nebam blew out his cheeks. 'Far too much.'

'And progress on the Gate?'

'Too slow. We're almost ready to fire the Amethyst Gate. The Lapis Lazuli Gate is next. Who knows what wonderful treats it holds? Any word on finding Uzza?'

'No. The Temples were our best bet.' Havilah pushed a loose strand of hair behind her ear, her eyes haunted. 'Losing so much food changes things. I'll call a meeting with the leadwuns.' She turned to Josenif. 'I'd appreciate speaking with the Kinleader first.'

Josenif pulled his wrap-around sarum tighter. 'I'll fetch the Kinleader. She's not far from the caverns.'

'Let me know as soon as you get back.' Havilah attempted a smile. 'Gilarth, find these raiders. More to the point, find the stolen stores.'

'I've a good idea where to start looking.'

'Then see to it. And Watcher Retza, I want Lady Zara to attend the meeting.'

'Yes, your Honour.' Retza jumped at the mention of his name, and jumped again when Josenif leapt into the air, shifted into eagle form and flew off towards the tunnels that led to the Cauldron.

Retza headed back to the duty rooms. Now would be a good time for Delvina to return with answers or Uzza to be discovered with the seal. Things couldn't get much bleaker.

Zara paused on the threshold of the meeting room, not sure why she was now included in the rebels' deliberations. Lead Hands and the section headwuns crammed the room and the air was thick with the smell of sweat-soaked felt, rock-dust and fear. In the centre of the podium, Havilah sat on a raised chair, her hands gripping the armrests. Secundwun Nebam stood beside her, legs astride and hands hooked into his belt. Next to him, a young woman with Greenstone South insignia held the long speaker's staff. On the other side Kinleader Telsima and three other shapeshifters towered heads and shoulders above everyone else present, their silvery-white skin picking up a faint luminescence from the glimmer lights. Only the Head Watcher, Gilarth, came close to matching them in height. Hand on his truncheon, Gilarth's iron-grey eyes skimmed the room.

'Lady Zara coming through.'

Retza shouldered his way through the crowd and guided her to a spot to one side of the podium. The tens of eyes watched her progress, some curious or confused, others hostile. Zara looked away and smoothed down the embroidered dress she hadn't worn for days. Maybe she should have declined Havilah's invitation. If it was an invitation and not a command.

The young Speaker stepped forward and thumped down the pole on the stone floor. 'Overseer Havilah speaks.'

Eyes turned to the Overseer. The hum of conversation faded away to a soft shuffling of feet and an occasional cough.

Havilah stood up, her care-worn face solemn. 'Lead Hands and Section Heads, thank you for coming. Despite averting disaster again and again, our realm faces a dire situation, one with few remedies. Difficult decisions confront us.'

'Is it true we've run out of food? That the Commissary has been raided?' a leadwun with a long blue-dyed beard called out.

A murmur ran through the room, some obviously unaware of the news.

Havilah held up a hand, waiting for silence. 'As you say Zirmon. We have enough at quarter rations for a day or two, but no more.'

Shocked silence descended on the room. Zara's chest tightened. She'd no idea things were this bad.

An older man with a mossy beard jumped up and waved his arms. 'The potato harvest is at least two rosters away. And almost as long for the reseeded mushrooms and algae farms. You've eaten everything else. You cannot expect to live on air and good wishes.'

Havilah lifted her chin, her face frozen into a forced calm. 'Yes, thank you, Farm Lead Gregan. The Tamrin's supply train is due to arrive outside our Gate at the King's Road even now. They have enough food to feed us until the harvests. But unless we open the Gate, we cannot reach it.'

Another shouted, 'What about the silverskins? Can they fly the food to us?'

'That's a good question. Kinleader, would you explain?'

'Gladly, daughter of the mountain. The koraktil shifters can fly into the area, not out. the terrain does not allow them to take off. Certainly not loaded down with supplies.'

The leadwuns glanced at each other, some nudging and whispering, others with blank stares.

'And what of the Gate?'

Nebam stepped forward. 'With Lady Zara's help,' he gave a small bow in her direction, 'we have managed to get through the first of the seven gates and are close to conquering the second. At this rate it will be over several ten-days before we reach the final gate.'

'So on the best scenarios, we'll be without food for at least that long?' Lead Hand Zimon said, one hand with a death grip on his beard.

Havilah nodded. 'Unless we can dig up some potatoes now, to carry us by, Gregan?'

'Your Honour, the tubers haven't formed yet and the leaves and flowers are poisonous.'

Someone called out from the back, a woman. 'We've been on reduced rations for over three rosters. Many of our oldwuns and littlewuns are already weak and close to dying.'

'Then maybe we should let them die and reserve what food we have for those who can survive,' shouted someone lurking in the far corner.

'Aye, and evict these Old Guard survivors and the other freeloaders in the holding cells,' another shouted.

'With less mouths to feed, more could survive,' the lurker said.

A hubbub erupted. Leadwuns jumped to their feet, some agreeing and some objecting to the proposal. Her baba wouldn't have allowed such insubordination. No wonder things were a mess.

'Quiet!' Nebam bellowed.

The Speaker slammed down her staff. Bang, bang, bang.

A stifled silence brooded in the room and inky shadows seemed to creep in the corners, dimming the glimmer lights.

Havilah's amethyst eyes blazed as she scanned the crowd. 'We will not sacrifice some to save others. We will not give up. We will find answers.'

'Yeah, and how long will you keep your worthless rebel son in the holding cells? He killed my brother,' the lurker said.

'Or her?' A balding leadwun with Ferrous South insignia pointed his bony finger straight at Zara.

All eyes turned to her and she shrank back into her chair. Retza stepped in front, as though to shield her, hand tight on his truncheon.

Havilah held up her hands. 'When we survive this crisis, which we will,' there was iron in Havilah's voice and stance, 'Putarn and the others will have to account for their wrongdoing. As for Lady Zara, you and I would be dead now if she hadn't revived the Crystal Heart, and without her, progress on the Gate would take many times longer. She has earned a place in this room.'

Zara's heart fluttered. A reward then, but one she'd be happy to forgo with all the hostile stares like loaded springs aimed her way.

Havilah stood like a bulwark. 'Kinleader Telsima has a proposal, I suggest you listen. And when she's finished, I'll be asking for your help to do the best by our people.'

All eyes turned to the shapeshifters' leader, Telsima, and Zara let out a breath, a bit dizzy from holding it in.

'You are afraid, and fear brings foolishness in its wake.' The Kinleader's grey-green eyes scanned the room, picking out the dissenting leadwuns. She held up an eagle's feather and let it twirl in the ventilation currents. 'You are out of time, dwellers of the deep. If you remain huddled here separated from the world you face starvation. We can lead you down the mountain to where the food awaits you.'

Zara's mouth gaped open. Leave the caverns? How could they? The caverns were their life, and besides, the Gate was still shut fast against them.

A rustle ran through the room, and the fragile calm seemed to fray.

'How could we survive such a trek? The sun burns our flesh, blinds our eyes. Where would we live? How could our littlewuns walk so far?' The woman at the back wrung her hands, eyes large.

'It would be difficult.' Zara jumped as Retza spoke. 'But my sister and I survived two ten-days trekking across the mountains.'

'I do not say it would be easy, children of the deep, or even safe.' The Kinleader's voice softened. 'We too had to leave to find a new home in the Wide Lands. These two koraktil shifters can take your younglings and elders and as many as possible on their backs to where the supplies await you. The rest, will need to trek down the mountain.'

'But we can't get out. The gate is shut and the walls of the Cauldron are too high,' the Copper Clan Lead Hand said.

Havilah spread out her hands. 'I've already sent toolwuns to erect ladders and add ropes. It can be done. If there was any other way, I would not ask this of you. Leadwuns, you must set the tone for our people, choose those in most need to be flown out, then prepare for the journey.'

'Why can't they bring the food to us?' someone else asked.

Nebam grimaced. 'A few Tamrin have agreed to risk themselves or their beasts on the treacherous mountain trail to meet us partway. Their lives are not at stake, ours are.'

A wail came from the back of the cavern. 'We are doomed.'

'This is what comes from defying the Dark Ones,' someone whispered near Zara, though all she could see was the watchers guarding the podium. Once she would have agreed. Now she wondered at the price the Dark Ones claimed.

So many spoke at once, it became hard to hear their words. The Speaker thumped the staff until it might shatter, but no one was listening.

'Be quiet,' Telsima roared, the volume of her voice hard to believe from her slight frame. 'Let your leader speak.'

Havilah lifted her hands. 'Over a hundred years of feeding the blood of innocents to the Dark Ones did not restore the Glimmer Heart. It is because of Uzza's ignorance and that of his father that we are in this dire situation.'

Telsima spread out her arms, seeming to encompass them all. 'Dwellers beneath the mountain, do not despair. By the Maker's favour, there is always hope, even in the darkest places.'

Havilah looked around the room, fire in her eyes. 'Leadwuns, can I count on you? I need you to stand with me.'

Eyes darted around the room and feet shuffled.

'Come on, come on,' Retza muttered under his breath.

The young Speaker bowed toward Havilah, her young face determined. 'Greenstone South supports you, Overseer.'

'Thank you, Karel, Secondwun of Greenstone South.'

The blue-bearded Leadwun stood and fingered the hammer hooked in his belt. 'Zirmon of Diamond North is with you.'

'Ferros of Pyrite Crew,' another with a red-plaited beard added.

Soon the room was full of affirmations.

Zara felt chill bumps mantle her neck and shoulders. The new Overseer and the Kinleader had won them over. Not through threats and truncheons, but by persuasion and good will.

'I thank you.' Havilah allowed a smile to spread over her face. 'Take this message to the crews and sections. Stay strong and we will prevail.'

Nebam stepped forward. 'Quartermaster Narval will ensure that your people are provisioned with ropes, blankets and other necessities for the journey. Now go prepare your people and be ready when the call comes.'

Zara waited on the podium as the leadwuns filed out of the room. Havilah approached her, a genuine smile on a face grey with tiredness. 'Zara, my thanks for joining us. This is a bitter pill to swallow, and many will find it hard to accept. I need your help with the Old Guard survivors. As Uzza's daughter they would listen to you.'

'They may prefer to stay here.'

'We're not forcing anyone to go, Zara. Is that what you want, for you and Jesson? To stay?'

One of the attending watchers brought them flasks of water.

Havilah nodded. 'My thanks, Watcher Manoah.'

Zara took one and gulped it down, her mouth dry as an ash pit. Leaving would mean giving up any hope of finding Baba and the members of her family who may have survived. Her throat tightened at the thought of her matu's death. She blinked back the tears, inadvertently catching Retza's pale grey eyes. Her shoulders eased at the sight of his honest face and she made a decision.

'We'll come with you, Overseer Havilah.'

Zadeki spread his flight feathers, fingering the wind currents above the steep-sided ravine. Baba's huge shadow glided over the terrain, blotting out the sunlight that bounced off red rocks and shimmered over the rippled waters of the fast-running stream. Sharp peaks, wreathed in clouds and topped with snow, rose in serried ranks behind the eastern ridge.

Zadeki dipped lower over the clumped spear grasses and rocky ground. Here and there, stone blocks butted against each other, forming a broken trail beside the river.

'Is that the King's Way?'

Baba nodded his great koraktil head. 'The King's Gate stands some twenty lek to the south of here.'

'Can we check to see if the yarma train has arrived at the Gate?' Danel yelled against the whistling wind.

'My regrets, son of courage. Landing would be difficult and the take off in koraktil form near impossible. You and Delvina would need to walk the rest of the way.'

'It's not that far. We could at least fly over and see if the Gate is open,' Delvina yelled.

'Not far, maybe. But the Cauldron is beyond those high mountain ridges and we've been flying for a night and a day now,' his baba's voice rumbled. 'From where I'm flying, every extra lek counts.'

'As you say, Highwun.' Delvina dropped her eyes, disappointment evident in her posture.

What his baba said was true.

'I could check it out,' Zadeki keened. If he found the Gate open it could save them time and he would like to see Delvina smile again.

He felt the gentle probe of Baba's thoughts. 'You are not too weary?'

'No, Baba.' He waggled his wings. 'If I need to rest, I can perch on your back in eagle form, once I catch you up again.'

'Be safe.'

Zadeki peeled off and headed south, following the ravine. The broken road running beside the fast-flowing river showed signs of recent travel with both yarma and human prints in the softer ground, along with the ash of old campfires and discarded food scraps. He banked as the river took a sharp bend and skimmed over a mass of white water swirling through jumbled rocks.

The sharp smell of dung and wet wool carried on the air currents and a strange whistling bleating overlapped the whine of the wind and gurgling roar of the river. On the near side of the river, a few hundred yarmas milled around in pens made from rough branches. Tamrin wrapped in colourful cloaks kept watch.

Zadeki's feathers ruffled with unease. The sun was still high in the sky. The yarma train should be winding its way to the Gate, not camped for the night.

Another sharp bend, and the river backed up, foaming and swirling over the broken road. A raw scar ripped into the eastern shoulder of the mountain. Boulders and broken trees sprawled in a tangled mess down the cliff face, half burying the ravine. A small trickle of water seeped through the piled debris and ran down into the stream on the other side. Copper-skinned Tamrin were clearing the rubble. They stopped and stared as he flew over.

Zadeki climbed higher in the sky. Past the landslide, the road hugged the ravine before zigzagging up the slope towards a small fold in the mountainside. A bridge crossed the trickle of water in the riverbed and led to a flat river terrace.

Vertical cliffs surrounded the area, casting it in shadow. Bits of masonry and broken beams spilled down the left side of the precipice. The debris displayed more weathered edges and some plant regrowth, indicating the older landslide Josenif had mentioned in his earlier report.

Whatever platform may have existed before was now shattered beyond repair. There was no suitable place for a koraktil to take off, barely enough space for such a great beast to land.

At the end of the road, two gigantic cracked statues of toolwuns holding lift-bars and pickaxes stood guard, and between them, a huge red gate carved into the sheer mountainside. A gate that remained firmly shut.

'Youngest son of Korak,' a voice keened on the wind. An eagle flew towards him from the east.

Zadeki banked to meet her. 'Greetings, Umbria Pathfinder.'

'What news from the Lonely Isles?'

'Mostly chaos and disaster. This doesn't look much better.' Zadeki followed the pathfinder's lead and alighted on the closest statue's head and folded his wings. 'How will the yarmas get past the landslide?'

'The Tamrin are clearing the path.' Umbria ran a hooked beak through her flight feathers. 'This landslide is extensive. It will make the trail between here and the Cauldron more difficult to access.'

And dangerous. Zadeki pushed down the heaviness in his gizzard. 'And the Gate?'

'Darane have made some progress. Where is Telsima's eldest daughter?'

Zadeki half-opened his wings and looked away. 'She has entered the Maker's undying song.'

'May she be at peace.' Umbria's neck feathers ruffled. 'And the others?'

'Flying to the Cauldron. I should join them now.' Though he'd rather not be the bearer of such disheartening news. What more could go wrong that hadn't already?

'Before you go. I was about to report this latest landslide to the Kinleader. Can you take this news to her?'

'As you wish.' They touched beaks before leaping into the wind.

'Fare you well, son of the Korak and Shama. May the Maker go with you.'

Retza stood on the threshold of the meeting room, balancing the laden tray. Havilah, Gilarth, Quartermaster Narval, Farm Lead Gregan, Kinleader Telsima, Nebam and some other leadwuns clustered around the meeting room table looking at lists, deep in discussion of logistics, priorities, people. The Forest Folk had left earlier to help facilitate a way out of the Cauldron.

Zara sat listening on the edge of the group. Her shoulders rounded and head drooped, understandable after such a long, weary day.

The gong for the third shift sounded and the glimmer lights dimmed, casting denser shadows about the room. Retza placed a steaming beaker on the table in front of Zara. 'You should drink, Lady Zara.'

'What is it?'

'A herbal broth. Not food exactly, but it fills the stomach for a while.'

Zara gave him a tentative smile and sipped the hot liquid. 'Thanks. It will be a big day tomorrow.'

Retza nodded. He passed the beakers around to leadwuns, watcher Natan stepping in to help him.

Once finished, he returned to stand by Zara. 'How did your meeting with the Old Guard survivors fare?' he asked.

'It took some persuading, but they saw the need. They are in a worse state than most and with Elim and the others in the holding cells, they have none to lead them.'

With a puff of air, Gilarth pushed aside the piled-up charts. 'That's the best we can do tonight. You should get some sleep, your Honour.'

Havilah sighed. 'Very well. Tomorrow we focus on evacuating the littlewuns and making sure the crews are prepared for the journey by second shift. I'll see you all here at first gong.'

Retza's stomach squirmed at the memory of the trek across the mountain; the burning sunlight, the ice and snow and precipitous pathways. He and Delvina had barely survived their trek. Ironic that he'd not gone with Delvina in part because of his determination to avoid repeating that experience. And now, all the crews had to attempt a longer one in their weakened state.

Gregan, Narval and the other leadwuns emptied their beakers and shuffled past, eyes looking down in sober thought. The door closed behind them.

'I should get back to Jesson. Get him ready for the journey.' Zara put down the beaker and stood.

Manoah saluted. 'Levim and I will escort you, Lady Zara.'

Retza glanced at Overseer Havilah, in muted conversation with Gilarth and Nebam. 'I will take her.'

'No need. We are still on duty, Watcher Retza.'

Retza gave Manoah a dubious look. 'We're all on duty at the moment.'

Zara touched Retza's shoulder, her eyes shadowed. 'You're dead on your feet. Go get some rest. I'll see you at first shift.'

Before he could protest, she marched out of the room with Manoah and Levim in tow. Retza pushed away the feeling of unease. He was tired. Manoah wasn't keen on the Old Guard, but he was a watcher first and foremost.

'Hey Retza,' Gilarth's big voice boomed out. 'If you're headed to the watcher crib, you can stop by the duty room and tell Secondwun Timon to prepare the prisoners for the journey.'

Retza sighed. 'Yes, sir.' First trywuns' serving duty and now back to being a messenger. But what he'd said to Manoah was right. Given the situation, they all needed to pitch in and do what was needed.

He headed out the door and into the corridor. Manoah and Levim disappeared around the corner in the opposite direction.

As Retza approached the archway that led beyond the Overseer's quarters, a low rumbling noise grew in volume. At first, it sounded like the ravine waterfall, perhaps swollen with rains from outside, but the volume increased to a low roar. Now, he could make out the rhythm of words and bootsteps in the tumult.

Not good, not good at all. Retza's stomach soured on the thin broth. Flattening against the wall, he peered into the long, broad hallway outside the Grand Cavern.

Down the far end, an angry crowd of toolwuns and crewless, even some Old Guard, rushed up the public stairs from the Great Causeway, poured out into the hallway and jostled against the archway leading to the watchers' rooms. They were heading in this direction. He had to warn Gilarth and Havilah.

Retza sprinted back to the meeting room and pushed past the watchers at the door. 'There's a mob on the concourse outside the Grand Cavern. Coming this way.'

Gilarth jumped up from where he was talking to Havilah. 'How many?'

'Hard to tell, but at least five tens.'

'Wuban and Nate, lock the door and keep the Overseer safe. The rest of you with me.'

Overseer Havilah stood. 'No, Gilarth, let me speak to them.'

'I don't like it, your Honour.'

Nebam pulled his beard. 'Maybe, the Head Watcher is right, Matu.'

Already, the clamour of the crowd swelled in the corridors outside the door.

'Not answering their concerns will only inflame the situation. Gilarth's watchers will protect me.'

'Then stand back at least.' Gilarth directed Retza and the other watchers to form a cordon in front of the Overseer. Once satisfied, he gave a nod to the watchers at the door. 'Crack it open.'

A roar of voices tumbled into the room.

'Death to the traitors.'

'Evict the Old Guard.'

'Putarn should die.'

'Why should Uzza's brats eat while we starve?'

The crowd surged forward, pushing against Retza and the watchers at the door. Retza's knee twinged as he planted his feet and pushed back.

He recognised faces that had rallied with Javot against Havilah. Now they were calling for Putarn's blood where once they'd supported him. Fear did that to people, clouded their thinking. A pity the Forest Folk were in the Cauldron. Josenif's powerful presence would be useful about now.

'Be silent!' Gilarth bellowed. 'Is this any way to approach the Overseer.'

'She won't listen to us lowwuns.'

'Well, she is listening to you now. Choose a speaker and present your grievances with proper respect.'

The crowd gaped at each other, suddenly uncertain.

A greybeard yelled. 'If Overseers can be toppled, why should we listen to her?'

Gilarth's neck corded. He used his greater height and width to be heard. 'Because without Havilah, your youngwuns would be thrown in the pit for the Dark Ones to feed on. Without Havilah, the Crystal Heart would still be broken. Without Havilah cave rats would already be gnawing on your mouldy bones. Without Havilah, those sadwuns—Uzza, Putarn and Javot—would have buried you in death and darkness.'

One of the Old Guard survivors pushed forward. 'What does that matter, if we die now. They say the food has been stolen and there is no more to eat.'

'We say the guilty should be punished,' a flame-haired woman shouted from the back.

'They should be dropped down a shaft.'

'Let the Dark Ones decide their fate.'

'I said, listen,' Gilarth roared.

An uneasy silence fell over the crowd.

'My people,' Havilah's voice rang clear. 'How will such revengeful actions bring us food? And who among us is without guilt? Tell me, which one of you stood up against the Old Guard's sacrifices of our youngwuns? By our silence, we all allowed them to take more and more power.'

'We were afraid. Uzza killed all who opposed him,' the grey-beard said.

'Yet, the twins and the young shapeshifter Zadeki didn't allow fear to stop them. When this crisis is over, the guilty will be dealt with. But what must concern us now is survival. Have not your leadwuns told you? Food awaits us at the bottom of the mountain. The Forest Folk have offered to fly our littlewuns and oldwuns there. The rest of us will walk.'

The flame-haired woman looked confused. 'We are crewless. We have no crib.'

She had a point. The crewless often missed out or were ignored. 'Maybe they could form their own crew,' Retza said under his breath.

Havilah looked at him askance, then nodded. 'Yes, why not? You,' she pointed at the woman, 'What is your name?'

'Lazra, your Honour.'

'Good, Lazra is now leadwun of this new crew. Choose a second and then come back and discuss with me the needs for your group. At first shift, you will be given necessities for the journey.'

'Yes, your Honour.' Lazra dipped her head.

'Someone's coming,' the greybeard called out.

A clatter of boots boomed down the corridor. Secundwun Timon, followed by a handful of watchers, pushed their way through the crowded corridor. His hair was disarrayed, his cheek dripping blood.

The protesters backed away, giving the watchers distance.

'Head Watcher.'

Gilarth held up a hand. 'A minute, Timon.' He turned to the crowd. 'You heard the Overseer. Disperse now, and send back your lead and secondwun with your concerns.'

Lazra glanced at Timon, then beckoned the others to follow. After some moments, the others drifted after her. Retza relaxed. At least one crisis had been averted for now.

Once the last one disappeared, Gilarth let out a gusty sigh. ' So you're here, Timon. What took you so long?'

'Some of that lot mobbed the watcher duty room. They had weapons and pinned us down for a while. They took over the holding cells and escaped through a back entrance.'

Havilah ran a trembling hand over her face. 'Did they harm any of the prisoners?'

'They released the Old Guard prisoners and some of the other rabble. We've rounded most of them up. Er ... the only two missing are Putarn and the former speaker Elim.'

'Perhaps the protest was a diversion.' Havilah blinked and touched her throat. 'We need to find them before ...'

'Or an opportunity.' Gilarth asked. 'Did you recognise any of them, Timon?'

'Yeah, that trouble-maker Fenna and some of his lot. And a few Old Guard survivors.'

'Not Darin?' Retza said. It could be hard to disentangle from the wrong company.

Secondwun Timon shook his head. 'No, nor his sibs.'

'I'm glad to hear it,' Gilarth said, his voice gruff. 'Given the lengths I went to persuade Secundwun Karel to take that troublesome threesome on as trywuns.' He scowled at Retza. 'Remind you of someone?'

'Not me and Delvina. We weren't into stealing stuff.'

'Humph. Couple of mischief-makers if ever I saw any.'

Retza's mouth dropped open. Secondwun Timon and Havilah looked bemused. Only Nebam nodded his head in agreement.

A laugh rumbled up and Retza gripped the table edge. After a moment Gilarth slapped him on the shoulder and joined in. Not that the joke was all that funny, yet sometimes you had to laugh to keep your sanity.

'Right,' Gilarth said, wiping his eyes. 'I want six guarding the Overseer at all times, the rest come with me to check the duty room and to track down these miscreants. We'll find them, your Honour.'

A thought flashed into Retza's mind and his blood curdled. 'What about Zara?'

Gilarth whipped around, eyes narrowed. 'Didn't she leave before the mob got here?'

'Manoah and Levim took her back to her rooms.'

Gilarth nodded, relieved. 'She should be alright then. Though if the attack is targeted ...' His bushy eyebrows contracted. 'Watcher Retza, better go check on her, to be safe.'

Retza didn't need a second urging. He saluted Havilah and Gilarth and took off down the corridor at a jog.

Zara placed her pen beside her journal and shook fine sand over the wet ink. She should be sleeping, but her mind buzzed with possibilities. The night seemed sharp-edged and full of strange noises—the distant slap of boots in the tunnels, the rumble of voices, a sudden outcry. Though surely she was imagining it. Havilah had calmed the fears of the leadwuns, won them over by her calm resolve. Zara fingered the embossing on her journal, remembering her own decision to commit to the rebels' plans. She still grieved the loss of her family, her matu and baba and siblings, but at last she'd let go of the past and somehow felt lighter.

An unbidden smile stole across her face. Half-closing her eyes, she could see Retza standing strong and stalwart, his serious eyes clear like water, the white-gold fuzz on his strong chin. No matter how uncertain the future, she felt safe when he walked beside her. She touched her lips, remembering the kiss. Maybe, she could make a new life with him outside the caverns.

The sound of hurried footsteps in the corridor sliced through her thoughts.

'Who goes there?' Watcher Manoah's voice came from outside.

Jesson rolled over and mumbled in his sleep.

A pause then another voice, she couldn't quite place, murmured a response.

She stood, her shoulders tensing. It wasn't time for the change of shift and too early to begin the days' duties. Could it be a messenger with bad news?

The door flung open with a bang against the wall. Two hooded figures stepped into the room, followed by Manoah and the other watcher, Levim.

Jesson sat up and rubbed his sleep-filled eyes, his white-gold hair awry.

'What do you want?' Zara gripped the chairback for support.

The stooped hooded figure turned to the watchers. 'Wait outside. Warn us if anyone comes.'

The voice was of an older man, one that niggled at her memory. 'Who are you?'

'Zara, have you forgotten me?' He pulled back his hood. His face had changed, now ravaged and framed by stringy grey hair, but there was no mistaking him.

'Uncle Elim!' Tears sprang to her eyes. She ran forward and took his hands. 'Did Havilah release you?'

'Come, child. I must take you and your brother to your father.'

'You know where he is?' Baba was alive! This changed everything. Yet all she could think about was what would happen to Retza, Havilah and the others.

Elim smiled benignly. 'Get your things now. We need to hurry.'

Zara frowned. 'Have you told Havilah where he is?'

'No,' the older man paused, his cool gaze assessing her. 'We will speak with her later, Zara, but for now speed is important.'

Did Havilah know Elim had come to her? But surely, Manoah and Levim wouldn't have allowed them in otherwise. And if Baba was alive and had the seal, he could open the Gate and the dangerous journey across the mountains would be averted. She could speak on the rebels' behalf. Surely, there would be no harm in finding out. Even so, the spider dance in her stomach didn't settle.

'Up and dressed, Jesson. Do you want to bring your diggers?' She grabbed her clothes and journal and shoved them in a bag.

Her brother clutched the covers, his eyes like glimmer lamps. 'I don't want to come.'

'Don't be afraid.' She knelt beside him. 'We'll see, Ma—' she swallowed hard, '... Baba. You remember, Uncle Elim don't you?'

Jesson wriggled back against the wall. 'I'm not going with him.' He pointed at the silent still-hooded figure standing behind Elim.

The hidden man stirred. 'No need to fear me.'

Chill bumps crawled over Zara's arms. Putarn!

It was Putarn who'd wanted to sacrifice Jesson to the Dark Ones. Putarn who would have slit her throat without thought or regret, Putarn who almost killed Delvina. The scene in the Heart Room felt as real as if it was happening there and then.

She stepped back, her whole body shaking. 'What ... what is he doing here? Get him away from us!'

'It's alright. He can be trusted, Zara.' Elim extended spatulate hands. 'Your father has need of him.'

'How can that be? He tried to kill us.'

Putarn lowered the hood, his mauve eyes not leaving her face. His voice nub flicked up and down. 'Forgive me, Lady Zara. I was wrong. I see that now.'

Acid burned her throat. 'No, no, no. Uncle Elim, you must tell him to go or we are not coming.'

'Wait.' Putarn knelt at Zara's feet. 'Lady, forgive me. I ... was mistaken.' Tears glistened on his hollowed cheeks.

'And why should I believe you?'

'Your father spoke to me in my dreams. It's important that you and Jesson go to him.' He lifted his head. His amethyst eyes, so like his matu's, pierced her. 'You too have the dreams. I have seen you in them.' He held a slither of a dark crystal that gleamed a pulsing purple.

Zara's skin went clammy, her heart squeezed tight.

She clutched the throbbing pendant around her neck. It was as though she were transported to a dark chamber and the dream-image of Baba stood beckoning her. 'Follow my messenger, my little light.'

Why would Baba speak to this mad toolwun, a rebel appointed secundwun? She stood welded to the stone floor, all her newfound certainties crashing down around her.

Elim's face convulsed. 'We don't have time for this. Get up, Putarn. And you, Zara, will come with us, willing or not. Guards.'

The two watchers and another slipped into the room, truncheons ready.

'Grab the littlewun. The girl will follow.'

No.' Jesson backed away. Manoah lunged for him. Jesson ducked between the burly watcher's legs and dashed for the door.

'Leave him alone!' Zara screamed.

'Catch him.' The other two thugs advanced, arms wide.

Zara grabbed her half-filled bag and threw it at them. Her things scattered in a wide arc and clattered across the floor.

Jesson slipped past, avoiding Uncle Elim's clumsy lunge. Zara rushed out the door after her brother.

Someone grabbed her hair, yanking her back. 'Stay with me, girl.'

Uncle Elim pushed her toward Manoah who captured her arms in a crushing grip.

'You two idiots, get after the boy,' Elim roared.

The clatter of running boots echoed from far down the corridor.

The one not dressed as a watcher hesitated, 'Someone is coming, Highwun.'

Could it be Gilarth or Retza? Zara stamped down on Manoah's shins. He yelped and lifted her over his shoulder.

'Get the brat.' Putarn stood and brushed the knees of his breeches. 'We'll be trapped here if we don't hurry.'

Elim frowned. 'No time. At least we've got the girl. Just don't lose her too.'

Putarn's eyes narrowed, then he shrugged. 'As you wish.'

Zara pummelled Manoah's back. 'Let me go.'

'Not likely.'

'Help, help!' she yelled.

'This way.' Putarn said. He replaced his hood and led them toward the maze of small storerooms in the other direction from the bootsteps.

'Come on.' Elim hustled them forward.

Zara's face bounced on Manoah's back as he ran, his arms like iron bands around one elbow and the back of her knees. She choked on his rank sweat and unwashed jerkin. At least Jesson had escaped. She knew Havilah would not harm him, but her skin prickled at the thought of the cost to others, Elim and Baba's plans would require.

Retza jogged down the corridor towards Zara's room, urged on by the unsettling conviction that she was in trouble. What if the rioters blamed the Overseer's children as well as the Old Guard for their troubles? Easily winded after so long on meagre rations, he took great lungfuls of air. When he neared the rooms set aside for Zara and Jesson, he slowed his pace and loosened his truncheon, senses alert for trouble.

The murmur of conversation echoed down the corridor. The voices rose and fell, just on the edge of discerning words. Then, as clear as a shift change, 'Help, help.'

His skin crawled. Zara's voice. She was in danger. He sprinted down the corridor, turning the corner. Something small and low hurtled into him. Retza staggered back a few steps, catching his balance, and grabbed the youngwun.

It was Jesson, still in his sleeping shirt, hair sticking out like a bird's nest, face streaked with tears, and eyes wide and dark with fear.

'Badwuns. They've got Zara,' the youngwun wailed.

'Hush, Jesson. It's going to turn out right.' He crouched and caught the boy's frightened gaze. 'Who has Zara?'

Jesson hiccoughed. 'Badwuns. That Putarn and ... E... Elim. They want to take us to Baba, but I don't want to go.'

Retza frowned. There were only storerooms further down the corridor. They'd have to head this way, sooner or later. 'How many badwuns? Just those two?'

'Jesson shook his head. He held up his small hand with five fingers raised.

Too many to handle on his own, but by the time he fetched help they could have gone anywhere. They could be hurting Zara.

Jesson grabbed Retza's hand and pulled him back the way he'd come. 'We've got to help her.'

'Stop.' Retza pulled him into a side room. 'Listen, Jesson. I'm going to keep them in eyesight. You go get help. Find Gilarth or the Overseer and tell them what's happened. Can you do that?'

The youngwun's eyes were as big as soup bowls. 'But ... I won't know where you've gone.'

Good point. He might need to follow them. He searched an open toolbox, finding a stub of chalk. 'I'll mark the wall with this. You know how to get to Overseer Havilah rooms?'

Jesson chewed his lip. He gave a small nod.

'It's simple. Keep to the wider corridors. Now off you go, as fast as you can, and bring help. For Zara.'

Without another word, Jesson took off down the corridor towards Havilah's ward room.

Retza rocked back on his heels. Taking a deep breath, he stood and ran towards where he'd last heard Zara's cry for help.

Zara stumbled as Uncle Elim hustled her along. He didn't allow her to stop or catch her breath. Manoah and the other two thugs hemmed her in at the back. She fretted about Jesson and was disgusted with how they were treating her. She'd tell Baba for sure. Even most of the rebels treated her better than this.

Putarn led them through the discarded clutter of abandoned storerooms, into shadowed areas unlit by the glimmer lights. The air was thick with dust and cobwebs and forgotten things.

Elim shone a torch over the rooms, glancing often over his shoulder back the way they'd come. 'Do you know where you are going?' he ran his hand over his face. 'All I can see is dead ends.'

'Yes! Now move these crates out of the way.' Putarn pointed to the long rectangular metal boxes stacked crookedly against the wall at the end of the corridor.

'Levim, Fenna, do as the toolwun says,' Elim barked. 'Manoah, keep hold of the girl.'

While the other two hurried forwards, Manoah folded his arms and glared at Zara as though daring her to make a break for it. She felt an itch between her shoulder blades and turned. Putarn stood to the side, one leg jiggling and his mad purple eyes fixed on her. Zara shuddered. What did the rebel Secondwun want? She didn't trust him, however much he might claim to work for Baba. She didn't trust any of them.

With a series of crashes, Levim and Fenna pulled and

shoved the storage crates to one side, revealing a gaping hole in the wall.

'How is that going to help?' Elim asked.

'It's an old goods lift,' Putarn said. 'We can take it down to the farm levels.'

Elim frowned. 'Is that where the Overseer is?'

An evasive look flickered in Putarn's eyes. 'I can't tell you that.'

Elim tapped his foot on the stone floor, glancing between the hole and the corridor. 'If you're leading us astray, Putarn, I'll roast you and eat your organs one by one.'

Zara could almost believe he'd do it. Still, the longer they lingered here, the more chance she'd be rescued. 'It could be a trap.' But didn't she want to find Baba?

'All in,' Elim said, ignoring her.

Manoah pushed Zara onto the rickety platform and the others crowded after them, the smell of sweat and fear rank in the air.

'Levim and Fenna pull the crates back in place, as best you can.'

Once the job was done, Elim yanked the lever. With a shudder, the cage descended into the dark. Zara's heart climbed to her mouth and her stomach followed. The shadowy walls slid past to the whirr of the cables. Her ears popped and the air felt different, more humid and lusher. She had never been lower than the level of the Gate before, never really thought of the many levels that reached down to the roots of the mountain. Why would her father be hiding deep below the living levels? And how could that slagheap, Putarn, know Baba's location? If only she could fly out of this net, that closed tighter around her with each passing level.

A screech, and the cage jolted to a stop. A solid wall covered with red fur and black slime faced them and, in the distance, the steady drip, drip of water and the muted roar of an underground river.

'Fool, this is a dead end,' Elim growled.

'Turn around,' Putarn countered. 'Look the other way.'

Manoah pulled Zara around with the others, his thick fingers none too gentle. A long, dank tunnel stretched out to the left and the right, the glimmer lights further spaced than in the higher levels.

'We could get lost down here,' Elim muttered.

Putarn gave a snorting laugh. 'If you highwuns can't find your way around on the farming levels, how will you cope with the lower levels? Follow me.'

'Why do you trust him, Uncle Elim? He means us harm.'

Elim met her eyes for a moment. 'We have no choice, girl. Come on.'

Manoah pushed Zara down the long tunnel, her feet slipping when she found it hard to keep up the pace. Their bootsteps echoed down the empty spaces. A little further on, the tunnel opened out into a huge cavern filled with dirt and neat rows of green shoots.

'Potatoes.' Fenna rushed forward and pulled up a plant, exposing button-sized lumps clinging to the roots.

Putarn swotted the plant out of the fellow's hand. 'Stop wasting time. Another thirty days before they're edible.' He led them through a maze of caverns and tunnels until they came to a high-vaulted entryway or lobby with lifts on each wall. Putarn brought them to the largest lift. The shaft was an open maw. The muted roar of the waterfall came from the opposite wall. This area must be directly under the hallway outside the Grand Cavern, four levels down.

'Now, what?' Elim asked.

'An empty lift shaft's not much use.' Fenna threw a rock at the cables, sending them swaying and twanging.

'Be quiet, you slug,' Putarn hissed. He moved to the control panel and prised off the cover. 'I can override the controls from here.'

Elim grunted. 'Be quick. This area is too exposed if someone comes.'

Putarn grunted. 'It's going to take as long as it takes. Why don't you eat while you're waiting, instead of grumbling?'

Manoah pulled out some provisions from his pack and divided the dried algae cake up into six and passed it around. He put the water flask to his lips, took a gulp, then gave it to Zara.

The water was sweet and refreshing. She hadn't realised how thirsty she was.

'Just one mouthful.' Elim nudged her and she passed it to him.

A soft scraping noise came from the tunnel entrance.

'What was that?' Elim asked.

Zara's heartbeat quickened, though now all she could hear was her own breathing. Just four levels above, Retza, Havilah and Gilarth might be walking along the concourse, except that it was deep into the third shift. Could it be someone coming to rescue her? Had Jesson gotten help?

'Probably just cave rats.' Manoah swallowed the shredded algae.

Elim hovered over Putarn. 'Have you figured it out yet, Secondwun?'

Putarn pulled a lever and the cables swayed and started to slide downwards, others going up. A large open cage dropped into view. Putarn pulled a switch and the cage slowed to a stop. 'Enough chatter,' he said. 'Pile in.'

This cage was much bigger than the last, it could easily hold a shift-crew of twenty toolwuns. It swayed under Zara's feet and in less than a second the floor fell away at a frightening speed. Faster and faster they rushed into the depths. All this time, Zara had wanted to find Baba, but not like this, pushed around like so much baggage. But if she could find the seal it might be worth it.

Retza ran down the corridors following the tracks left in the dust by Zara's abductors. Every hundred tanis or so, he marked the walls with chalk. Some distance past the room she shared with Jesson, their whispered but heated discussions echoed along the abandoned corridors and he slowed his pace despite his urge to charge at them and rescue Zara. The challenge was to keep enough distance to remain undetected without losing them.

Several moments later, the crash and scrape of heavy objects replaced the whispers and he sped up again, his fingers tingling at the thought of what they might be doing to Zara.

He arrived at the corridor in time to glimpse Fenna pulling a stack of crates behind him. Panting heavily, He shoved and pushed the stack aside to reveal the old abandoned lift. Retza operated the lift controls and noted the time the lift took to return. Ten minutes indicated the Farm levels or maybe the workshop level before it. It didn't seem likely that Uzza could be hiding in levels that in normal times would be teeming with farmwuns and toolwuns.

Rubbing the sweat from his eyes, Retza jumped onto the platform even before it drew level with the floor and sent it downward to the Farm level. He stepped out of the lift and looked around. The scuff of bootprints seemed fresher heading north and their voices a faint echo, so he headed in that direction.

Following the trail of the abductors was harder on the more well frequented, less dusty, farm levels. He lost all trace of them in the interconnecting caverns of the potato farms. They could go anywhere—perhaps hiding in a hidden cavern or even finding an uncollapsed tunnel to one of the other nodes. Defeated, he backtracked, looking for a missed clue.

A sudden twang of the pit lift cables echoed along the corridors. He pulled to a stop. He should've thought of that. The main lifts led to another twenty levels or so, even more places to hide or possible hidden escape routes. Spinning around, he raced through the tunnels, approaching with more caution only as he neared the big lifts. Sweat beading his temples and dampening under his arms, he edged closer, flattened himself against the wall and peered around the corner into the staging area.

The group huddled close to the north lift, sharing a meagre meal while Putarn fiddled with the controls. He moved closer and flinched as his boot sent a rock skittering along the concourse. He ducked back and held his breath.

'What was that?' The voice sounded like the old Speaker, Elim.

'It's just cave rats,' a familiar voice boomed out, some moments later. Retza's heart skipped a beat. Manoah teaming up with Putarn and Elim. The treacherous blackguard. Who else had turned against them?

No bootsteps came his way. He started breathing again.

A quick exchange of more muted conversation was followed by a clank. The whistling whine of the cables set Retza's neck hairs on end. He could hear the scrape of stealthy shuffles as the group moved onto the platform.

He risked another look. Manoah pulled back the safety gate, glimmerlight falling on his face. Elim pushed Zara onto the lift platform and the others piled in after them. Levim had also defected, it seemed.

Retza ran his hands down his breeches. He had to follow them, but how? He couldn't board the lift, couldn't step into the waiting area without exposing himself to discovery. If he launched an attack on them, he might slow them down a little, but with five against one, they'd soon overpower him. Though maybe he could distract them long enough for Zara to escape.

Putarn glanced in Retza's direction, a faint smile on his ravaged face, and pulled the lever. The lift shuddered and the platform moved downward. All he could see was Zara's frightened face, pale as a beacon, sliding down, disappearing into the shaft.

He ran out on the concourse. The cables whizzed past, speeding up as the lift covered more distance. They were going deep. Maybe he could wreck the controls. But what if it caused the lift to career out of control, killing those aboard including Zara?

He smacked his head. Of course, the emergency ladder. He first chalked the stone concourse, 'taken the lift down', then raced to the recess. Bashing open the gate, he gripped the rung at shoulder level. He sucked in air and swung onto the fragile metal construction. Not looking at the abyss beneath his feet, he climbed down one rung at a time. If he fell … but Zara's face and the memory of her sweet lips on his, strengthened his resolve.

The cables whizzed past him, only an arm's length away. He climbed down faster, counting the levels as the passed them. His arms ached and the air grew heavy and stale the deeper he went. Beneath him came the occasional sound of voices, and the soft grumble of the platform's descent grew fainter.

His breathing grew more laboured. His hands burned on the metal rungs. Five, ten, fifteen levels. How far were they going? He had to stop soon, catch his wind. He was lagging behind, he could hardly see them, but still the cables continued moving. He was losing them. Perhaps, this hadn't been such a smart idea. At least he knew that the old Overseer was in the lowest levels. Though by the time he got back to Havilah and Gilarth, they might well have moved on to another lair.

By level eighteen, the walls radiated heat. Sweat rolled down his face and his hair stuck to his forehead. His lungs heaved and his muscles screamed for him to stop. But he had to keep going. He and Delvina had climbed the Cauldron, fingers squeezed into tiny cracks in the rock face. He could do this. Just one foot after the other, shift to the next rung down, move his hands down, and repeat, step one foot down then the other. Keep going–

His hands, slick with sweat, slipped on the grimy rung. He stumbled, lurched to catch metal and was suddenly sliding downward. His back bounced against the protecting loops, agony screamed through him. The rungs, he had to grab the rungs. *Maker help me.* He grabbed wildly, found air. Grabbed again, his fingers brushing metal. He closed his fist and his arm jerked, almost pulling out of its socket. He came to an abrupt stop. Pain lanced through his shoulder as it took his full body weight and he groaned.

He hung from one rung, twisting first to one side, then the other.

Biting down on his lip to stop the scream tearing through his throat, he moved his foot in search of the lower rung, hooked onto it and hugged the ladder. His heart thundered in his ears and his stomach clenched tighter than an overwound winch. How far had he fallen?

The levels only went down to twenty-one below the Great Causeway. No, there had been twenty-two levels etched on Gilarth's copper-foil map. A secret level that no one knew about. Was that where Putarn was leading them?

The lift cables hummed and slowed to a stop.

The kidnappers had reached their level, but which one? His muscles dragged like heavy buckets of stone, his mouth dry. He had to keep going, he couldn't stop now.

He screwed his eyes shut and forced his foot down, one after the other.

Voices echoed back up to him.

'So, we leave the lift at the bottom?'

'No, I'll send it up half way.'

A hum and the cables reversed. Moments later the cage rushed past Retza.

He kept climbing down. He'd go as far as the ladder took him. Hand over hand, one foot down, then the next. In a daze, his foot slammed into the floor. He couldn't go any further. He looked up. Level twenty-one.

Retza collapsed against the wall, his muscles shuddering, and caught one long wheezing breath.

In the pale shine of glimmerlight, multiple fresh footsteps trailed through the thick dust heading off to the right.

Pulling the stub of chalk from his jacket, he scribbled a message on the floor before following the trail. He only hoped Jesson had warned the Overseer. He was a long way from help, and he was on his own.

An icy wind whipped Delvina's hair about her face and into her eyes. The tip of her nose and chin were stiff with cold. She pulled the Tamrin cloak tighter about her and snuggled closer to the sleeping koraktil's furnace-like flank. Curled up beside her, Danel mumbled a few words, before settling back into a restless sleep.

If she'd had a choice, they'd have continued flying through the night. The caverns of her birth were so close she could almost taste them on the wind. Still, she could not deny Korak's need to rest after flying a night and day across the rolling hills that separated the high mountains from the coast. He'd decided not to expend the energy shifting for the sake of a few short hours of sleep. Now his wings folded along his back and his long tail curled around her and Danel, forming a barrier to the dizzying drop beyond the narrow ledge.

The sky lightened in the east, the rim of the sun sliding above the ranks of frosted peaks like a golden topaz in an intricate silver setting. Stars winked from the sky. Hard to believe that her people could be in dire strife beneath such serene beauty.

Danel rubbed the sleep from his eyes and yawned. 'Amazing sight, isn't it?'

'I only hope our journey wasn't for nothing.'

'We sailed across the ocean, survived shipwreck and the machinations of the Vaane. Today we'll walk inside the caverns again. Somehow, I don't think our time will be wasted.'

Danel's hand brushed against hers and Delvina smiled. He was a good man, strong and brave. 'By the Maker's favour,' she said and calm settled inside her like a chick snuggled under its mother's wing.

With a flurry of feathered flight, an eagle swooped down from above and landed on the koraktil's shoulder. The great beast stirred and cracked open a coal-black eye. 'You took your time, youngest son.'

Zadeki fluffed out his feathers and lifted his wings. 'Slept on the wing,' he keened. 'I met up with Pathfinder Umbria.'

Korak shook himself. Delvina and Danel grabbed hold of his fur as they began to slide down his side.

'Watch out,' Danel yelped.

'Sorry little ones. Not a lot of room up here. Grab your things and mount up. You can tell us the news as we fly, youngest son.

Delvina scrambled onto the koraktil's back, Danel following after her.

The great beast pushed up on all fours, and spread out his vast wings in the warming sun.

'Do you need to wait until the thermals, Baba?' Zadeki asked.

Korak swiped his tail, thumping it against the cliff face. 'The drop should be deep enough. Besides, I'm getting hungry enough to eat everything in sight.' He twisted his head around and opened his great mouth, showing a forest of sharp, curved teeth. Smoke wisped from his nostrils.

Delvina shivered. 'You wouldn't eat us, would you?'

Korak let out a great rumbling laugh. 'No, but the longer I stay in this form, the more like a koraktil I think. Ready?'

Before Delvina could reply, Korak launched himself off the cliff. She gripped the koraktil's fur and buried her head between his great shoulder blades. Danel hung on to her waist. They plummeted like a lead weight, the wind whistling past.

Down, down, down they went. One mighty downward thrust of his mighty wings, two, three, and still they fell.

The sour taste of fear crept up her throat. She couldn't breathe. Had Korak misjudged, his koraktil thoughts confusing him? What would it be like to smash into the sharp rocks at the bottom of this ravine? Her vision mottled, and Danel gave a soft whimper.

The sound of the river rose to meet them, the cliff sides rushing by on either side. On the sixth downstroke, they began to rise a little, then a little more.

Now the rocks rushed by in the opposite direction and they shot up into the pink-gold glory of the dawn.

Exhilaration rushed through Delvina. 'Woohoo!'

'And I was beginning to enjoy flying,' Danel moaned behind her.

'It was close,' Zadeki keened. 'But Baba knows what he's doing.'

'Ha,' Korak responded. 'Just got my claws wet. We'll be at the Cauldron before the sun touches the lake. So, what did you learn, son of my heart?'

'Not so good, Baba. A landslide has delayed the yarma train, but they've almost cleared the blockage at ground level. Damage higher up will make access from the Cauldron harder.'

'But is the Gate open?' Delvina asked, her chest tight.

'Secundwun Nebam couldn't salvage the tunnel—and so far, they haven't been able to find the seal or open the Gate.'

This was terrible news. Delvina's stomach heaved, and then a new thought niggled at her. Danel was right, each time an obstacle had seemed impossible to overcome, a way had opened. She put her arms around the koraktil's soft neck and whispered, 'Bikan's sacrifice won't be for nothing'.

The sky flared with reds, and oranges and yellows, before blending into teals and purples and blues. The white-headed mountains rushed by beneath them, blue-gold shadows lengthening as the sun rose higher in the sky. Mount Pelee expanded on the horizon and before she knew it, the rim of the Cauldron glowed beyond it like a golden bowl. Soon the silver mirror of the lake and the dark green of the pines became visible on the Cauldron's floor. On the western rim, toolwuns were working on a contraption abutting the cliff wall.

Before she could see what it was, Korak skimmed over the lake. In the newly cleared areas closer to the entrance, tender leaves of half-grown potato plants rippled in a breeze. Now, the ground rushed toward them and Korak came to a running stop in front of the entrance to the tunnels. He lifted his head and roared. The sound rolled out like thunder and echoed off the sunlit cliffs in the west.

Delvina and Danel slipped off his broad back and removed the harness. Zadeki landed, shifting seamlessly into human form beside them.

'Come, let's find out what's happening in the caverns.' Korak transformed, his face gaunter and wilder than two days ago. 'And doesn't anyone have anything to eat?'

Danel threw him a stale bread loaf from his pack.

'Thank you.' Korak's teeth ripped into the hard bread, demolishing it in seconds. 'Lead on, Thirdwun.' The way he stalked and the sharpness of his teeth retained the shadow of the koraktil.

Delvina ignored her own stirring of hunger and hurried toward the entrance to the caverns, Danel close behind her. Her heart beat a rhythm of anticipation, of fear, of dread. What would they find? Who would be left? Would Retza be there to greet her?

No one spoke as they made their way through the tunnels to the central levels. At last, they emerged into the huge space of the Grand Causeway. Delvina's stomach gripped tighter. The familiar chuckling rush of the river in the central ravine cloaked a deeper silence. Glimmer lights beamed down on the empty concourse, casting dark shadows.

It had to be the start of the first shift, usually the busiest time with duty crews milling about on their way to the lifts and others lining up at the commissary for food rations and supplies. Instead, the thoroughfare was as depleted of life as a mined-out ore seam.

'This isn't right,' Danel said, his eyes crinkling with concern. 'Where is everybody?'

'No dead bodies, like last time at least,' Zadeki said. 'Where should we go? The Great Cavern?'

It was a good call. That was where they usually gathered in times of trouble.

'I need to report back to Havilah,' Danel said.

Delvina nodded. 'She'll be with the people.'

'Let's go then.' Korak strode down the concourse, angling toward the bridge over the ravine.

Delvina ran after him and caught his arm. 'There's a shortcut the messengers take. We could go that way.'

Korak looked down at her, his forest-dark eyes unfathomable. He gave a sharp nod. 'Show the way, daughter of the mountain.'

She led them past the food and clothing outlets, most still boarded over with the crisis. It felt surreal, to be home again after so long away, to get used to the dim light and the closed-in feel of stone walls. The stores, which once looked fine to her, now looked serviceable and clunky. The musty odours of damp rock and lichens tickled her nostrils. An abandoned pallet lay against a wall. Surely everything wouldn't have fallen apart so quickly? There would be some food left, some sense of order, some survivors.

The outline of the archway to the restricted flight of stairs emerged from beyond the sprawling commissary.

'What's that sound?' Zadeki asked.

'What?' Delvina strained to listen. A barely audible sniffling came from behind them. Chill bumps dimpled her skin. Whatever it was, it didn't sound like cave rats.

'It's a youngling.' Korak said.

'Back this way.' Zadeki turned and loped back towards a shadowed laneway.

Delvina eased the weight of her pack. What would a youngwun be doing in here, alone and abandoned?

'What if it's a trap?' Danel said from behind her.

'Then they will have caught more than they bargained for,' Korak said, amusement tinging his voice.

The dark lane opened up into a service area to one of the outlets, with metal crates and pallets stacked against the wall. The sniffling stopped.

Zadeki stood still, tilting his head. His eyes lit up.

'Behind those crates.' He ran forward and pushed them to one side. 'Here he is.'

A small boy crouched against the wall, thin arms wrapped around his legs, tear tracks running through grimy cheeks. Delvina's eyes widened at the sight of the fine facial features and white gold hair.

'Jesson!'

The boy looked up. Eyes darkened with fear slowly turned to wonder. 'Zadeki!' He shouted and launched himself at the abovegrounder, hugging his knees. 'Delvina!' he added, his face splitting into a grin. Then a shadow slipped over his face. 'They took Zara. You've got to help her.'

'Who did, child?' Korak slipped past Delvina and touched Jesson's narrow shoulders.

Jesson's face crumpled and his chest heaved. 'The badwuns. The badwuns took her from our room.'

'Which badwuns?'

'Uncle Elim and ... the madwun with the purple eyes. I tried to find the Overseer, like Retza told me. I got lost.' Jesson hiccoughed and scrubbed his eyes.

Retza was alive then. Delvina sucked in a breath, put a hand to her chest. But the madwun with the purple eyes? Did Jesson mean Putarn? Why would Putarn be working with Elim, the old Speaker? Was the boy confused?

'Elim?' Danel rubbed his beard. 'The Old Guard survived? He wouldn't hurt Lady Zara, surely?'

'They want to hurt Zara,' Jesson wailed. 'You have to save her. Help Retza too.'

'How long ago was this?' Korak asked.

Jesson's face scrunched up. 'I don't know.'

Zadeki stood still, staring into the shadows. 'The trail will get colder, the longer we delay. Jesson, can you show us where they took her?'

The boy shook his head, his bright eyes clouding with

confusion. 'We were sleeping in our new room in the storage area.'

'That's okay, I can follow the scent trail.'

Danel cleared his throat, his expression torn. 'We should report to Havilah.'

'I'll come with you, Thirdwun.' Korak bent down and scooped Jesson up. 'Don't do anything rash, youngest son.'

'I'll go with Zadeki,' Delvina said. It wasn't just Zara, but her twin in imminent danger.

Zara could feel the weight of the mountain pressing down on her like a pile of rocks. The glimmer lights seemed weaker here and inky dark shadows gathered in the corners of the cavern. With a soft clank and hum of the cables, the lift slid back up to the higher levels. Despite the oppressive heat, a shiver ran down her spine.

'So, where is the Overseer?' Elim's intense gaze flitted from the roughhewn walls, to the dust encrusted stone floors, to the discarded machinery and rubble in one corner.

Rather than answering, Putarn moved away from the lift and headed to the right.

'Putarn?' Elim's face wobbled and doubt seeped into his posture.

The former Secondwun kept going. Anger, then fear, then resignation flitted across Elim's gaunt face. After a moment he gestured the others to follow. Zara needed no urging to keep close. The last thing she wanted was to be lost and alone down here.

Putarn stopped at the back corner of an alcove that looked like another dead end. After a short search, he knelt, grabbed a metal ring recessed into the floor and pulled. Whatever it was didn't budge.

'Help me lift the cover.'

Manoah sauntered over and pulled. His arm muscles bulged and his neck corded, but again the cover didn't move. 'Is it locked?'

'No.' Putarn frowned. 'It's rusted. We need a lift-bar or something like it.' Striding over to the machinery, he prised out a long rusted pole. 'Here, use this.'

'What's down there?' Elim asked. Then his skin took a greyish tinge. 'The forbidden twenty-second level.' He glared at Putarn, his eyebrow bristling. 'You fool, don't you know what's down there? Would you reawaken the shadows?'

Putarn's lips flattened. 'I remember well enough, Speaker, but you said you wanted to find Uzza. Not scared, are you?'

Elim huffed and his eyes strayed back to the lift. Zara's skin crawled. Was Baba really down here or was Putarn leading them all into some kind of snare?

Scrape. Clang. Crash. Manoah applied the makeshift lift-bar and the trapdoor smashed open.

Putarn smiled like a bat swallowing a plump moth. 'This is where the answers lie.' A look of confusion flashed through his eyes and then the mad certainty returned. 'Come with us, Speaker, or go crawling back to my matu, it makes no difference to me. Zara and one other are all he requires.'

'Down here?' Manoah shone his torch on a ladder disappearing into the shadows.

Zara edged backwards, her heart turned to ice. There was something in Putarn's voice and manner that triggered the warning gong in her mind. And the further down she went, the harder it would be to escape.

Elim grabbed her arm and pulled her forward. 'Come, Zara my dear.'

She planted her feet on the stone floor. 'No!'

Putarn snagged her other arm. 'Come, Lady Zara. Your father is anxious to see you again.'

'I ... I need to rest.'

'Soon. It's easier to climb the ladder if you turn backwards.'

Putarn helped her down, his hands gentle, his skin icy cold.

At the bottom of the second ladder, they rested. Elim handed around the water bottle and some algae cake shavings.

A scraping noise came from above them. More cave rats. Zara squeezed her eyes shut and swallowed the few strands of dry algae Elim passed to her.

She didn't like it down here and the closer they came to meeting Baba, the more doubts clouded her mind. Would he be angry that she hadn't brought Jesson with her? Would he demand a sacrifice to the Dark Ones as he had before? He said sacrifices had to be made for the good of the realm, but why was it always someone else who paid the price? Delvina, Retza, Havilah, that strange shapeshifter Zadeki, and even Gilarth were all prepared to put their own lives in danger for others. But Baba would have a reason, surely. Her shoulders slumped and her eyelids fluttered shut with the desire to forget it all in sleep.

Another scraping noise, this time much closer. She jerked her head up, suddenly alert. Dust drifted down from the square hole above.

Elim brushed his hands off and jumped up. 'That's too big to be a cave rat.'

'Depends on the rat,' Putarn said with a knowing smile.

Elim opened his mouth and then closed it as Putarn put his finger to his lips and gestured for Fenna and Levim to hide behind the ladder.

'Let's keep going,' Putarn hefted up his pack.

Zara's heart thudded a beat and her fingers tingled. Who would have followed them and how? He was setting a trap, whoever they were. She opened her mouth to give warning.

Elim grabbed her from behind, pressing his hand over her mouth. 'Be quiet, girl,' he hissed in her ear, and he gave her arm a warning squeeze. Manoah took her other arm, the smell of stale sweat overpowering.

They pulled her down the tunnel after Putarn, but two thugs stayed behind. Stealthy boots scraped on the metal rungs of the ladder. She bit down hard on Elim's bony hand and screamed a warning. Too late. The sound of a scuffle erupted from behind them.

Manoah let go of her and rushed back with Putarn to the trapdoor.

Elim slapped her face. 'Blasted she-bat, you'll spoil everything.'

So much for the kind-uncle routine.

Fenna and Levim were trying to subdue another figure in the shadows, far too big to be Jesson and in watcher bat-leather besides. He was putting up a good fight, dodging and wielding both truncheon and whip, keeping his attackers busy.

'Manoah, what are you doing with these scoundrels?' he asked between breaths.

A wave of cold drenched through Zara. It was Retza. Now they were closer, she could see his face, pale hair sticking out beneath his helmet, eyes narrowed in concentration.

Please, please don't let them hurt him. She twisted against Elim's surprisingly strong grip and he whacked her on the ear. The room swirled and she staggered.

Manoah hawked and spat. 'Havilah can't save us. The Old Overseer is our only help now.' He lifted the abandoned metal bar and lunged forward, closing in from the other side.

'You're wrong.' Retza ducked behind the ladder to put distance between him and the relentless blows. Now there were four of them, tightening a circle around him. He dodged, spun, thrust and kicked. But as soon as he avoided the blows of one, the other three moved closer until Fenna came up behind and grabbed his arms. Manoah smashed the flat of the bar against Retza's chest and he doubled up with a grunt of pain. Fenna kicked behind his knees, and Retza fell to the floor. Soon three of them pinned him down.

Tears sprung to Zara's eyes. Please, don't let them hurt him.

Putarn rubbed his hands, long fingers interweaving. 'Tie him up and bring him here.'

Elim drew a long knife from his belt and put the point under Retza's chin. 'Are you alone, scum?'

Retza's bloodied lips tightened. His eyes flicked from Elim to Putarn to Zara. 'Secondwun, why are you helping the Overseer?'

Putarn gestured to Manoah. 'Take one of the others, go check if anyone else is in the level above.'

Manoah hesitated, then nodded. 'Come on, Fenna.' They both disappeared up the ladder.

Elim gave Retza a shake. 'Tell us. Who else knows you are here?'

'You don't think I'm mad enough to come on my own, do you?'

Putarn laughed. 'Yes, you and that crazy sister— though she's left you behind, hasn't she?'

'She's gone to get help from the Vaane.'

'Right, but there's none coming. We're on our own with the shadows. And there is no one here to help you.' Putarn's mouth twisted into a smile. The sooner you accept it, the better it will be for you.'

Manoah bellowed down the hatch. 'No one up here, boss.'

'Are you sure?' A shadow passed over Elim's face. 'Good. We need to keep going. Better get rid of the excess baggage.' He grabbed Retza's hair and yanked his head back.

'No,' Zara shouted. 'No, no, no' echoed down the tunnel and bounced back. She met the former Speaker's icy stare. She had to persuade him somehow. 'I mean, we … we might need him, Uncle Elim.'

'I can't see how.'

'Besides, a body leaves a messy trail.'

Putarn caught Elim's arm. 'The girl makes some good points. Let the Overseer Uzza decide what to do with him.'

Elim shook off Putarn's grip, then shrugged. 'If he tries to escape, we'll shove his corpse in the first crevice we find. Does that meet your approval, Lady Zara?'

Zara's fingernails dug into her palms. She smiled. 'Perfectly, Uncle.'

Her heart hitched at the look of betrayal in Retza's grey eyes, but whatever happened, whatever it cost her, she had to ensure these madmen didn't kill him. She could no longer imagine a future without Retza.

Danel took the last stair and stepped into the hallway outside the Grand Cavern. Korak followed with Jesson snug in his arms. Before Danel had taken three steps, six watchers in bat-leather surrounded them. All of them were little more than skin and bones.

'Why are you here?' Timon demanded, then with the look of recognition, he scratched his balding scalp, 'Oh, sorry Thirdwun Danel, Highwun Korak, I didn't realise you were back'. His gaze lingered on Danel's face, no doubt taking in his burn scars, though he was too well trained to comment.

Suddenly self-conscious, Danel resisted the urge to rub his mangled eyelid. 'Where is everyone?'

'In their cribs preparing for the trek across the mountains. We leave at the start of second shift.' Timon nodded at the tear-stained Jesson asleep in Korak's arms. 'You should take the littlewun to the Grand Cavern to be flown out.'

Havilah was evacuating the Caverns. Then it was worse than he'd imagined.

'So, where is the Overseer?'

'She's with Gilarth in the holding cells. I'll take you to her.'

Danel raised an eyebrow at the destination. 'Lead the way.'

Crossing the length of the concourse, they ducked through the archway and headed up the stairs to the watcher's duty room. On seeing Secondwun Timon, the two watchers at the door allowed them to pass through without challenge.

The duty room was a mess, with furniture smashed and overturned, maps and cylinders scattered in piles on the floor. The young scrybe from Lapis East crib bandaged an injured watcher. Others sported bruises or cuts. Danel's pulse quickened. Was it the unrest that precipitated Havilah's decision to leave?

'What happened here, son of stone?' Korak asked.

'A rabble attacked the Overseer's quarters after a meeting of the leadwuns. Overseer Havilah calmed them down, but part of the group diverted here and released the Old Guard prisoners.'

Danel shook his head. 'Old Guard? I thought them dead.'

'Gilarth discovered a remnant hiding in the northern node. We've recaptured most of the prisoners, but the old Speaker is still missing.'

'Including Putarn?'

'Yes. How did you know?'

'Young Jesson here said that both Elim and Putarn attacked Lady Zara.'

This made the littlewun's story more credible, though no more explicable. A frisson of worry unsettled Danel. He hoped Delvina and Zadeki wouldn't find themselves in more trouble than they could handle. Both were inclined to rush into danger if they thought someone needed help. Though Zadeki was a formidable opponent and would do all he could to protect Delvina. Danel sighed and rubbed the itching skin around his eye.

'This way,' Timon indicated the stairs down to the holding cells.

In the first cell at the bottom of the stairs, Head Watcher Gilarth and Overseer Havilah stood in front of a kneeling figure. Two other watchers and Secondwun Nebam stood behind him.

'I don't know why he went with them.' Danel knew that nasal voice, like metal scratching a rock wall. So Javot, Putarn's second in crime in their costly attempt to overthrow Havilah, had been left behind. 'He kept talking wild stuff, like the Overseer was alive where the shadows lie.'

'Maybe they took Putarn as hostage,' Gilarth said. 'To use as leverage against you.'

'We have to get him back,' Nebam said.

Havilah rubbed red-rimmed eyes. 'Yes. Though the evacuation must take priority.'

'He's your son, Matu.'

'I know that, Nebam.'

Secondwun Timon cleared his throat. 'Your Honour, Thirdwun Danel is here.'

Nebam looked up, startled, and both Havilah and Gilarth swung around to stare at him.

Havilah hurried forward and threw her arms around him. 'It is good to see you, sister's son. We were beginning to wonder if you'd return, it's so long since we've heard word.'

Embarrassed, Danel patted her back. 'We ran into ... complications, Ma-Sestru.'

She pulled back and her mouth flattened into line. 'So I see. Are you hurt?'

'Mostly healed.' He shrugged and looked away. Scars of honour, Zadeki called them.

Havilah glanced at Javot. 'We should talk somewhere more private.'

'Yes, come to my ready room.' Gilarth threw a key at Timon. 'Secondwun see if Javot knows anything further.'

They trooped up the stairs and into Gilarth's room.

'What news from the Lonely Isles? Did you find some way to overcome the seal and open the Gate?' Nebam demanded even before the door was fully shut.

Danel's cheeks flushed and he stared at the stone floor, polished by countless boots over the ages. 'There is a way to bypass the seal, but the Grand Technician refused to divulge it before he died and now the Lonely Isles are in chaos.'

Havilah's shoulders drooped. 'Our food stores were raided. Our only option is to evacuate.'

Gilarth peered behind Danel and Korak. 'Retza will be happy to see Delvina. Where is she and the rest of your party?' His bushy eyebrows shot up. 'Is that Jesson you're holding?'

Korak placed Jesson on the ground. 'Yes, son of rock. We found him hiding in the Great Causeway. He claims Putarn and Elim took Zara and that Retza followed them. Zadeki and Delvina search for them.'

Nebam shook his head. 'That's madness. Putarn wouldn't work with the old Overseer's minions. Not after what Uzza did to our father.'

'And who would have said he'd rebel against your mother? But he did.' Gilarth folded his arms.

With a weary look, Havilah held up her hands as though used to mediating between the two. 'Why is not important now. My eldest son's actions are no longer those of a sane man. Jesson, how long ago was this? Where were they going?'

Tears leaked down Jesson's translucent cheeks. 'Badwun said he'd take Zara to Baba.'

Gilarth shook his head. His iron-grey eyes narrowed. 'I sent Retza to check on Zara at the beginning of third shift. It's now …' he rubbed a hand over his face.

'First shift.' Danel said.

'After sunrise,' Korak said at the same time.

Havilah's face hardened and she sighed. 'This is indeed worrisome, but the evacuation must take priority.'

Danel's gut wrenched. He couldn't have heard right. Surely, Havilah wouldn't abandon Retza and even Zara to Putarn's whims. Delvina would never leave her twin behind, and he couldn't imagine leaving without her.

She turned to Korak as though the subject was ended. 'We need your koraktil shifting skills to help transport the more fragile wuns.'

'In time, but I've flown a long way and it will be a few days before I take on the koraktil form again. Is the Kinleader nearby?'

'She's in the Cauldron.'

Danel blurted out, 'Let me look at least.'

Gilarth met his eyes for a second, then took a step forward. 'Your Honour, if these fugitives can lead us to Uzza we might be able to find the seal and open the Gate.'

'We've been down this tunnel before, Gilarth. Putarn,' her voice hitched, 'my son is not rational. Nor, from your reports, is Elim. They may believe they know where the Overseer is, but we might still come up with a bucket of air. The journey across the mountains is a perilous feat we've never faced before. Each day, each hour we delay, more of our people will die. I need you all.'

'But we can't just abandon them,' Danel said, bunching his hands against his side.

Gilarth didn't budge. 'Havilah. We … I … can't abandon Zara, or Retza. Look, we're not planning on moving out until an hour or two into second shift, when the sun begins losing its heat. The trek will need to go at the slowest person. We can catch up if need be, even if we walk through the day.'

Havilah's face shuttered. She looked from one person to the next, stopping at Jesson's wide-eyed, tear-stained face. 'Very well, you have until the start of first shift tomorrow. No more.'

Danel closed his eyes. It had to be enough.

'Move it.'

Manoah jerked the rope and Retza stumbled forward, just managing to get his feet under him before sprawling on the floor. His head throbbed and sharp, breath-stopping pains shot through his chest at the slightest movement. And his injured knee was getting in on the act.

Smart move getting caught when no one knew where he was. Caught, in fact, on this secret twenty-second level he'd only ever seen marked on Gilarth's map. He glanced at Zara walking straight-shouldered, her eyes fixed ahead and her sweet mouth in a firm line. Had the kiss been a lie? She'd almost said as much. His chest felt as hollow and emptied out as his belly. What a fool to believe Uzza's daughter could love him.

Maybe, just maybe he could salvage something out of this, if Putarn was really leading them to Uzza. If he could steal the seal and escape, bring it back to Havilah, then they just might be able to open the Gate. He frowned. But would Zara also be needed to open the panel and would she be willing to help now that she'd found her father again?

Elim put a bony hand against the tunnel wall, and caught a ragged breath. 'How much further?'

'Here's the entrance now.' Putarn pointed with his chin to a dull shape in the grimed stone walls past piles of cleared rubble. A thick metal door stood ajar, twisted out of shape and its titanium-steel surface marred with scorch marks and small gouges.

Levim gave the door a shove, but it wouldn't open any further, even when Fenna and Manoah joined in. Instead, the party squeezed through the gap.

'That's built to keep something out.' Manoah grunted as he squeezed his bulk through, pulling Retza after him.

'Or in,' Putarn's face split into a mad smile, his mauve eyes glittering. Then a look of hollow grief distorted his face. He caught Retza's eye. 'This is where they died. My father and the others.'

Retza shivered at the tone in the Secondwun's voice.

More wreckage was cleared to the sides, the support beams with warped temporary struts assisting them. The roof and walls showed signs of makeshift repairs. The place held the faint taint of decay and despair.

Sudden realisation hit Retza like a rockfall. 'My parents died here? This is the cave-in?'

Zara made a small noise, her blue eyes widened with emotion. 'Oh, how terrible.' She frowned. 'Why have you brought us here?'

Elim shuffled his feet. 'This better not be a trick.'

But Putarn paid them no mind. 'No, slug, your mother died here. Your father died in the temporary crib. But it was the shadows.' His eyes swept around. 'And your great heroes—Havilah, Gilarth. They did nothing to help. They just stood by and watched them die.'

Anger boiled through Retza. 'How can you know that,' he yelled. 'You're making it up.' This couldn't be the place. His parents weren't murdered. They saved the lives of others in a cave-in.

'I saw it with my own eyes. Rather ironic that Uzza chose this place as his lair, isn't it?'

And with that he turned and strode down the dark corridor.

'He's mad. It's pure madness to follow him,' Zara whispered. 'Uncle Elim, let's turn back.'

Elim hesitated then threw his arms up in the dank air. 'We have no choice. Get a move on, you lot. Keep your eyes sharp. And you,' he smacked Retza's ear, 'keep up.'

Chills ran down his spine and black splotches mantled his vision. What fate lay at the end of this tunnel? He had a sinking feeling that this little expedition would not turn out well; not for him, or Putarn or even for Zara, whatever she believed.

The corridor stretched out in a straight line that went on forever. The further Zara walked, the more she doubted the wisdom of coming with Uncle Elim to find her father. Not that they had given her a choice. A spiderweb of cracks and divots mantled the rough stone walls. Some areas were more heavily damaged and propped up by newer struts. At least the damage wasn't as extensive as around the door.

'Must have been a massive explosion,' Manoah muttered. 'Is it safe?'

Putarn shrugged and kept walking.

Zara stole a glance over her shoulder at Retza. Blood trickled from the cut above his eyebrow into a bruised eye. He favoured his left side as though nursing damaged ribs and he was limping again. She wanted to help him but that might draw attention to him. What would Baba do with him? Zara took a sharp breath and half-choked on the thick, hot air. The thought of Retza dying left her tight and breathless, the day's events weighing her down.

Sometime later, Zara stumbled into Elim's back.

'Watch it, girl,' he growled.

The others shuffled to a stop behind her. In front, Putarn stared at a door flush with the wall.

'So this is where Uzza is?' Elim asked.

'Hush.' Putarn's pale eyebrows furrowed. He tilted his head as though listening. With a sharp nod, he hammered the metal surface. The door swung open. He and Elim stepped inside and Manoah pushed Zara forward into a long narrow room.

Half-emptied crates were stacked against the front wall. A rotting felt curtain screened off part of the room to the right. A small food preparation area sat beyond it and then another door in the back wall. A maze of cracks spread across the side wall on the left.

'Overseer,' Putarn called out. His hand hovered at the gap in the decrepit curtains on the side.

The door at the end burst open, and a robed man stepped into the room. Despite his wide chest, his arms were bone-thin and his face hollowed out.

'Best leave the dead undisturbed.' The voice was hoarse and throaty.

Putarn turned, eyes wide. 'As you wish, your Honour,'

'Overseer Uzza,' Elim said.

Shocked, Zara realised that this stranger was her father. No longer ample to overflowing, he was stick thin and what little was left of his once thick hair was white. Baba, alive and standing in the same room she was, despite what everyone had said. She should be overjoyed, excited, but she felt nothing but a growing apprehension.

'You have done well, Putarn,' Baba said. 'Elim, sister's

partner, good to see you. Who else do we have here?' Baba turned slowly examining each of them in turn, quickly dismissing the other watchers, eyes lingering on Retza then settling on her.

His eyes crinkled. 'Nomi, my child. Is not your brother Jesson with you?'

Zara swallowed hard. Nomi was her older sister. Tears blurred her vision as she briefly wondered what had become of her. 'Baba, sir. It's Zara. Jesson ran away and there wasn't time to go after him. Are you alone?'

'No, never alone.' He waved a hand and his gaze wandered back to Retza. 'And who is this?'

'An over-brave, foolish, disloyal watcher,' Elim said with a shrug. 'I would dispose of him, though your new servant seems keen to keep him.'

Putarn folded his arms, bony elbows sticking out. 'That's Retza, son of Zalell and Holima, of the Greenstone South Crew.' Putarn stopped. 'But that means little to you, Overseer. His parents died with the rest of the crew in the search for the dark crystals. It was him and his twin sister who incited Havilah to rebel. Havilah thinks highly of him. So, I think, does your daughter.'

Baba's eyes flickered. 'Well then, better keep him close. Zara, attend to his wounds. Putarn, Elim come with me into the ready room. You,' he pointed to Fenna. 'Prepare a broth, and you other two louts can watch outside the door.'

Baba re-entered the far room, with Elim and Putarn close behind and the door shut with a solid clunk. She'd been dismissed.

Zara stood with arms by her side. She didn't know what she'd expected, but it wasn't this—to be shooed away like a small child, while the adults discussed matters of importance.

With his heightened jaguar senses, Zadeki found Jesson's meandering trail easy enough to follow despite the confusion of older footprints and lingering scents. Delvina tagged behind, not interrupting his focus and not questioning whenever he backtracked or set off at a sharp angle. The boy had taken a rather circuitous route, often retracing his steps or resting in hidden nooks, no doubt distressed at the taking of his sister and losing his way in the maze of tunnels. Even so, it didn't take long to find where Jesson's trail crossed Retza's stronger scent.

Zadeki sat back on his haunches to orient himself and match their route with his limited knowledge of the caverns. This wasn't an area he'd been in before.

'Are we at the back of the messengers' cribs, Del?'

She screwed up her light grey eyes in focused thought, face like a pale moon in blue-white glimmerlight. 'Yeah, I'd say so, though I thought Zara was in the Heart Room. This area doesn't get much use anymore.'

There was a wistfulness to the feel of her thoughts. Zadeki's tail twitched and he resisted the urge to groom his ears. He hated knowing he'd hurt her, but at least they were talking again.

'Perhaps Havilah moved them to their own rooms?' He put nose to ground, tasting the air and sensing the space with his whiskers.

The tunnels here had the faint odour of neglect, yet there were multiple footprint trails that suggested more frequent use over recent days, and it was harder to tease out separate scents. His friend Retza's signature was easy to recognise, though. At least one other scent was familiar and not one he'd soon forget—Havilah's eldest son, Putarn. His fur ruffled on the back of his neck and his tail lashed at the memory of the former secondwun's previous betrayal.

Retza's trail came from the direction of Havilah's new quarters and the messengers' cribs and led off to the quieter, more neglected areas. Retza's tracks was straight and purposeful, a steady jog, and overlaid with Jesson's more tentative footprints going the other way. Further down, both had paused for a while, perhaps talking together. Beyond this point, Jesson's stride was longer, more urgent as though running. Retza's footprints also showed a sudden increase in length. Putarn's scent lingered underneath both, along with a couple of others less familiar. Yes, this was definitely the direction to explore.

His lip curled back and a low growl rumbled in his chest. 'Jesson was right about Putarn. I fear Zara is in danger.'

'Then let's find them.' Delvina's face was set in determined lines, her hands curled in fists.

Bunching his leg muscles, he bounded down the corridor, following the trail to an open door. Inside was a table, a couple of stools, and bowls. The adjoining rooms contained sleeping mats and a small ablutions area. A book and other personal effects were scattered on the floor. Zara and Jesson's scents were strong here, as though they'd spent many days in this place. There were signs of a struggle, that Zara had not gone willingly.

Zadeki moved out of the door and down the other end of the corridor, where the trail in the dust was heavy with the passage of multiple feet.

'This way,' he called.

A solitary glimmer-light caught a chalk mark on the wall. He paused to investigate, then froze at the whisper of sound in the corridors they'd just left behind. 'Someone's coming.'

'Trouble?' Delvina asked.

Zadeki tilted his head, his ears forward. He noted the

rhythm of his baba's loping stride first, then Gilarth's heavy tread, followed by Danel's lighter step and that of two others, watchers most likely.

He sat back. 'Friends.'

Moments later, the party came around the corner and skidded to a stop.

Gilarth's shaggy eyebrows shot upwards. 'How did you get here?'

'Zadeki traced Jesson's trail back to here. Is the littlewun safe?' Delvina asked.

'Yes, he's in Scrybe Barekia's care. What of his story about Zara being abducted?'

Baba crouched, his eyes following the patterns on the floor. 'That's the story written in the dust.'

'And chalk,' Zadeki said. 'They went down that way.'

Gilarth pushed at his helmet. 'It's just storerooms back there.'

'Yet that's the direction the arrow points.' Danel hunkered down and traced his finger along the chalk mark. 'Maybe, we're in luck and we can corner them.'

'Humph, maybe Thirdwun Danel, but they've had several hours' head start. Let's get moving,' Gilarth said.

Zadeki needed no further urging. With a flick of his tail, he twisted around and followed the trail. The others hurried after him.

After several left and right turns, he came to a roomy corridor ending in a blank wall.

'This doesn't look right,' Gilarth growled. 'Maybe they backtracked.'

Frustration welled up inside Zadeki. There hadn't been any side trails. They couldn't just disappear. 'What about the chalk marks?'

'Here's an arrow. It's pointing downwards.' Delvina pushed aside a stack of crates at an angle to the wall. 'Hey, is this a lift?'

Danel hurried to her side. 'Yeah, looks like a small goods lift.'

'How far would they go?' Baba asked.

'Probably as far as the farm caverns, though it could also stop at any of the three levels in between.' Danel's eyes lingered a moment on Delvina's troubled face before he turned towards Gilarth and Baba.

Gilarth tapped his thigh. 'Depends on where they're headed. The Cauldron and the Gate seem unlikely options. Let's take the lift to the farm levels first, then work our way up if need be.'

'A worthy plan, son of rock,' Baba said.

Delvina nodded once. 'Let's go.'

They crammed into the lift. Danel pulled the lever and the cage plummeted down past solid rock and tunnel openings. Even before it came to a complete halt, Zadeki bounded off into the tunnel. It took only seconds to pick up the trail again and the chalk mark led the way through the intersecting caverns of potato fields and tunnels, only occasionally backtracking. After half a lek, a familiar tunnel opened out into a lobby-like space.

Delvina caught up with him, breath whistling, the others panting behind her. Baba came last, guarding the rear.

Zadeki's fur ruffled. 'More lifts.'

A chalk mark pointed to the lift in the north wall with the words 'taken the lift down' hastily scrawled on the floor.

'How many levels does this one access?' Baba asked.

Danel leaned forward, hands on knees. 'Too many.'

'Eighteen levels below this one,' Gilarth shook his head, 'and they might stop at any of them.'

'We need to check every one?' Sudden exhaustion settled into every crevice and cranny of Zadeki's being. He was already running on nerves and hope.

Danel walked to the controls and pulled the lever. The cables tugged and juddered, but did not move. 'It's not working.' He ran his hand over the console. 'Someone has jimmied it.'

'Blast it.' Delvina scuffed the floor with her boots. 'Every minute we delay puts Zara and Retza in greater danger.'

Danel rested his hand on Delvina's shoulder for a fleeting moment, 'We'll do everything we can to save them, Messenger Delvina.' His ash-grey eyes softened with a tender look, framed by the pull of the scar tissue on the left side of his face. 'I might be able to fix the lift controls.'

Zadeki's long whiskers quivered, a new thought stirring. Did Danel care for Delvina in a special way? His fur ruffled with territorial jaguar senses. He wasn't sure if he liked that idea. Yet, was it really fair on Delvina when he wasn't ready to pursue a future together? Not yet, at least, with a wide world out there ready to explore and experience.

'We've got until the start of first shift,' Gilarth's tone was grim. 'Havilah's right, she can't delay the evacuation for a handful of people, however precious.'

Delvina spun around to face the big watcher. 'I'm not leaving without Retza.'

Zadeki wasn't about to leave his friend in danger either. 'I'll check every level if I have to.' Though it had been his refusal to follow commands that had resulted in Bikan's death, this was different.

'By which time, they may be long gone.' Gilarth sighed. 'But we have to try. I couldn't face Jesson, or myself, if we don't save his sister.'

Baba placed a hand on Zadeki's head. 'Peace. There may be other ways to tackle this puzzle in the time allotted. There's little point in us all collapsing with exhaustion. Let's take a brief rest and think through our options while Speaker Danel looks at the controls.'

'Sounds fair.' Gilarth shrugged out of his watcher jacket. 'I can help Danel.' He beckoned to one of the watchers. 'Report our progress to the Overseer and then come back here.'

Zadeki sprawled out, belly along the floor, the toils of the long flight and little rest with two shape changes, hitting him like a landslide. Hunger roared through him and his energy reserves were too meagre to waste on an unnecessary shapeshift. He could only hope Retza would appear to report on the location of the fugitives.

Retza slumped against the wall, his head throbbing with exhaustion and unanswered questions. The former Overseer, a mere shadow of his old bulky self, disappeared into the ready room with Elim and Putarn. Zara hovered in the centre of the room, her blue-eyed gaze flitting around dim musty fittings.

Retza turned his head away and closed his eyes. Could it be true that his parents died here, cruelly murdered and not in an accidental cave-in as he'd been told? Had Havilah and Gilarth misled him? But then how far could he trust Putarn? The pretentious toolwun was mad, and even when he'd been sane, he'd been nasty. Ready to make his and Delvina's start as Greenstone South trywuns a misery. Ready to sacrifice Jesson to restart the Crystal Heart. Ready to kill Delvina to make his plans a reality. An unseen hand gripped Retza's heart and squeezed tight.

Somehow, he had to survive this and find her again. Now Zara had turned on him, his sister was all he had left to fight for. Zara seemed a willing part of her father's plans. Had he been a fool to think Uzza's daughter cared? His mouth twisted and he tasted bile. Right, a lowwun like him.

'Retza, drink this.'

Retza pulled away from the gentle touch on his shoulder. The soft rustle of a dress and a hint of sweet caramel twisted his heart like crumpled wire.

Zara settled down beside him. 'Retza, please, let me check your injuries. This cut looks deep.'

Her hands were soft and cool as she rolled up his sleeve and dabbed at his arm. He could almost imagine concern in her voice and touch.

'Ow.' A stinging pain lanced through him and his eyes flew open.

'Sorry.' Her nose was wrinkled in concentration. Purple shadows circled her eyes. 'Is Jesson safe?' she whispered, her sweet lips a hair's width from his ear.

'I sent him to find Havilah,' he said, before remembering her betrayal. Though her words had saved his life. Perhaps she did care. And whether she did or not, he cared about her. He lifted his chin and met her lapis-blue eyes. 'Why are you following Uzza?'

'Maybe Baba will make things right.' Small lines crinkled between her golden eyebrows, as though she found her own words hard to believe.

He suppressed a sigh. 'This isn't going to end well. Not for me, Zara, probably not you. Not for anyone.'

He grimaced and shifted so his ribs didn't ache so much. At least, with so few followers and this far down, Uzza couldn't do too much harm to Havilah and the others.

Doubt flickered across her face like a sputtering candle. 'I ... I can ask him about the seal and the Gate.' She glanced at Fenna, muttering as he threw things in a pot bubbling on the hob, then lowered her voice even further. 'I won't let anyone hurt you. Now, hold still while I bind your wounds.'

She leaned closer and dabbed his scalp with a moistened cloth. Retza's heartrate sped up and his cheeks warmed at the memory of their kiss. Despite everything that had happened since, he ached to take her in his arms and feel her soft lips on his chafed ones. No matter how deluded she might be, he knew with a certainty he loved her. Somehow, he needed to protect her from herself and those she trusted most.

Before he knew what he intended, he leaned forward and pressed his split lips to hers. She froze like a frightened rock-rabbit, then she returned the kiss with a hunger that took his breath away. His blood roared in his ears.

A door banged open. Zara pulled back and scrambled to her feet. Retza sucked in a sharp, agonising breath and cradled his ribs.

Uzza stood framed by the ready-room door, Putarn lurking behind him.

'I would suggest you not get too attached, my dear,' Uzza drawled. 'Though in the circumstances, it might make things easier.'

A chill slipped down Retza's back at the undercurrents in Uzza's voice. Make what easier?

Zara twisted her hands in front of her. 'I was ... attending to his hurts, Baba.'

'So I saw.'

She took a big breath. 'Baba, I need to talk to you about something important.'

'Later, my dear. We've no more time to waste. We're moving out.' He flicked Fenna's ears. 'Leave that mess and secure the prisoner. And you, Secondwun Putarn, son of Havilah, lead on.'

Zara's mouth gaped as her father brushed past her, with Putarn and Elim at his heels. Only when Fenna hauled Retza up and pulled him along after Uzza, did she follow.

Retza swallowed a feeling of unease. He was about to find out what the old Overseer's plans were, plans likely to bring destruction and sorrow rather than salvation from their food crisis.

Delvina paced the length of the lift lobby, too tense and unsettled to rest. She could feel time slipping like ash through her fingers. At one end, Zadeki lay sprawled out in jaguar form, with Korak asleep against his flank. Danel fiddled with the wires and cogs inside the lift control panel, while Gilarth handed him tools from the metal box between them.

The sensible part of her mind could see the need for delay, but that didn't make it any easier to accept. Why hadn't Retza returned with the information about the kidnappers' whereabouts hours ago? Though with the lift not working, he was probably stuck somewhere down there as surely as they were stuck up here. They'd been chasing mirages and shadows for days and seemed further from answers than before. Delvina kicked a loose stone, sending it skittering across the floor and down a secondary shaft.

'Looks like the circuits have been rerouted and the floor relays rigged so the lift can only go down from this point,' Danel grumbled.

Gilarth stood up and stretched his back. 'So that makes it easier to determine which level they stopped at.'

'Maybe, but we can't get to that level without the lift.'

'What about emergency access?' Delvina asked.

Danel's scarred face lit up. 'Now, that's a possibility.'

'Might be a long climb,' Gilarth said. 'But we could climb down one level and see if the control panel is working there. Still going to take time checking each level to find their trail.'

'Yeah, though give me some minutes. I think I can override the blockage.'

The sudden hum of cables sent Delvina's hopes soaring, until she realised it was from the main goods lift on the west wall of the lobby. What now?

The lift cage slowly descended, revealing a small cluster of people. Overseer Havilah flanked by seven watchers, two Forest Folk and Nebam. Delvina's stomach cramped. As long as the shift felt, they hadn't run out of time yet, surely. She tensed for the inevitable argument that would ensue.

Korak stirred awake, instantly alert, and shook Zadeki.

Kinleader Telsima walked toward Danel, beckoning Delvina to follow.

'Welcome back Holima's daughter, son of Shuzza. Your mission wasn't successful?'

Danel lowered his spanner and grimaced. 'It was a long way to go for so few answers.'

Delvina couldn't meet the Kinleader's gaze. 'The seal is soul-bound. There are ways to transfer the link but,' she shrugged, 'we don't have the seal or knowledge of how the transfer can be done.' And that wasn't the point now. 'Highwun Bikan ...'

'Umbria has told me what happened. In truth, I felt her passage, but I didn't want to believe it. It is too cruel a thing for a mother to survive her daughter.'

Delvina studied the scuffed patterns on the floor stamped by constant use. Her face burned with shame. Had Zadeki passed on her betrayal? Is that why Telsima singled her out? Silence stretched out—the soft roar of a nearby underground river and waterfall, the hum of the ventilation outlets, the accusation of her own heartbeat.

'Look at me, daughter of sorrow.'

Delvina raised her chin, expecting condemnation in the Kinleader's grey-green eyes. Instead there was only compassion.

'I allowed my hurt feelings to blind me,' she stuttered. 'I'm sorry about Highwun Bikan.'

Telsima's eyes clouded for a moment. She let out a soft breath. 'As am I. The Maker takes his children in his own time.'

'Da-Matu, she died by the Grand Technician Iulien's hand, but by Princess Avardin's intent and will, and now she sleeps in the Ravine of our Ancestors,' Korak murmured.

'We will talk of these things once the Darane are brought to safety. What of that other matter I sent you on?'

'Cantor Jossi and the crystal singers confirm your suspicions about the shadow crystals.' Korak tapped Danel's shoulder. 'Son of courage, give the Kinleader the message Eldar Bikan entrusted to you.'

'In all that happened in those last days of the island, I almost forgot.' Danel hunted around in his jerkin and pulled out a piece of paper.

'Shadow Crystals?' Havilah's face drained of all colour.

The Kinleader unfolded and scanned the message before lifting her eyes. 'You have heard of them, daughter of Elad?

Havilah briefly met Gilarth's gaze. 'Twenty years ago, but they were all destroyed.'

Twenty years? Delvina's breath caught. Around the time of the cave-in when her parents were killed.

Kinleader Telsima's lips tightened. 'Not all destroyed. I felt their influence as soon as I re-entered the caverns.'

Havilah's face took a greyish tinge. 'Impossible.' She closed her eyes. 'Even so, it no longer matters since we are leaving.'

'If only it were that easy. The ones that took Uzza's daughter, what do they seek?'

'We don't know. Neither Elim or Putarn are rational. The evacuation ...' Havilah's words trailed off under the Kinleader's steady gaze. '... we don't know where the fugitives have gone.'

'What lies that deep, daughter of the mountain?'

'The crystals. The Dark Ones,' Havilah whispered. 'But that horror is buried under tons of rock.'

'No longer, it seems. The crystal's influence is malignant to all who approach them. Should they be uncovered, the future of more than your realm will be imperilled.'

Highwun Korak stood beside the Kinleader. 'And now, the daughter of Dragon Kings, Avardin, seeks to gain access to them.'

Delvina felt a weight press down on her. Were the Dark Ones more than shadows or the cruel imaginings of mad Hezikah? Then Retza and Zara were in far more danger than she'd thought. More than that, this was bigger than her concerns for those she loved.

Kinleader Telsima rested the palm of her hand for a moment between Havilah's collar bones. 'We cannot keep running from this, daughter of Elad.' There are still five hours until your people set out on their journey. And even then, others can ensure their safety.'

'How can we fight nightmares?'

'We have to,' Delvina said. 'It's what we've been doing all along.'

Havilah gave a faint smile. 'You are your mother's daughter. Courageous to the end, but you have no idea what's down there.'

Unbidden tears rolled down Delvina's cheeks. It's what she'd always wanted, to live up to her mother's heroism. Now she'd settle for life with a man who loved her, a family and a future for her people, though they all seemed to hang on the thinnest of threads.

'I'll go, Matu. The people need you and Gilarth to lead them.' Nebam's unusually quiet voice reminded Delvina of his presence.

Havilah gripped her son's shoulder. 'You and Timon can lead them, if need be. The Kinleader is right, this is my unfinished business.'

'Where are these dark crystals?' Danel closed the

control panel and wiped his hands on a cloth. Zadeki prowled behind him.

Havilah squared her shoulders. 'On the forbidden twenty-second level, roughly five lek northwest of the lift shaft.'

'North-west.' Danel combed his fingers through his beard. 'That would be below the Sunken Temple.'

'I did wonder,' Havilah said.

'Temple's Rest,' Zadeki's rounded jaguar ears perked up. 'Could that be what it means? Where what is thrown in the pit comes to rest?'

Delvina took a deep breath. 'Then what are we waiting for?'

Gilarth raised an eyebrow. 'The lifts? Or I suppose we could just all clamber down over a lek of ladders.'

Danel grinned. 'I'm finished.' He gave a little flourish, pushed a button and pulled the lever. The lift cables in the main shaft jerked and the hum of the lift sounded from far below.

Relief flooded through Delvina, and with it, apprehension of what dangers waited for them below. Though with the watchers, four Adelphi, Gilarth, Havilah and not least, Danel, maybe it would be Uzza and the shadows that needed to fear them.

'If you encounter the shadows before I return, remember darkness feasts and breeds in darkness, but retreats before the smallest light,' Telsima said.

Havilah looked shocked. 'Are you not coming with us, Kinleader?'

'I must check something out first, daughter of the mountain.' Telsima beckoned to her companion. 'Come with me, Umbria. Korak and Zadeki, help the mountain dwellers. Do not take unnecessary risks.'

Placing her hands on her chest, she bowed. Then with an upward sweep, she leapt into the air, shifted into her

bat-form and flew up the lift shaft. Umbria followed in
the form of an owl.

Some of Delvina's confidence leeched out. Where
could the Kinleader be going?

'Don't worry,' Zadeki gave her a nudge with his furry
head. 'She'll be back.'

'Besides,' Danel added waving a wrench. 'They've still
got us to contend with.'

Delvina smiled, glad to have such stalwart friends.
And maybe that was what mattered, that they were
friends. Anything else could sort itself out in time.

Zara's clothes stuck to her skin and sweat
beaded on her forehead only to roll down her face. Putarn led
them through the tunnels at a brisk trot. Temporary glimmer
lights were strung along the tunnel. These walls showed less
damage than the ones closer to the metal entrance door, but
it was still unsettling. If she let her mind wander, she could
almost imagine a dark malevolent presence batting against
her mind like a moth against a light.

She glanced back at Retza being yanked along
by a scowling Fenna. Manoah and Levim formed an
impenetrable barrier at their rear. The thought of more
harm coming to the young watcher set her pulse racing.
She had to find a way to free him, but there was nowhere
to escape along this long narrow corridor.

Baba moved closer to her and tucked her arm into his.
'Don't worry, sweetling. I have a plan to put things back
the way they should be.'

Wasn't that what she'd been hoping ever since she and
Jesson had been left behind in the rebels' hands? But he
gave her a pinned-on smile often bestowed on littlewuns.
His palms were moist on her skin and it was all she could
do not to pull away. Did he even remember her name?

'What will happen to the re...' she bit her lip.

'The rebels.' Baba's eyes hardened. 'The traitor Gilarth and that she-bat Havilah and all who helped her will be cast out, just as she cast me out. But I can be forgiving. The lowwuns need only swear their allegiance and I will overlook their rebellion.' His fingers brushed her cheek. 'You, my dear, shall be rewarded for your loyalty. I'll even grant you that misguided fool back there, if you want him. But you must do everything I say, without question. Do you understand?'

The image of Havilah's tired honest eyes and Gilarth's resolute ones hovered before her. Whatever their faults, they were only trying to save the realm and its people. Not for the first time, Zara doubted that the Glittering Realm would truly be better off under her father's rule.

'Baba,' she said, her voice cracking. She cleared her throat. 'Baba, what happened to Matu and Asrab and Nomi and the rest.'

His fingers tightened on her arm. 'Oh, don't concern yourself, my dear. They are safe and well cared for. You will join them soon.'

A chip of ice settled in her chest. Had the serving woman lied about her matu's death, or was Baba lying now? What had happened to all those people? Or maybe more to the point, how had the others survived? Did Baba have hidden stores that no one else knew about?

'Do you doubt me, girl?'

'I ... I don't understand. How will you feed all our people?' Nothing but dust and cobwebs and suffocating heat grew down this far. This tunnel was as barren as any other.

'All will be revealed soon.'

Zara took in a deep breath and wet her suddenly dry mouth. This was her chance. 'Baba, Havilah has made arrangements with the Tamrin. There is food enough for all waiting on the other side of the Gate. We only need the seal to open it.'

Baba's eyes narrowed and he waved an impatient hand as though batting away an annoying insect. 'That awful woman is a liar. Only destruction awaits outside the Gate. The Dark Ones have promised to restore the realm to its former glory.'

How could she be sure that Havilah was telling the truth? She hadn't seen the food trains. Yet surely she or Retza would not lie to her. 'But can the Dark Ones provide food for the people, Baba?'

'You ask too many questions, daughter. The Dark Ones will supply what we need, but first we must follow their instructions and open Temple's Rest.'

Putarn stopped in front of them. 'Almost there, your Honour.' A look difficult to interpret crept into his purple eyes.

'Good lad,' Baba gripped Putarn's shoulder. 'You've proven yourself more worthy than your mother.'

The former Secondwun flinched under Baba's touch. He bared his teeth, though the expression was so fleeting that Zara wondered if she'd imagined it. His mouth stretched into a wide smile. 'Are you sure you want to do this, Uzza, son of Hezikah? This was where it all started.' There was an odd note in Putarn's voice.

'Of course, get on with it.'

'As you wish, your greatness.' Putarn strode down the tunnel with a smug look.

Baba patted Zara's hand. 'Come, girl, I'll show you something that you'll not forget. Something Havilah could never have achieved.'

After walking several tanis, they heard muted voices and the tapping sound of metal on rock drifting toward them from where the tunnel ended into the side of another. The closer they got, the dimmer the glimmer lights seemed and the harder it became for her to move. A feeling of dread trembled inside her. What was this thing her father put so much faith in? Was it a machine or monster, tool or weapon? What did he intend to do with it? Shadows flickered and moved in the pale-blue glimmer light spilling into the tunnel from the doorway.

They were much closer to the opening before she realised the shadows were cast by a group sitting and standing around at the end of the tunnel.

'What is this?' Baba roared beside her, making her jump. 'No rest until the door is open.'

A taller figure wearing a stained robe rushed forward. He smoothed down his grey plaited beard with fading blue tips. 'Overseer.'

The melodious voice belonged to High Priest Beltain, though it was hard to recognise the once heavy-jowled priest. She had never liked the man from the time she was a littlewun.

She counted five other people. None of her siblings, not even her older brother, Asrab. She shivered despite the heat. Was this all that was left of the group Baba had brought here?

Further down the corridor stretching off to the right side, there were signs of collapse, though a makeshift shelter offered some privacy.

A broad-shouldered woman moved forward, holding her hands to stop their shaking. 'Your Honour, it's taken us two rosters to dig through the tunnel collapse, but we have exposed the door as you ordered.'

Baba grinned and rubbed his hands together. 'Good, good, show me.'

The people moved aside, revealing the outlines of an oval door of polished grey metal, much like the broken wreck of a door near the lifts.

Baba let out a hiss. 'That is it, the door to Temple's Rest.'

Danel watched as the Kinleader and her companion disappeared up the lift shaft. Now that was unexpected. He went to throw the spanner in the toolbox, then tucked it into his belt instead. It might be needed if … when they found the miscreants who had taken Zara.

'Are we going?'

Overseer Havilah beckoned the others. 'We haven't much time. Pile in and then take it to the bottom, Danel.'

Zadeki bounded across the lobby. The others followed. Once all had positioned themselves, Danel adjusted the lift control and pulled the lever. With a jerk and hum, the platform plummeted down, speeding up as it went. His injured left eye watered at the brisk updraft, yet despite the circumstances, it felt good to be in the caverns again. Even better to be with friends.

Delvina was lost in thought, though she gave him a tired smile. Zadeki settled down near the edge of the platform, his sprawling jaguar form taking up much of the space.

'Do you remember the way, your Honour?' Gilarth asked.

'It's etched in my memory like a hot iron,' Overseer Havilah replied. She half-turned. 'I thought your teams searched all the levels.'

'We did. But the access was locked and given that the entrance was buried in a ton of rock …' He shrugged. 'Better to leave sleeping shadows undisturbed.'

'If only Uzza thought the same way,' Havilah sighed. 'I guess we'll work out how to get past the debris once we get there.'

'With any luck, Uzza will have shifted it for us.'

The levels whizzed by with the minutes, each level taking them deeper into secret places buried beneath the mountain's roots.

Danel frowned. It was the first time he'd heard of this lower level. He'd never really thought the Dark Ones were real and didn't understand how these shadows could be a threat. He'd never seen Havilah or Gilarth spooked like this before, either. Apprehension tightened his shoulders. Easier to face familiar dangers than the unknown.

At last the lift slowed and the platform came to a shuddering rest on solid rock.

Zadeki lept out. 'There are footprints here,' he said. He spun around. 'And chalk marks. They came this way.' Without waiting, he prowled off to the right.

Delvina strode after the shapeshifter and Danel followed close behind. He only hoped they could find Retza and Zara in time.

Chills ran up and down Retza's spine as though some malignant force was watching him. The door gleamed in the dim glimmerlight, reflecting distorted images of those gathered around it. The longer he looked, the more convinced he became that there was something behind the silver door that should stay hidden.

'Why is it called Temple's Rest, Baba? Is it a shrine?' Zara's clear voice rang as sweetly as a bell.

'Yes, or a home of the Dark Ones. The pit in the Sunken Temple leads to the chamber beyond the door.'

Retza shuddered. This is where the sacrifices ended up. 'Then it is a tomb,' he said.

'Blasphemy.' Beltain linked his hands and rested them on the grubby golden sash across his withered chest. 'The Dark Ones, and their shadow crystals will save us.'

Retza swayed, struggling to stay upright. 'Listen, there's a yarma train of food waiting at the King's Road outside the Gate. Lady Zara is right, we need the seal to the Gate.'

Uzza clicked his tongue. 'You are deluded. No one from the outside would help us.'

Zara caught her father's arm. 'But they have agreed, Baba. If you spoke with Havilah—'

'Enough! I will hear no more of such nonsense.'

Retza's mouth twisted. 'I thought the Dark Ones required sacrifices for their help.'

'The Overseer said to shut up, slug.' Fenna whacked him over the ear, sending him sprawling against the wall.'

'Yes, well, it would seem the Dark Ones have provided all we need to please them.' Putarn folded his arms and smirked.

Retza shook his head to clear the ringing in his ear. Did Putarn mean him? But the sacrifices were always in pairs. Cold dread settled in his limbs. His heart hammered like tongs on metal. They couldn't mean Zara. He could take comfort that whatever happened here, the evacuation would go on without him. But if there was some way to rescue Zara, he had to take it.

'We're wasting time.' Uzza stood in front of the door and studied it carefully. 'Have you worked out how to open it, Beltain?'

'Not yet, my lord. It needs a key.' He pointed to a small slot in the door's smooth surface.

A look of frustration passed over Uzza's face. 'You need to bypass it.'

The woman who'd spoken before bowed low. 'Your Honour, we've tried. The door is hardened metal and fitted snugly into the frame with phalanges. Our finest chisel cannot find a gap wide enough to exploit.'

Retza bit down on a smile. 'Why not knock. They might let you in.'

'Silence!' Uzza spun around and thrust his face close to the priest. 'So you're saying you have no idea how to get in?'

Beltain threw up his arms. 'Without the key, your Honour? No.'

Uzza's face darkened. He paced back and forward, mumbling. 'This is another test.' He stopped in front of Putarn. 'Do you have you any ideas?'

Putarn ran his hand over the rock wall, probing a few of the cracks. 'Anderite,' he said. 'Hard rock but softer than your door.'

'You're not suggesting we dig our way in?' Beltain asked.

'No, but if you dig around the hinges, loosen the frame, it should work. Manoah, get your muscles into it.' Putarn waved his hand.

Manoah looked to Uzza, and when the former Overseer nodded, he grabbed a pickaxe leaning against the wall and swung. The metal blade bounced off the wall and landed ninas away from his boot, the tip sinking into the floor.

'By the pit.' Manoah yelped. His face glowed as red as a rusted chain.

Zara stifled a giggle.

'Call yourself a miner,' Uzza roared.

'I'm a watcher, not a rock digger.'

Putarn let out a chuckle. 'That much is obvious. Let's try something more subtle. Grabbing a chisel, he pushed Manoah out of the way, and chipped at the wall. 'This could take a while.'

The longer the better as far as Retza was concerned.

Uzza glared at Beltain. 'I'd expected it done already old friend.'

'Yes, yes, come and make yourself comfortable down here while you wait, your Honour.' Beltain's eyes gleamed. 'I have some more provisions.'

Uzza rubbed his hands together. 'Good, good.' He pointed to the woman. 'You, tie the prisoner up down there. Zara, see to his needs. We don't want him dying just yet. The rest of you, take half-hour turns at the door and don't stop until it's accomplished.'

The woman grabbed Retza by his bound hands and dragged him down the left tunnel. Retza's vision darkened with the renewed stabs of pain. He sighed as she tied his hands to a metal ring protruding from the wall.

'I need to relieve myself,' he said.

The woman snorted. 'Your problem, not mine.' She pinched his cheeks and showed sharpened teeth. 'Glad you've joined us.'

Zara stood some moments staring after her father before she manoeuvred past the cluster around the door and walked toward Retza. She looked lost, her face troubled.

'Lady,' the woman sketched a bow. 'I'll send the food when it's ready. She pushed past Zara, re-joining her companions.

Zara attempted a smile when she met his gaze. She pulled out her water flask and dribbled a few drops into his mouth.

He licked the moisture off his skin and leaned back against the wall, eyes half-lidded, lips taut. 'Funny, last time I was chosen as a sacrifice I was treated like a highwun.'

Her eyes widened into two blue fathomless pools in a pale face. Her mouth made a perfect circle. 'That's not what Baba plans to do.' She closed her eyes.

'He did last time.' Did she really believe that? Whose side was she on? But she must have some feeling for him, to kiss him the second time.

Zara's hands trembled as she checked the bandages. Tears beaded on her golden lashes and rolled down her cheeks. He wished he could take her in his arms and make this horrific situation go away.

He glanced down the corridor. Uzza had disappeared with Elim and Beltain into the shelter. The others were clustered around Putarn and the door, some munching on strands of smoked meat and other rations.

'Zara, you should escape while you can. Get out of here. Take the emergency ladder up to the higher levels. It's next to the lift.'

Her stance stiffened. 'Not without you.'

At least she hadn't protested the need to escape. 'It's all I can do to hobble. I'd only slow you down.'

'Shush.' Putting down the healing box, she searched among the ever-present rubble until she found a narrow, sharp-edged rock. Hooking under the bounds, she sawed until they gave way. 'You go. I'll delay them,' she whispered. 'He won't hurt me.'

He took her arm, as much to lean on as to bring her with him. 'Don't you see. You are in as much danger as I am.'

A pebble pinged beside them. 'Be quiet you two.' Manoah shouted down the tunnel at them.

They stood stone still, clinging to each other. No one looked. No one came.

After several heartbeats, Retza put his mouth to her ear. 'I am not leaving you behind.'

'Which way?'

Creeping past the crowd around the door was too risky. They'd have to chance that this tunnel connected up with the exit somehow. He pointed further in.

Together they eased their way along, taking the turn to the right, though it would have been better if the tunnel had turned left, if he'd kept his sense of direction.

Each step took all his concentration. Retza leaned against the wall to catch his breath. 'This leads away from the exit', he mouthed. But at least they were hidden from direct sight.

'It's the only way. We can backtrack later.'

He nodded and they continued on, her hand warm in his. The chip, chip, chip of the chisel blows followed them. Rubble lay scattered on the floor. Cave-ins blocked the branching tunnels to the left. Soon the line of temporary glimmer lights came to an end. Black shadows twisted like roots seeking water through a cavern roof and black spots mottled his vision. His temple throbbed, and pain gripped him whether breathing or walking. He didn't know how much longer he could go on or whether he could protect Zara from attack, if it came to that.

Zara stifled a sob.

'What is it? We'll find a way out.'

'It's not that.' She took a big shuddering breath. 'If ... if you're right and he intends to offer both of us, I can't shake the idea he intended to use Jesson. I think I could be brave enough to risk my life for the sake of the realm.'

'You already have.'

'But what father would do that to his children, just to save his own skin?'

What could he say? He pulled her closer to him, breathing her in, wanting to linger.

She held him tight. 'Why did you come alone? You should have gotten help.'

'I was afraid I'd lose your trail.' A louder clang came from down the corridor. 'We should keep going or find somewhere to hide.' Though all he could see was the cracked tunnel walls.

'Just in case I don't get another chance,' she said, 'I love you.'

'I love you too,' he whispered and then laughed for the absurd joy of it. She loved him.

She leaned her head on his shoulder and he caught the wall to stop toppling over. They held each other close, safe if only for a moment in each other's embrace.

Who cared whether she was Uzza's daughter? She was his beautiful, brave Zara and that was all that mattered. That and making sure she escaped this nightmare.

Zara wanted to shout the words, to dance and laugh and tell all who would listen. He loved her, and she loved him. But she couldn't just yet. Once they'd found a way out or a place to hide, she would be able to savour this fragile new thing between them. For now, she needed to focus on escaping. The tunnel took another sudden turn, once again to the right.

'We seem to be going in a circle,' Retza said.

'It's like we're skirting a large box.'

'Temple's Rest.' He pushed his sweat-soaked hair from his face. 'Maybe we should backtrack, check one of the side tunnels.'

'None of them looked promising.' She chewed her bottom lip in frustration. 'They'll miss us soon.'

'If we keep going this way, we'll end back where we started. We could do with some outside help at this point.'

'You mean, like the Maker the Adelphi call on.' She hadn't meant her tone to be so dismissive.

He didn't answer at once.

'Retza?'

He squeezed her hand. 'One thing is certain. I don't mean the Dark Ones. Whatever happens,' he turned toward her, his face half in shadow, 'it was worth it.'

'Don't give up now. If there isn't a way, we have to make our own.'

They shuffled down the dark corridor. Retza counted their paces under his breath. After a while, he pulled her to a stop.

Putting his mouth to her ear, he whispered. 'The turn should be fifteen tanis ahead if it encircles the shrine.

Something moved up ahead, a play of light and shadows on the walls. She could hear a mumble of voices. Someone laughed. Her knees felt like soggy felt. She knew that laugh.

'That sounds like, Baba.'

Retza nodded. 'Let's go back the other way.'

Together they crept back along the tunnel. The voices rose louder behind them. A high-pitched pleading lifting the hairs on Zara's arms. Someone was in trouble. The desperate words changed into a choking scream then silence.

They looked at each other, the horror she felt reflected in Retza's eyes.

She licked her lips. 'We should help.'

Retza shook his head. 'She's beyond help.' And she knew he was right.

When they reached the corner, Zara stumbled into a run, with Retza just keeping up.

She stopped at the first side tunnel, clutching her aching side. Retza leaned against the wall behind her, gasping for breath.

The flash of a glimmer torch came from further up the tunnel accompanied by the soft whisper of stealthy steps. They were trapped.

Two figures with drawn truncheons turned the corner and stalked down the corridor towards them. 'There you are,' Manoah's voice boomed down the corridor. 'Overseer Uzza is not happy.'

Retza pushed himself off the wall and launched himself at Manoah pummelled him, taking the bigger watcher by surprise. 'Run, Zara!' he shouted.

Levim dashed out from the other side and grabbed Retza, twisting his arms behind his back.

'Don't hurt him,' Zara said.

Manoah grabbed her arm. 'If you come with us nicely, Lady Zara, we'll be gentle.'

He pushed her down the corridor after Levim and Retza.

Retza looked behind him. 'Manoah, you do understand what he intends to do to us? Are you okay with that?'

'Maybe it's not what I expected, but you've got to understand, if we don't bring you two back, then we'd be taking your place. Nothing personal, but if it's a choice between your life or mine, then I'm choosing mine.'

Levim spat on the floor. 'The Overseer, doesn't take failure kindly. That woman got iced for not keeping guard.'

'Don't you see, you're only staving off trouble. If you join with us, we could stop him now.'

'Not going to happen. If you don't shut your mouth, I gag you.'

They walked the rest of the way in silence. And each step Zara retraced felt like a defeat.

Back where they started, Baba stood in front of the door. A door now deeply chipped around the hinges but still firmly shut.

Zara held out her hands. 'Baba—'

Before she could say more, Manoah shoved her forward and she fell on her knees, her crystal pendant swinging out from under her dress. Levim pushed Retza down beside her.

'Baba, please. You can't intend to do this.'

He stood stock still, arms folded, and eyes following the swing of the pendant. With a grunt, he lunged forward, and pulled the crystal until the golden chain snapped.

'Where did you get this, girl?' he spluttered.

'I found it in a box in an old storeroom.' She withered under Baba's penetrating stare. 'In ... in Da-Baba's old room. It's just a trinket.'

'It's the seal. I can't believe how long I looked for this and you had it all this time.'

'But Baba, we tried it on the Gate. It didn't work.'

'Foolish girl, of course not.' He closed his fingers over the glowing crystal. 'It responds only to the true heir.'

Hope sprouted. 'Will you use it to open the Gate?'

His face turned a bright magenta. 'Havilah has corrupted you.'

Turning his back on her, he strode towards the gleaming metal door and inserted the crystal in the slot. A humming noise filled the corridor, followed by a clunk, and the door swung outwards.

A smell of sulphur and decay wafted outwards. Zara's blood turned to water at the pulsating purple black, like a living, breathing hallucination, a dense darkness with sharp black teeth.

Taking a breath, she reached across the distance and took hold of Retza's hand.

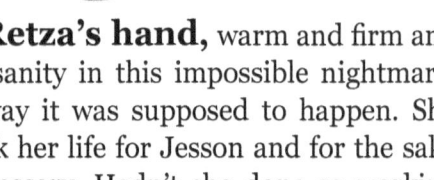

Zara gripped Retza's hand, warm and firm and alive. A lifeline to sanity in this impossible nightmare. This was not the way it was supposed to happen. She would choose to risk her life for Jesson and for the sake of the realm, if necessary. Hadn't she done so working with Nebam to open the Gate? That at least made sense. She took a breath of fetid air. Retza and Delvina had been right. Her faith in her father was horribly misplaced. And that was the saddest thing of all.

The darkness in front of them felt alive, full of whisperings of despair. Misty faces, eyes, hands seemed to writhe and reach toward her from the swirling blackness, *You have lost. You belong to us now. There is no point continuing the struggle.*

Retza pulled her close to him and squeezed her hand. 'We have to resist the voices.'

'You go in first, Beltain, you're the priest.' Baba hovered beside them, eyes wide and staring.

Beltain gave a choked gurgle, then cleared his throat. He held up shaking arms.

'Dark Ones, we come to you to seek your wisdom and power. We have not forsaken you, like some. Tell us what you want from us.'

Come to us.

Baba stepped forward and pushed Beltain in. The shape of the priest shimmered as though he'd stepped into a cloud of dark smoke.

With a grunt, Beltain fell to his knees, bowing low until his forehead hit the stone floor. He gave one great shudder and lay still.

'This is crazy,' Fenna said, backing down the corridor. Others followed.

Manoah's fingers dug deeper into Zara's shoulders. 'Shut up, Fenna. We've come this far, we might as well see it through.'

A sigh like a wind ran through the tunnel. Beltain stood up and turned. His eyes went dark and his face blank. 'The Dark Ones have heard you. You are favoured, Uzza, son of Hezikah. They find your ... gift ... acceptable. Do not despair, all that you have lost will be given back to you.'

'Thank you, oh great ones.'

'Now, give us the girl and her companion.'

Zara licked dry lips. 'Baba, this is madness.' One thing she was sure of, whatever the Dark Ones promised, this was a poisoned chalice.

'Uzza, she's your own daughter,' Retza said.

Baba blinked, almost as if he saw her for the first time.

'It was never too high a price when it was someone else's youngwun or the lives of your toolwuns you put in danger.' Putarn leant against the wall, arms folded. He hawked and spat on the floor, his spittle sizzling on the stones. 'Coward to the end.'

'They died doing their duty. Your father ...'

'My father, Retza's parents, the others, died to fuel your ambition while you played with forces far beyond your comprehension.' His purple eyes narrowed. 'We're all doomed. Nothing can save us now. One satisfaction before I die is to watch them take you, like they took my father.'

'You're wrong, Putarn.' Havilah's voice rang out from the connecting corridor. 'The shadows didn't defeat Ozier. He and Holima and Zalell died fighting them. They lit the explosion that sealed them in.'

'Let them go,' Delvina roared. Behind her, a huge jaguar growled.

Zara lifted her head and felt hope rise like an injured bird escaping a trap. Perhaps, help had come in time to save them from the shadows.

Delvina was shocked at the appearance of her twin. When she'd left the caverns, he'd been strong and healthy, if a little thin. Of course, all those who stayed behind looked gaunt, with hollowed-out cheeks, shadows beneath their eyes, and collarbones sticking out like tree roots. But Retza's skin was grey, he had a dirty bandage wrapped around his head, and he cradled his chest with every breath.

Zara knelt beside him, while a ragtag bunch, led by a ravaged oldwun with stringy white-hair and patchy beard, stood clustered around a metal door. Shadows flickered across the ceiling and blackness pulsated beyond the door. Putarn, she recognised, the old speaker Elim, and Fenna, but not the watchers restraining her twin and Lady Zara or the others stretched out down the corridor.

Her hands curled into fists. 'Let him go,' she roared. 'Let my brother go.'

'And who would you be?' The oldwun moved closer

to Zara, a crystal dangling by a broken golden chain clutched in one hand. Something about his face and stance reminded her of the once dazzling and corpulent Uzza, Zara's father.

Delvina lifted her chin, refusing to be intimidated. 'I am Messenger Delvina, daughter of Holima and Zalell. Retza's sister.' She'd left without telling her twin and against his wishes and she hoped he would not still hold it against her.

'Back away, if you don't want your friend and brother hurt,' the watcher holding Zara snarled.

She almost laughed. She counted eight opponents to their twelve. Fourteen if she included Zara and Retza, and they had the two Forest Folk on their side—formidable foes able to change form at will into great beasts with sharp teeth and claws. Only the cramped corridors would work against their advantage in a fight.

The need to attack, to crush these feeble opponents, ripped through her like dark lightning. Delvina dug her fingernails into her palms to counter the desire's unexpected pull.

'What do you want, rabble?' Uzza backed towards the door and Elim edged toward him.

'The seal to the Gate would be a good start.' Overseer Havilah said, her face set like rock. 'To let in the food supplies. And Retza and Zara returned to us unharmed.'

Uzza's lip curled. 'Pitiful. You don't know what powers you deal with.' He beckoned the watchers holding Retza and Zara. 'Bring them.'

'No, Baba.' Zara pulled against the bigger watcher.

'Son of fear, do you seek your heart's desire in that tomb of darkness?' Highwun Korak pointed at the open doorway. 'You would trust yourself to that?

Uzza wet his swollen lips and flicked a nervous glance behind him. 'Why, what can you offer me that the Dark Ones can't? Will you give back what you took from me?'

Havilah folded her arms. 'I can't reinstate you as Overseer, Uzza.'

'If you set me in the northern node, return my followers, and share the food with us.' Uzza tilted his head to one side and stared at Havilah with half-lidded eyes. 'I might consider a deal. I'll include Retza along with the seal.'

'And Zara,' Gilarth said.

'Putarn maybe, if you want him back, but Zara is my daughter. She stays with me.' He dangled the crystal by its chain, light spearing from its rotating facets.

Retza lifted his head, eyes stricken. 'No.'

Delvina flexed her jaw. It would be a deal made in perdition, but many lives might be saved if food could be brought into the caverns and the perilous trek across the mountain averted. And it would return Retza to them. But at what cost with Uzza still free?

Overseer Havilah's lips thinned into a flat line.

Uzza smirked. 'You need this, Havilah.' He swung the crystal. 'You need me.'

Black mist like a hundred fingers writhed and twisted out through the doorway.

'Do you mean to cheat us of what you promised us? Fool!' A figure emerged from the centre of the shadows and plunged an obsidian knife into Uzza's side.

Uzza screamed, the eldritch sound bouncing off the walls, and collapsed to the ground. The crystal flashed liquid light as it dropped from his hand. Beltain melted back into the gloom.

Zadeki barrelled into the watcher holding Retza. The man sprawled sideways, and as his grip loosened, Retza fell forward.

Gilarth grabbed the neck of the watcher holding Zara, pulling him back and to the side before bringing his truncheon down on the watcher's arms. 'Give it up, Manoah.'

Manoah yelped. He released Zara and spun round to grapple with the Head Watcher. Delvina rushed in to help Gilarth.

Korak took hold of Putarn and Elim, immobilising both with what seemed little effort. Zadeki kept going, landing among Fenna and the rest of Uzza's followers and sending them scrambling down the corridors. Gilarth's watchers joined the chase.

It was over in an instant.

Danel grabbed some ties and bound the watcher Zadeki had knocked over, then moved on to Manoah, Elim and a smirking Putarn.

'Baba.' Zara staggered up and rushed toward the threshold, where Uzza lay clutching his side and moaning.

Delvina hurried to her twin, hardly believing that after all this time they were together again.

He grinned. 'Delvina. A bit on the late side, aren't you?'

She pulled him into a hug, relieved to be at peace with her twin, and then, when he squawked, let go.

'Maybe someone should close the door,' he said.

Too late. A dark shape loomed out of the shadows.

'Zara, watch out,' Retza screamed. 'Behind you.' He jumped up, pushing past Delvina and staggered towards the door. Delvina picked herself up and followed.

She recognised the dark figure, a hollow husk of his former self, as the bloody-handed priest, Beltain. She'd never wanted to see him again after the fiasco at the Sunken Temple.

'We take what is ours.' Beltain kicked Uzza to one aside and wrapped his arms around Zara. Retza threw himself at the priest, pummelling him with fists. Beltain accepted his blows without flinching. Dark shadows whipped around them, pulling Zara and Retza through the doorway into the dark maw.

'Noooo!' Delvina launched herself through the closing gap.

The door slammed shut behind her and the light winked out, leaving behind a stygian black. She crouched, blinking at the dense heaving darkness soaked with a sickly-sweet odour of death.

'Delvina, no!' Danel dropped the ties and rushed to the door. 'By the pit, bring them back you mealy-mouthed priest.'

Highwun Korak put his hand on Danel's shoulder. 'Calm yourself, son of courage. The shadows will only feed on your emotions.'

Danel wheeled around, anger like molten metal rising up inside him. 'What, we just leave them in there?'

Putarn snickered behind him and waved his bound hands. 'Good plan, cousin, let the Dark Ones out again. Lost sight of the bigger picture, haven't we?'

Danel rounded on him. 'You! Don't you lecture me. She ... they wouldn't be in there, if it wasn't for your stupid, selfish machinations. You brought Zara here. What were you thinking?'

Putarn shrugged and looked away.

'Settle down, Thirdwun.' Gilarth picked up the cables and continued binding the prisoners. Korak bent down to examine Uzza while Havilah stared at Danel, face grim.

Danel closed his eyes then opened them, not sure why he felt so unhinged, except that Delvina had become his bright light in the dark and this place unsettled him.

'Delvina and Retza wouldn't leave someone behind. Your Honour, we can't abandon them,' Danel said, making his voice calmer.

'We won't, Thirdwun, if we can help it, but we need to secure the seal and get it to Nebam.'

Danel breathed deeply. And time to avert the evacuation was bleeding away and the seal would open the Gate.

'The son of darkness dropped the seal over here somewhere, when the shadow-taken priest attacked him,' Korak knelt beside Uzza. 'I can't see it here.'

'Perhaps he fell on top of it,' Gilarth said.

A greenish-grey tone tinged the old Overseer's face and bright blood seeped through his clothes. 'He's injured. Let me stop the bleeding and we can move him.'

Korak ripped strips of cloth from Uzza's robe, making a wad to stop the bleeding and pressed it into his side, then bound it fast with more strips. He lifted the wounded man in one smooth movement, and laid him close to the makeshift shelter down the corridor. A red stain spread out across the stone floor where he'd been.

'Thanks, Highwun,' Havilah gave him a quick smile. 'Let's see if we can find this seal.'

Danel searched around the door's threshold. Gilarth and a couple of watchers joined him. Nothing.

'Someone else may have picked it up.' Danel looked at each face in turn. Which of them would have motive to take it?

'Or perhaps they kicked it in the middle of the struggle.' Gilarth moved further down the corridor, eyes searching the ground.

Zadeki, still in jaguar form, filled the tunnel as he herded two terrified looking escapees back towards him. 'Kicked what?'

'The seal, that crystal that Uzza was holding.' Havilah said. 'Better search the prisoners too.'

'Zara's crystal,' Zadeki nudged the trembling prisoners towards the watchers. 'Where is Zara? Or Delvina and Retza?'

'In there.' Danel pointed with his chin at the closed door.

Zadeki growled. 'Then what are we waiting for, we need to save them.'

A low groan came from the floor. Uzza's eyes fluttered open.

Havilah knelt down beside Korak and turned Uzza's face toward her. 'Where is the seal?'

'They asked for everything and still, the Dark Ones betrayed me,' Uzza wheezed.

Havilah gave him a shake. 'What else did you expect, given their demands? Where is the seal? We need to open the Gate.'

Uzza gave a breathless laugh. 'I don't have it.'

Anger flashed in Havilah eyes. 'Then who does?' she asked, her voice as calm as the eye of a sea-storm. Despite himself Danel shivered.

'I don't know.'

Zadeki prowled over and leaned close to Uzza. The former Overseer scrambled backwards, his eyes popping. 'I don't know, I don't know. Get that foul beast away from me.'

'Beltain took it,' Putarn said. 'It's in there, in Temple's Rest, behind that locked and sealed door.'

'It's gone then. Besides only I can use it and I'm dying.' Uzza's laugh wound down to a splutter as Zadeki nudged him with his head. 'Ah! Havilah, don't let the beast hurt me. We were friends before you married that boring toolwun Ozier. I took you to see the hidden waterfall, remember? Didn't know that, did you Gilarth?'

'Ozier was worth more than a hundred of you.' Havilah's voice hardened to tempered iron.

One side of Gilarth's mouth ticked up in a crooked smile. 'Harsh, but fair.' He eyed the door. What next?'

'If Beltain has the seal,' Havilah stood and glared at the door, 'seems we're not done with the Dark Ones.'

So they had to get in some other way. Danel fidgeted

with his spanner. 'Is there a back entrance somewhere, a delivery hatchway, a ventilation shaft we could access?'

'We found no other entrance last time Ozier and ...' Havilah swallowed, 'last time we were here.'

'It's true, I've been right around,' Zadeki said, his long tail lashing from side to side. 'Some cracks in the wall but nothing otherwise.' He padded up and down along the crowded corridor. 'There has to be a way to get in. What about gouging around the door?'

Danel ran his hands over the seams of the door and explored chisel marks chipped around the rock circling the hinges just a few tinas deep. 'It would take hours to get through this way.' Who knew how much time Delvina had or what dangers she and the others were facing?

'Could we override the door controls?' Gilarth asked, tugging his beard.

'The controls are on the other side or hidden in the wall.' An artery ticked in Danel forehead. His throat burned with acid. They were back to where they'd started. 'We could use firepowder to blast a hole in the wall.'

Putarn sniggered. 'And risk injuring those inside or destroy your precious seal or maybe bring the roof down on top of us all? Didn't work too well for Nebam, did it?'

Gilarth rounded on the former Secondwun. 'Maybe you could keep your opinions to yourself.'

'There is a risk, but being trapped in there isn't good either.' Havilah joined Zadeki in pacing before the door. 'We need that seal. Highwun, Korak, what about the danger of releasing the Dark Ones.'

'A concern, daughter of sorrows. Certainly. Though, the Kinleader suggested a confrontation is necessary. A locked door won't hold the shadows forever. Nor should you abandon those three brave younglings to their power, if there is a choice to save them.'

'We could do it.' Danel rubbed his hands together.

'With two explosions, your Honour. One to get in and then another set up and ready to go, to collapse this access tunnel. That should shut them in.'

'If you are quick enough,' Putarn snickered.

Gilarth beckoned. 'Nate, take the prisoners and secure them in the crib closer to the entrance.'

'We'll need some rations if you can find them,' Korak added.

'Food? I would've said firepowder and firewire.'

'That too, but Zadeki and I need to revive if we're going to be of effective help. You should get some rest too, daughter of Elad.'

'Right,' Havilah stood still, rubbing her chin. 'Gilarth, if Nate takes the prisoners, you're in charge of getting the firepower and blasting wire from the crib. Send someone topside if you have to. Highwun Korak, would you ensure Uzza gets to Barekia or another scrybe safely?'

'As you wish. Zadeki can help down here until I get back.'

'I'll start working out the timings and where to place the firepowder,' Danel said, 'Unless you wish to, Overseer?'

'No, you're the most qualified present, Thirdwun Danel.'

Putarn pulled against the watcher leading him away. 'I'm better than any of you. Let me help.'

Danel started at the former Secondwun, his cousin and Havilah's son. What he said was true, but how could they trust him after all he'd done. They couldn't.

'Your help is no longer needed or wanted, Putarn. You accuse Ma-Sestru of doing nothing while her crew died, yet all you've done is plot against the best Overseer we've had in a long while, while she has worked shift after shift to keep this realm together. You're a joke, Putarn, and a sick one at that.'

Danel looked over at the other kidnappers— Manoah, Fener, Levim and Elim—standing cowed and tightly bound. He nodded to Gilarth. 'Take them all away, we have work to do.'

Zadeki shifted into human form. 'Show me what I need to do.'

Their eyes met and Danel nodded.

If there was a way to blow the wall down without bringing everything down with it, then he would do it. Every minute, every second could make the difference between life and death for those taken by the shadows.

Though there was no light, the darkness seemed to shift and writhe like a living thing. Delvina rolled over and pushed herself up. Beneath her hands and knees, the ground felt hard in some places and spongy in others. The strong smell of sulphur burned the back of her throat and stung her eyes. Somewhere nearby came the soft tinkle of dripping water and the sighing of heavy breathing.

Her skin crawled and she resisted the urge to run. The door had closed behind her, and she had to find Retza and Zara. She wrapped the edge of her shawl over her face to ease her breathing and wobbled upright. Stretching out her arms in the darkness, she moved forward with a flat-footed shuffle.

Her eyes slowly adjusted, blurry outlines and strange shapes became visible. Several paces away, a shadow stood beneath an archway, his outline suggested against a dark glow behind it. He lifted a dark crystal in his hand. Dark light stabbed her eyes. Splotches of purple-black and shadows drifted across the roof and ceiling. It was like seeing and not seeing at the same time.

She backed against the rough stone wall of the grotto. Swathes of long bruised-purple crystals jutted out from the uneven roof with a strange alluring obscene beauty. Inside her head a thousand voices sang, soft, sibilant and insistent, like tired carewuns singing off-key lullabies of despair. The words crept into the crevices of her mind, sapping her energy, distracting her.

The figure standing in the archway beckoned to her.

'Come,' the former priest's voice purred. A thin tendril of shadow caressed her cheek. 'You must come with us to the sacrificial pool.'

'Beltain, what do you want with me?'

'My name is Legion and you are in my domain. Beltain has become one with us. Join us.'

'I don't think so.' Delvina struggled to stop her legs from moving. Maker help her, she had to resist the pressure of the voices' compulsion.

'Don't you want to join your friends?' Beltain gestured to his feet. Two figures huddled behind him, enmeshed in tentacles of dark smoke.

Relief flooded through her. Retza and Zara were alive. Together they could fight this monstrosity.

She stumbled forward. 'Retza, Zara, we have to escape.'

Beltain gave a contorted smile. 'They can't hear you, sweet morsel. They are trapped in the dark dreams of their own longings. As are you.'

Delvina bit her lip until the sharp-iron taste of blood came. 'This, this is not a dream.'

'Everything is a dream, all knowledge an illusion, all attachments are shadows. You think there is light but there is none. This is all there is.'

She shook her head against the insistent voices. 'No, I've seen the light, the wide blue sky above, the living, breathing ocean, I've felt the warmth of my mother's arms, the bond of friendship.' She pictured the faces of those she loved—her parents and Retza and Zadeki and Havilah and old Barekia ... and Danel.

'Pretty fantasies. You are but a commons-rat, lost and deluded that you can make a difference. You are alone. No one cares. Come with us.'

One pale long finger beckoned.

Her legs felt like boulders and, despite her resistance, she took one dragging step after another. The more she fought against it, the more she felt the pull.

In front of her, Retza and Zara stood up, their eyes wide open but unseeing. Zara's blue eyes flicked from side to side, as though caught in a bad nightmare. Retza's mouth twitched as he stared into the distance.

Beltain giggled. He turned and walked through the opening. The other two followed.

Delvina gritted her teeth. Going heedlessly to the slaughter block would not help her brother or friend. Dark coils slipped around her wrists and pulled her with the insistent tenderness of a lover. Shadows swarmed in the dark crystal light, but there was no real light down here.

She ducked under a low arch, gagging on the even stronger stench in the next chamber. In places, black and green glistening sheets mottled the wall like stained rags. Purple-black crystals bulged in between, like the glistening seeds of a rotting fruit, and long strings of gelatinous globs hung from the stone roof over the milky white floor. A faint mist drifted across its smooth surface.

Beltain walked along a worn track leading to a raised dais in the middle of the cavern. Only when his robe dragged over the side of the path and sent ripples fanning out and criss-crossing, did Delvina realise that a series of intersecting fuming pools formed most of the grotto's smooth white floor.

This was like no cave she'd ever seen before.

Beltain walked up the two stairs encircling the central platform and sat in a seat carved out of the living rock. Retza and Zara sank to their knees in front of him.

The whispering voices battered against her mind, Despair, like the biting burn of acid, ate away at her heart.

He crooked a finger again. 'Come, sweetwun.'

She planted her boots into the sludge, locking her knees. Yet, tinas by tinas she was drawn closer. The warning toll of her heartbeat clamoured in her ears. Shadowy feelers wound round her shoulders and legs and she slid towards him.

'Brave Delvina. Plump little bird. Why do you continue to struggle?'

'Because this is not real.' She curled her hands into fists and her jaw clenched hard. She would not give up. 'Retza, Zara,' she yelled. 'Wake up. Wake up.'

'Hush, my little dumpling.'

She pulled her head back and yelled harder. 'Help, somebody help. Retza, Zara, wake up! Ret—'

Smoke tentacles arched and curled around her face, into her mouth, choking her with their freezing touch. Her muscles could resist no longer and she knelt on the floor before him.

Help me. Please help me.

The gravel or something else on the rough floor dug into her knees. No, not rocks, but shattered crystals. Snatching up a broken shard from the ground, she hurled it at the shadow-taken priest. It smashed into Beltain's cheek bone, leaving behind a bead of bright blood, and deflected, glanced off Retza's shoulder.

Retza's eyes snapped open and he looked around wildly in every direction until he saw her. 'Del. Where are we?' Pulling against the shadow bounds, he tumbled sideways into her.

The dark coils loosened from her throat and she sucked in the stinging air. 'Quick, get Zara. We need to escape.' They would be stronger together.

They each took one of Zara's arms and pulled her up with them.

Zara looked around her in a daze. 'Where are we? What's happening?'

'We have to escape,' Retza said. 'Which way is out?'

'Back that way.'

'Fly little birds.' Beltain sat back on the stone chair, one leg dangling over the other, and laughed. A dribble of dark blood trickled down his cheek.

They ran along the path, past the fuming pools and slimy walls and through the archway to a smaller crystalline cave. Dense mist rose from the smoking pools, closing in and obscuring the walls.

'The door should be here somewhere.' She hadn't come far from the door before she'd seen Beltain.

Together they ran and hobbled through a series of small grottos. No sign of a metal door among the rough stone and jagged crystals. After what seemed a whole shift but was probably only moments, a dark archway appeared. Delvina sobbed with relief. The doorway would be there.

She staggered through the archway into a cavern with walls coated in slime and crystals mixed with black slime and the ground covered by pools of milky water. On a roughly carved platform to one side, Beltain sat in a chair, his shadow-filled eyes lit with malicious amusement.

He sat back and slow-clapped. 'Brilliant.' His face seemed fuller, the clothes no longer hanging on his frame. 'Come now, join us as is your purpose.' He curled his fingers and beckoned to them.

Delvina saw her own despair reflected in Retza's and Zara's eyes. They were trapped and far from help.

'By the Maker,' Delvina whispered. 'There must be a way to defeat them.'

Zara lifted her chin. 'If we are trapped here, surely the

shadows are too. Whatever happens to us, our friends are safe and they have Baba's seal.'

Delvina squeezed Zara's hand. A poor, frayed comfort perhaps, but it was true.

Beltain smirked. 'Thanks to your precious baba, little hawk, we now have the key.' He pulled a shining crystal from his tattered robes and let it dangle from his fingers. The crystal twisted at the end of a golden chain. Sudden flashes of blue-white light stabbed into the gloom. 'We are no longer locked in this prison. And when the time is right, we will rule your people, the diggers of the deep.'

Zara stepped forward, her eyes fixed on the swinging crystal. Had she succumbed so quickly?

'Zara, no!' Retza lunged to grab her, but she eluded him and he hurried after her.

This couldn't be a good idea. 'Zara,' Delvina called, following behind. 'Retza! What are you doing?'

'We must take the crystal from him. We can't let him use it,' Zara said, not turning around or stopping.

Beltain's smile widened and he settled back in the chair. 'You can try, my sweetlings.'

'Don't you see?' Delvina said. 'It's a trap.'

But neither of them was listening, rushing along the path between the smoking water. The crystal twisted and shimmered. Delvina blinked at the sudden flash of light and an idea broke through her shadow-muddled thoughts like sun parting the storm clouds. 'He can't use it. The seal is soul-bound to one person only.'

At last Zara stopped just paces away from Beltain's smug form and turned to face her. 'Is that what Baba meant, only the designated heir can use it.' She let out a peal of laughter, a little high-pitched, and she hugged herself. 'Brilliant.'

Beltain sat straighter and his white eyebrows dipped. 'What trickery is this?'

Zara grinned. 'I couldn't use the crystal on the Gate. It only works for him, for my father.' She caught hold of Retza's hand and faced the dark priest.

'You are trapped, Beltain, just as much as we are.' Retza stood side-by-side with Uzza's daughter, his shoulder brushing up against hers. She smiled and linked her arm with his.

So that was the way of it. Delvina bit down on a smile. She went away for a couple of rosters and looks what happens. She'd have to quiz her twin about it when … if … they escaped this madness. She stepped onto the island.

'You lie,' Beltain roared. His fist closed over the crystal, his face twisted with rage. 'I am Legion and … but wait, how do you know about the seals, toolwun?' His dark shade-filled eyes locked onto Delvina's and she staggered back a step at the force of the tidal wave of darkness that crashed down into her mind, probing its weakness. Her momentary pleasure at her twin's romantic leanings shredded like an old algae cake.

'There is a way to transfer the bond,' Beltain-Legion said. 'Show me how it is done.'

'We don't know how to,' Delvina shrieked.

'But it can be done. I see it in your mind.'

'Only Uzza or, I suppose, Princess Avardin can do it, so far.' Delvina felt arms around her, supporting her. Retza's familiar smell and Zara's sweeter scent on the other. She drew in a ragged breath. 'One is across the Lapis Ocean, the other you struck down. Both are beyond your reach.'

Dark fingers probed into every crevice of her mind, pulling and twisting and searching. Without warning, he ripped out of her, releasing her. She gasped in pain and slumped forward.

'No! No! No!' The shadow priest howled. 'Useless. Useless.'

He flung the crystal away. It curved in a flashing arc and landed with a small splash on the edge of the island. He stood, smoke curling and weaving around his torso, arms and mouth. 'If we cannot have those above, at least we have your very beings to feast on.'

Telsima's words came back to her. 'Guard your heart and the shadows have no real power to harm you.' But how could that be? She could see her doom in Beltain-Legion's mad-wracked eyes. They were at the creature's mercy.

Her heart shuddered and her limbs turned to slurry. Zara was right. Whatever ever else happened to them, Havilah, Zadeki, Danel and the others would be able to leave this place and survive. She closed her eyes and clung to the arms of her beloved brother and to his friend, who perhaps might one day have been her sister.

Cold mist curled around her and from somewhere high in the roof came the buffeting roar like the wind of an oncoming storm. All Delvina could hope was that the end would be quick.

Zadeki placed the keg of firepowder on top of the others the piled up against the wall in the makeshift shelter, careful to heed Danel's instructions. He was beyond tired, but he and the others couldn't stop, not until they'd broken into the Temple's Rest, rescued his friends and found the seal.

'That should do it,' Danel said. He took the fuse wire and, backing into the tunnel, rolled it down the corridor.

Zadeki smothered a yawn. 'Why stack it in this shelter and not just against the wall.'

'Ideally, we'd drill holes in the wall and insert the firepower that way. But we don't have time. The shelter should contain the initial explosion, directing its force for greater effect.' Danel rubbed his forehead with his arm and flashed a grim smile. 'Good of Uzza to build it for us. Let's fall back to the access tunnel.'

Zadeki's stomach tightened. Hadn't firepowder caused the first cave-in that destroyed Nebam's attempt to tunnel out? 'I hope the explosion doesn't bring everything down at once.'

'Don't sweat it.'

They edged past the door and smaller stacks of strategically placed kegs placed at the entrance to the connecting tunnel, rigged ready for the second explosion.

Gilarth appeared from the other direction, a sledgehammer over one shoulder, and two watchers following behind. 'The struts you marked are weakened, Thirdwun.'

Danel raised a thumb. 'Good. I'll give them a look-over and rig the second fuse, so we can fire it as soon as we get Delvina and the others out. Gilarth, let Overseer Havilah know we're ready and get the team in place.'

'As good as done.' Gilarth and the watchers strode past them, heading back down the branching tunnel that led to the abandoned crib room and the tunnel to the lifts.

Danel checked the struts. Zadeki paced the corridor wishing he was in his jaguar form. No doubt such caution was necessary, but his friends were in danger and every moment could make a difference between rescue or disaster.

'Will this take long?'

'It will if you keep distracting me.' Danel moved to the next strut. 'How about you check the tunnels around the shrine and make sure everyone's out before we blow this thing.'

Zadeki would rather be doing something than not. He turned and sprinted along the tunnels encircling Temple's Rest, checking the blocked secondary tunnels as well as the main one to be certain no one remained behind. They were empty except for dark fantasies, the impression of shadows seeping through the walls and prowling at the edges of his vision, only to disappear when he looked straight at them. If he could have bashed a hole in the wall with his bare hands, he would have. Delvina was in danger, he could feel it. Retza and Zara too. He could sense their terror, their pain, their despair throbbing through the walls. They had to get in there and help them.

Resisting the urge to shift into jaguar form too early, he raced back to Danel. 'All clear.'

'Come on then, the others are in position.'

They sprinted to the rough barricade part way down the connecting tunnel. In its shelter, Gilarth, Havilah, Baba and a handful of watchers huddled together, eyes wide and tense. Zadeki jumped in and edged past Gilarth to crouch beside Baba.

'Let's rumble.' Danel lit the fusewire and scrambled behind the barricade. The wire fizzed and fizzled along the tunnel.

The rapid breathing of ten or so people and his thudding heartbeat sounded like thunder in his ears.

'You sure this will protect us?' Watcher Natan asked.

'As long as the explosion doesn't bring the roof down,' someone else muttered.

'Shush,' Havilah said.

'Why's it taking so long?'

'Maybe, the fuse didn't take.' Danel half-rose before Gilarth pulled him down.

A pressing silence, then baboom. Boom. Boom. Boom.

The walls and floor shook. A growling sound like thunder echoed down the tunnels and the bones inside Zadeki's ears rattled. Then the slither and clatter of rocks falling and rolling that continued for long moments until at last all was quiet again. Dust drifted down the tunnel, but the roof overhead and walls in front were still intact.

'That was bigger than I expected,' Danel said, looking a little dazed and relieved.

'Didn't bring the roof down at least,' Gilarth said, wiping dust from his face. 'Shall we go?'

At last. Zadeki jumped over the barricade and ran out into the corridor, Danel at his heels. The sound of the others' boots and Baba's softer footsteps rang on the stone behind him.

Zadeki skidded around the corner. The shelter was gone, scattered and crumpled sheets of metal the only sign it had been there. Piles of rubble buried the floor and a grey-black powder coated everything. Inky shadows seem to slip and slide along the roof like a shoal of flesh-eating fish.

Gilarth, Natan and the other watchers pulled away the rocks, revealing a gaping hole ringed in a spiderweb cracks. Mist curled around the edges and the sulphurous smell of rot and decay seeped into the corridor.

'Remember, focus on the task, guard your minds against the shadows and stick together,' Baba said. 'Our priorities are to find the seal and get Retza, Delvina and Zara out of there.'

Gilarth nodded. 'Nate, you and one other keep guard out here. The rest of you, listen to the Highwun Korak.' He turned to Overseer Havilah. 'Your Honour, you won't reconsider staying behind.'

Havilah drew herself taller. 'We've come full circle. The Kinleader is right, we need to face this.' She turned to the two watchers positioning themselves on either side of the hole. 'Remember, set the second explosion off if we are not back in an hour and then tell Nebam to start the evacuation.'

'Yes, your Honour.' The watchers saluted each one as they approached the gap. 'Be safe.'

Baba bowed his head. 'By the Maker's favour, we will prevail. Remember, keep together.' He stepped into the hole, disappearing into the thick fog beyond the wall.

Zadeki stared at the dark maw and shivered, a sudden feeling of unease and doubt washing over him. It was like entering Avardin's pit again only bigger and this time by his own choice. The shadow-forged chains had sapped his strength and made it hard to shapeshift. They had almost broken him.

He met Danel's steady ash-grey eyes and nodded. Whatever happened, they had to save their friends and the people of this realm. It didn't matter what the shadows would throw at them. And he wouldn't be doing it on his own. Taking a deep breath, he ducked his head and stepped into the darkness.

Twisted black cables of smoke curled around Retza, entangling his limbs and distorting his vision. Zara huddled closer to him, her breath catching in a sob. Delvina stared at the pulsating roof, shudders racking her sturdy frame. He put his arms around them both and edged them away from the dais, even though he already knew distance would only delay the inevitable, if it did anything at all. Already he could feel the probing of his mind, the freezing touch as the tendrils wrapped around his limbs. What horrors did Beltain-Legion have in store for them?

A great gust of wind came from above them and a throbbing sound like great wings. A huge pulsing shadow swept across the surface of the milky pool.

Legion jumped up from the chair, his obsidian eyes bulging. 'No, no, no. You can't have them.'

Above him, the buffeting sound of wings grew louder, more insistent. A great bat swooped down over them from the dark opening in the cavern roof. Could it be the shaft that connected Temple's Rest to the Sunken Temple?

Delvina rubbed her eyes. Could it be? 'Telsima, is it

you?' Then her face crumpled. 'The voices are inside,' she whispered.

'Don't despair, children of the mountain. Help is closer than you think.' Smoke whips slashed out at the Kinleader and she swerved and dodged. 'Go now. Don't look back.'

The pressure on his mind eased. This was the miracle he'd hoped for. 'Come on.'

Baboom, boom, boom, boom.

A sudden explosion shook the cave and he stumbled. Zara caught him and the three of them clung together, propping each other up as the floor buckled beneath their boots. Crystals showered down with a discordant tinkling followed by splashing. Waves sloshed across the surface, acidic spray stinging his skin.

'Run toward the light.' The Kinleader swooped past them again. She stretched out a wing-claw toward a faint blue glow now lighting up the mist beyond the archway, then dodged more of Beltain-Legion's writhing smoke whips.

The dark mist thinned and weakened and the blue glow beyond the arch widened.

'Come on, Zara, Delvina. Let's go.'

'But what about Legion?' Zara said, looking nervously toward the dark figure walking toward them.

'Don't worry, I'll distract him,' Telsima said, flapping higher and swooping away. 'Keep to the path and follow the light.'

Retza stumbled along the path between the waters, Zara and Delvina walking close beside him. Only a few more steps to go and they'd reach the archway and the strange blue light. He could hear voices echoing from outside. Warm human voices.

Delvina stopped suddenly. 'What about the seal.'

'No point,' Retza said. 'It doesn't work for us.'

'There might be a way. If the Overseer ...' Delvina's voice faded.

'I'll get it.' Zara pulled her hands free and, before he could stop her, ran back toward the central island.

'Zara, no! We have to get out of here,' Retza called, but she didn't look back. A band tightened around his chest. He couldn't let her face that horror alone. He took a step backward.

Another tremor shook the floor. With a high-pitched rending sound, part of the roof in the far corner collapsed. The milky liquid sprayed upwards, before collapsing into a wave that sped across the pool towards the path.

'Zara,' Retza screamed. 'Come back.'

Too late. Instead of turning, she ran faster, back to where Telsima and Beltain-Legion dodged and swooped in a strange part-aerial dance.

Retza started after Zara, but Delvina pulled him back. 'Look out!'

The milky wave ran over the path and past the edge of the pool, until it lapped against their boots.

Zara gasped. 'The water burns.' She jumped the last section, landing in a sprawling crouch just below the dais. Rolling to the side, she crawled toward where they'd last seen the crystal.

Beltain had eyes only for the great bat swooping at him and twisting and dodging his whipping tentacles. The milky water streamed off back into the pool. Maybe Zara could get the crystal and escape in time.

In the next cavern, the sound of many footsteps and panting came closer. Korak emerged from the archway, followed by Zadeki, Danel, Havilah, Gilarth and a bunch of watchers.

Retza's legs went weak with relief. Help was indeed close, and finally here. Soon this nightmare might end.

Her heart thundering in her ears, Zara crawled along the pool's edge, eyes fixed on the lapping water. The crystal had to be around here somewhere. A bright glint flashed beneath the rippling surface. Nearby, the end of the gold chain stuck out onto the shore. She raised a fist, silently signalling her find to Retza and Delvina. But how could she protect her hands from the burning acidic water? She looked down at her ruined clothes. That might work. She ripped a strip from the skirt and wrapped it around her hand. She plunged her fingers into the pool and snatched the crystal out. Then, as quickly as she could, she pulled the soaked cloth off her stinging and reddened skin. At least it wasn't blistering. She edged back from the pool and crept towards the path. So far so good.

With a squealing shriek, another section of the roof shifted and fell, the edge of the spray splattering over Telsima and Beltain-Legion. Zara was sheltered by the raised dais and chair, but the great bat wobbled and lost her dancing rhythm. Beltain-Legion seemed unaffected by the acidic spray. He thrashed whip after smoky whip at the Kinleader. The bat was driven back behind a hanging pillar.

Zara sped up. Without the Kinleader's constant attacks, Legion-Beltain might turn his attention to her. She neared the start of the path as another bigger wave swept across it. Heart pumping, she jumped back, landing on her rear. Near where the roof had caved in, the water bubbled and boiled and a gurgling, rushing noise filled the cavern. When the wave receded, the now streaked, murky water still lapped over the path and narrowed the small rocky circle surrounding the dais.

Zara took a stinging, choking breath, terrified to twitch a muscle or even take another breath. Mist curled up around her ankles and stinging water lapped against the tips of her boots. She was trapped. Her path to safety was submerged in fleshing-eating acid.

The twins stared back at her, horror etched on their faces. Behind them were the people she'd grown to trust, Gilarth and Havilah, even the strange shapeshifters and a handful of watchers. She looked again at the water. The level hadn't fallen, if anything it had risen higher. And at any time, more of the roof could fall down, maybe crushing or trapping them in here.

'You have to go. Leave me,' she yelled across the churning pool.

Another light flashed on the edge of her vision. A bejewelled headdress lay half in and half out of the clouded water near the latest cave-in. Her blood turned to acid sludge.

The vision of the twenty-four chosen sacrifices filing into the sunken Temple, dressed in white and decorated with jewels flashed before her. Baba had said it was necessary to save the Crystal Heart and their realm. To feed the Dark Ones. To feed this abomination. To feed their own hates and fears.

Legion whirled around and saw her. Despair slapped into her mind and she ducked below the edge of the dais. How could she fight such a corrosive power? But she had to, at least for a moment, to do one last thing.

'Retza, catch.' She lobbed the crystal in a long, high arc towards her love. He met her eyes, and following the flashing, spinning rock and its glinting chain, dove to one side to catch it.

Beltain's purple-black eyes narrowed. 'Did you lie to us?' Tendrils shot her way, pinning her, pulling her, drawing her to him. 'Never mind, the way is opened to the outside. Do you think a handful of puny meat-and-offal beings will stop us?'

He reached out and caught her hand, pulling her up

and towards him. Biting cold seeped into her fingers. Pain seared through her arm.

'Come sweetling. It only hurts if you resist.'

'You would destroy our people. Why? What have we done to you?'

'Foolish little chick. What has the timid agouti done to the eagle, the peccary to the jaguar? There is only the predator and the prey. But we can help you save them if you submit to us. You could be our Queen.'

The cold crept past her knuckles to her palm. She felt the pull of power, the dark promises of status and recognition. She understood its allure, but she fought back, desperately.

'Zara no,' Retza's agonised voice broke into her daze. 'We have to reach her.'

Why was he still here? 'Go. Go now.'

'I have an idea. The debris from the shelter.' Another voice, Thirdwun Danel's. 'You three. Come with me.'

'And bring the powder.' The Kinleader swooped down, one wing skewed a little. Her claws wracking over Beltain's head. Two eagles dived down from behind her. Legion-Beltain shielded his eyes with his arm, but he didn't flinch or turn away as sharp beaks raked his flesh. His hold hardly loosened.

And it struck her like a blow. Legion didn't care about Beltain's form. It could take another, and another, perhaps had already done so over the tens-of-years. *We will take yours.* The thought dripped like venom in her mind. Maybe, but not her friends, not her people.

'Get out now!' she screamed. 'Follow the light.'

'Yes,' Legion purred. 'Let them run. It's you I need. You are bonded to this realm. You are the key. And so strong and young and delicious.' He batted away another swooping attack. 'These shapeshifters are a nuisance.'

With a wave of his free hand, mist poured out and

surrounded them, enfolding her into a shadowy cocoon with Legion. The walls of the cavern dimmed, and the sounds of her friends' shouts sounded as if coming from underwater. She could only hope they were escaping.

She had to distract him. 'You want sacrifices.'

'Sacrifices are always necessary, but we are not greedy. Besides what are these lowwuns to you? No one has really cherished you. Your father's forgotten daughter, your mother too busy to notice or care, hated and feared by those beneath you. We know you. We can give you all you deserve.'

Invasive, insidious, insistent. She felt the cold creep up her left arm, closing in on ... where? Her heart? She shuddered. How could she trust this entity not to harm Jesson or Retza?

'We will not hurt your brother or the young watcher. Whoever you love, we will protect at least until you tire of them.'

'Zara, let the light in.' Telsima's voice sounded distant. 'Don't allow the shadows to win.'

She blinked. 'And what did you promise Beltain?'

Legion took a step back, 'What? He asked to live forever. We gave him that.'

'You ate his soul.'

'We are legion. He is part of us now. But you. You are alone. No one loves you, no one cares.'

There was truth in what Legion said. Her baba had never loved her, she realised that now. Zara pulled her arm from Legion's grip and hugged herself, remembering the feel of Retza's arms around her, supporting her. And the feel of his lips on hers, and the way he looked into her eyes, as though she was so much more than she really was.

'Such love is fleeting. Everyone will let you down in the end. But we will be with you until the end of time itself.'

The mist wound tighter around, as though they were floating in the void.

How, how could she let light into this place of darkness? She had no light, no way of making it. She was unloved, unwanted, uncared for.

'With us, you will never be lonely again.'

She hugged herself tighter, tears rolling down her cheeks. It would be so easy to let go now, to be sucked down into the darkness. 'How do I let the light in?' she cried, flinging both arms out in entreaty.

Daughter of the mountain, you are loved more than you know. The voice came from within and without at the same moment. A great, warm assurance that she was loved by something so big, so glorious, so wonderful, the mind could not comprehend it. Joy bubbled up inside her and she gasped. 'I choose light, I choose life, I choose to be free.'

The cold tingling stopped moving up her arm, the mist thinned and dissolved, and the sudden return of sound imploded over her in waves. The shouts of her friends, the beating of wings, the putrid odours of this place, the feel of the air ruffling her hair and brushing her skin. And inside, a golden glow.

'Then you will die,' screamed Legion. 'Dead or alive, you will still serve our purpose.' It raised its hand, threads of purple-black light playing up and down its palm.

An eagle swooped from above and rammed straight into it. It staggered backward, falling into the acidic water, the ragged ends of its robe fizzing and writhing.

'Run, Zara,' the eagle keened and something in the rhythm and tone reminded her of Zadeki.

'This way, Zara,' Telsima pointed with her bat wing-claws to the group standing on the edge of the pool in front of the archway. And Retza was limping towards her on the surface of the smoking waters.

Beltain-Legion emerged from the pool. With each step, the milky acid-water pouring off the ragged ends of its robe, newly formed holes revealing red blistering flesh on legs and abdomen.

'Zara!' Retza reached her and gripped her by the waist. 'I've got you.'

'How are you walking on water?' A giggle escaped her burning throat.

Retza grinned at her. 'Danel had the brilliant idea to lay down pallets and sheeting to make a bridge across the water.' He turned and they walked together towards the stony shore where Delvina and Havilah stood, arms outstretched. At the edge of the cavern, Gilarth, Danel and the watchers were piling small containers against the walls of the grotto.

Legion-Beltain howled. 'You cannot escape me.' He held out a blistered hand, blacks wisps gathering in his palm.

Two eagles swooped down, driving him back further into the pool.

The great, silver-streaked bat rose high in the cavern. 'You have no more power here, legion of shadows.'

'Do you think to kill us,' the shadow priest mocked. 'We cannot die.' Tendrils reached out to grab her, and frayed like smoke as the eagles slashed them with their talons.

'Perhaps—as long as greed and fear and hatred live on.' Telsima landed before the chair, her bat form stretching and forming into the lithe Adelphi woman, long dark hair curling to her waist with a single silver streak. Her white flowing tari was ripped and singed near her shoulder. 'We will not attack you, stealer of souls. But we will destroy the dark crystals that allow you to feed on the thoughts of the unwary and give you power over them.'

Zara and Retza staggered onto the shore and Havilah and Delvina caught them.

Legion raised his hand, his eyes glowing. Small threads of dark light gathered and then fizzled. He took a step backward, even deeper into the milky acid, his borrowed face distorted with rage and hunger and despair. 'No, you cannot leave us here all alone. Havilah, please.' His voice changed and his face took on a different cast. 'Don't let them do this to me.'

Havilah's face drained of blood. 'Lead Hand Sami?' Then her face hardened. 'You killed him. You killed my crew, my husband, the twins' parents, you and Uzza's greed. This madness ends now.' She turned her back on Legion and signalled the Thirdwun Danel. 'Are all the kegs in position?'

He raised two thumbs. 'All set.'

Telsima stood taller. 'Go. We'll hold the rear while you escape.'

'Come Zara,' Retza said, and they all hurried through the archway towards the glow of blue-white glimmerlight.

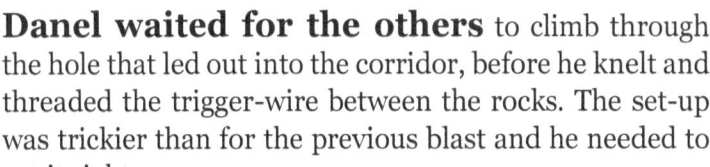

Danel waited for the others to climb through the hole that led out into the corridor, before he knelt and threaded the trigger-wire between the rocks. The set-up was trickier than for the previous blast and he needed to get it right.

The others paused where the shelter had been, catching their breath.

Delvina threw her arms around Retza and then pulled Zara into a tight hug before releasing her. 'I can hardly believe we're free from that nightmare.'

'We did it together.' Zara turned and hugged Retza. 'Thank you,' she said.

'Orf, careful of my ribs you two.' Retza's cheeks turned rust-red, but for all his complaints he moved in closer to Zara and slipped her arm through his own. She leaned her head against his shoulder.

Danel glanced at Delvina, who was smiling, and raised an eyebrow. So that's the direction those two were heading. Definitely a couple. Perhaps both twins would have life-partners soon. The thought left Danel feeling bereft. He ducked his head and focused on the task at hand.

Ahem, let's keep the tender reunions until we're all safe,' Havilah said, her voice gruff.

'Do you have enough firepowder?' Delvina moved towards Danel.

'The explosion will release the stored energy from the dark crystals. So, yes, it will work.' Overseer Havilah rubbed her forehead, a sheen to her eyes. 'It did last time when Ozier and I blew the entrance.' She beckoned to Lady Zara. 'We need to get the seal up to the upper levels.'

Zara glanced at Retza, her face falling. 'Only Baba can use the seal and ... that thing ... killed him.'

'Injured, yes, but he's alive.' Overseer Havilah clasped Zara's free hand. 'Highwun Korak and Natan took him and the other prisoners to the upper levels. If you could persuade him to open the Gate.'

'I will try.' Zara took a ribbon from her hair and tied the crystal to it and slipped it in a pocket.

Danel pulled the wire through into the corridor. He rubbed his hands on his breeches and picked up the roll of trigger-wire, ready to reel it out down the tunnel.

The sound of beating wings came from inside Temple's Rest. He looked up at the dark gap in the wall. Zadeki and Korak flew out in eagle form. Telsima climbed out after them, her long hair flowing behind her.

'Quick, block it off.' Gilarth signalled some watchers and together they piled the rocks in the gap.

When the last rock was placed, Danel cleared his throat. 'If you can clear the area, your Honour, I can finish setting up and blow the grotto.'

'Of course, Thirdwun. Today is a great day to bury the past.' Havilah beckoned the others to follow and laid a hand in the crook of Gilarth's elbow. Together they worked their way around the rumble. The watchers and the others fell in behind them.

Only Delvina and the Forest Folk didn't move. Korak and Zadeki settled on a pile of rubble and raked hooked beaks through their smudged and ruffled feathers.

'I'll help you,' Delvina said.

Danel blinked. His heart careered, faster and harder than when he'd been racing to lay the panels in the acid lake. Her eyes were red from the fumes, her clothes stained and dishevelled, yet she was beautiful. More so since he'd feared he'd lost her. He took a ragged breath. 'Thank you, Messenger Delvina. Perhaps—'

'Should I ...' Retza looked over his shoulder, the dirty bandage on his head slipping a little.

Delvina gave a wistful smile. 'You're injured and look half-dead. You'll just get in the way.'

'If you are sure Delvina?' Zara asked. 'I'd like him to come with me, but do come back safely.'

'Go, shoo, all of you.' Danel said, though he didn't mean Delvina.

Telsima touched his shoulder. 'Korak and Jazadek will guard the corridors. The shadows are a spent force for now, but better not to take chances.'

And perhaps it was better he wasn't left alone with Delvina. It was growing harder and harder to remember that her love had been given to another.

Once the others had left, Zadeki and Korak flew along the corridors. Delvina helped Danel lay down the firing wire he repurposed from the originally planned second-stage explosion. It wasn't quite long enough to reach the barricade, but it would have to do.

'Ready?' Danel called out.

Zadeki swooped out of the right corridor, followed by Highwun Korak from the left. Both flew down the tunnel towards them, their wing tips skimming close to the wall.

'All clear.' Korak keened. They glided over Danel and Delvina's heads and landed on the barricade behind them.

'Set it off, Del.' Danel handed her the trigger.

She smiled up at him and he smiled back. Whatever happened now, things would not be the same as before. He was going to miss the easy camaraderie they'd had together during their adventures.

'Sure you won't bring the whole mountain down on top of us?' Zadeki said, tension in his normally carefree voice. He lifted his wings and fluffed out his feathers.

Delvina looked up. 'Wait by the lifts, if you're worried.'

Zadeki turned an eagle eye to look at her. 'We're going to be here to protect you, in case Legion breaks out through that rubble. Just hurry up and do it.'

'Well, if you don't keep interrupting,' Delvina muttered under her breath.

She pressed the button.

'Run!' Delvina grabbed Danel's hand, bolted down the corridor. The thrumming sound of the two eagles close behind them.

A muffled boom was followed by a cacophony of rolling explosions. The ground shook beneath them, knocking them to the floor. Rocks and dirt rained at the end of the tunnel, advancing toward them until the corridor behind them disappeared in a cascade of rocks and clouds of dust.

They staggered to their feet and bolted.

Another roaring growl, the grinding sound of falling rocks and brush of wind against the back of Danel's neck lent speed to his strides. Small rocks pinged against his back. The floor rolled like the deck of the White Rose, and he and Delvina staggered into each other.

Tightening his grip on her hand, Danel ran faster than he ever thought he could, a rumbling roar at their heels.

Only once the sounds petered out, did Danel look back. There was no sign of the barricade. The tunnel was crammed with large rocks and rubble, now completely blocked.

'I hope the levels above are fine.'

Danel shrugged. 'Mostly worked out and abandoned tunnels. Right up to the Sunken Temple. But yeah, we'll need to check those areas. If we get to stay ...' Would Uzza cooperate. No doubt Nebam or Gilarth would manage to persuade him if Zara couldn't.

Zadeki flew down the tunnel and glided close to the sloping wall of shattered rock still creeping forward at a slowing rate. He banked and came back down the corridor towards them, landing awkwardly on the floor. 'Nothing is getting through that.'

Delvina shuffled her feet. 'Then maybe you and Highwun Korak should head on up. You both need to eat and rest. We'll be safe enough.'

Highwun Korak swooped down and folded his great wings. 'Are you sure, daughter of the mountain?'

Zadeki's neck feathers ruffled, his coal back eyes looking from one to the other. He spread out his wings, taking up most of the width of the corridor, and tilted his head. His flight feathers brushed Danel's shoulder. 'Look after her, or I'll be having something to say.'

Highwun Korak's laughter rang down the corridor. 'He knows what he's doing, son of my heart.' With two mighty down thrusts, Korak rose in the air. 'Your flying skills are improving, son of impetuosity, but can you keep up with a master?' With that, he hurtled down the corridor towards the lifts.

Zadeki whistled. 'Just watch me, father of years.' He turned his head, the glint in his eagle-eye. 'Be safe.' With that he flew off down the tunnel after his father.

Danel shook his head, feeling somehow obscurely happy. 'We'd better keep moving.'

Delvina reached up and rubbed some grit off his shoulder. He looked at her, coated in grey dust from the top of her hair to the soles of her boots. He supposed he looked the same.

'Look good together.' He chuckled. 'At least we match.'

He suddenly became aware they were still holding hands. He pulled to disengage, but she tightened her grip.

She leaned closer and before he knew it, he pulled her in and kissed her. He inhaled a load of dust coating her face and she must have done the same as they both sputtered and wheezed like oldwuns. She took a step back and mopped streaming eyes.

'Sorry,' he said, his face flaming.

'No,' she whispered, a new look in her eyes. As though it were the first time she'd seen him. 'No, I think I quite liked it.'

He cleared his throat. 'But what about you and Zadeki?'

She thought for a minute. 'We'll always be friends, but ...' She lifted a shoulder. 'Maybe I've found treasure closer to home.' She glanced at the pile of rubble behind them. 'Shall we head up, Thirdwun?'

'Wise idea, Messenger Delvina.' And he grinned so widely his cheeks ached.

Zara's thoughts swirled as fast as the lift slid upwards. Thoughts that were too numerous and fleeting to hold on to; relief that they'd survived the horrors of the grotto, delight to be with Retza, a lingering joyful glow, concern for her father, hope that at last the Gate would be opened. Retza's warm, solid if somewhat battered, presence anchored her. She relaxed against his chest, resting her head against his shoulder. He grunted then put his arms around her, his rough cheek against hers.

Glimmer lights flashed by with the levels, illuminating strained and silent faces then eclipsing them again in shadow. Each seemed lost in their thoughts. Gilarth stood close to Havilah, the watchers at a respectful distance and eyes averted in the huge lift. Telsima stood with grey-green eyes alert and a relaxed readiness in her stance.

As they neared the farm levels, an immense thundering boom rolled over them. The lift gave a huge bone-jarring shudder. The glimmer lights far above them winked out into darkness. The cables whined and screeched, their momentum upwards slowing.

Several heart stopping moments later, the lights winked back on, the sudden glare blinding her for a moment. The lift sped up again.

'That was massive.' Retza let out a slow breath. 'I hope Delvina and the others got away safely.'

Zara squeezed his fingers. 'I'm sure they did.'

Several moments later, the platform came to a gentle stop at the top of its run. Gilarth slid aside the protective cage, and they headed toward the Causeway.

The roar of the waterfall tumbling down into the ravine filled the breathless silence in the Causeway. Zara followed the others to the stairs sweeping up to the Grand Cavern and the Overseer's quarters.

'Has the trek across the mountain started already?' Retza asked.

Havilah stirred. 'Serafin and Perdak, the other two koraktil shifters, started flying small groups of youngwuns and frailwuns to the Gate at first shift. It will take a few days to ferry them all out. The crews should be preparing for the journey in the cribs.'

'The burning sunlight will be as much a threat as the

icy heights, so they'll wait until closer to sunset to move out,' Gilarth said.

'It may be wise to delay the trek until the son of Hezikah has tried the seal,' Telsima said.

Havilah nodded and kept walking.

'Less than fifteen hours since they took you,' Retza breathed in Zara's ear. 'It felt like forever down there.'

Their footsteps echoed along the empty hallway outside the Grand Hall. Retza stumbled. He was flagging, his limp more pronounced, and she moved closer to support him. He'd suffered much in his determination to protect her.

Her footsteps waivered at a sudden thought. 'Has Jesson been flown out or is he still here?' How could she have forgotten him, if even for a moment?

'Jesson refused to leave until you were found. He was helping Barekia last I saw him.' Havilah turned and smiled at her. 'He'll be overjoyed to see you again.'

'Matu!' Ahead of them a harried looking Nebam walked through the archway leading from the Overseer's new quarters, followed by one of the messengers. 'Er ... Overseer.' Relief washed over his face. He scanned the group, lingering on Retza and Zara. 'You got them back—and the seal? When the ground shook the second time, we thought the worst.'

Havilah hurried over as if to hug him and, at the last moment, brushed his shoulder. 'We subdued the Dark Ones and Zara has the seal. Send messengers to the leadwuns that we'll delay the start of the trek.'

Nebam gave an awkward smile and patted Overseer Havilah's hand before burying his own in his jerkin. 'Ahem, yes, good idea. The prisoners are secured, as requested.'

'Take us to Uzza. And then have water and some food, if you can spare any, sent to my Ready Room and a scrybe to tend to these youngwuns.'

'Kailah, see the messages are sent. This way then, Matu.' Nebam led them to a room just past the messengers' crib and Havilah's offices.

Empty shelves lined the walls. Baba lay on a pallet in the middle of the small room. He thrashed about, gasping for breath. Old Scrybe Barekia looked up from where she hovered over him. The sour-sweet odour of sweat and the hint of something putrid turned Zara's stomach.

'What ails him?' Zara rushed into the room, Retza limping behind her.

Barekia shook her head, her wrinkles deepening 'The knife wound is shallow, yet he's taken a turn for the worse.'

Telsima stopped beside Zara. 'May I see?'

Barekia pulled up Baba's once-white shirt and unwrapped the bandages, exposing a purplish wound along his ribs. The smell intensified and Baba groaned, whipping his head from side to side. His face was flushed and sweat beaded his upper lip.

Telsima knelt beside him and touched his forehead and chest. 'Be calm, son of Hezikah.'

Baba flinched and moved to the side. 'Hot. Why is it so hot?' His crusted lids fluttered open to reveal dull and sunken eyes. He blinked. 'Ruhanna's daughter, I thought you dead.'

'So, someone remembers me?' Kinleader Telsima said with grim humour. She probed the raised area with her fingers. 'The wound is infected.'

'So I think,' Barekia threw up an arm, 'But how can it be, it's less than an hour since it was inflicted.'

'Had it been an ordinary weapon perhaps.' Telsima's fingers traced a black line across his pale skin, a line creeping from the wound along the line of the rib towards the centre of the chest. 'But it was shadow-wielded. The tip may have broken off or the blade poisoned so that even a scratch could be ....' she glanced at Zara and the Kinleader's grim apologetic look said it all.

Only an hour ago, she was happy at the thought of never seeing her baba again. Not after everything he'd done to her, to her friends, to the realm. Now, she realised it was not so easy to cut the ties that bound parent to child. She wasn't going to make excuses for his behaviour, or to say what he'd done was acceptable. Yet despite all, she loved and grieved for him, as much for the might-have-beens. As simple as that. Tears scalded Zara's eyes.

Retza took her hand, the feel of his strong fingers comforting. 'What can you do?' he asked, voice subdued.

Barekia rubbed her chin. 'What would you advise, Kinleader? Not ten minutes ago, I probed the wound, rinsed it out and packed it with stagmoss.'

'Such things would help an ordinary wound. Do you have wind's breath leaves?'

Barekia's shoulders drooped a little. 'No. My store of herbs diminishes every day with no way to replenish them.'

'No matter. This infection is shadow driven. It's more of the mind than the body.' Telsima lay her hands-on Baba's chest, but he pushed them away.

'Leave me be,' he growled.

'Uzza, the Kinleader is skilled in healing,' Havilah said from the doorway.

Zara shivered. The purple-black streak appeared to have grown even in the short time since they'd entered the room. The skin around Baba's mouth had a mottled bluish tinge. He clutched his chest and his breaths came in grunting pants.

'Hush, I'm not going to harm you, son of Hezikah.' Telsima placed her hands on Baba's forehead and sang in a soft, sweet voice.

The sound washed over Zara, calming her and bringing hope in its wake.

Baba's thrashing eased. He licked his dry flaked lips and stared first at Telsima, then Barekia, and then at Zara.

'Why are the glimmer lights not working?' his voice a hoarse whisper.

'Baba?' Zara leaned forward, a little breathless. The glimmer lights shone at full strength with no pity for his ravaged face.

'Who is that?'

'Zara.' Her voice hitched on her name. Did he even remember her?

'You are alive.' He reached up and touched her face. 'You must escape. It's too late for me. I've been a fool. Go! Go while you can.'

'It's never too late to embrace the light,' Kinleader Telsima said. 'Though the long shadows of some actions are hard to undo.'

Baba shuddered and turned his head away. 'What have I done?' He moaned.

Havilah cleared her throat. 'Not to be callous, but can we carry him to the Gate? To use the seal?'

Barekia threw up her skinny wrinkled arms. 'Moving him would speed up the progress of the infection. He'd not survive it. His life is in the hands of the Maker now.'

Zara's heart convulsed. If he survived at all.

'Ask him about the seal, child,' Telsima said.

Baba struggled to raise his head. 'The seal. Do you have it?

'Yes, Baba. Only you can use it, remember.' She held it out to him in her acid-burnt hand, the crystal swinging gently on its golden chain. Barekia was right though, he'd not survive the distance between here and the Gate a level down and five lek away. 'But only you can use it.'

'The link can be transferred. The crystal-singers of the Lonely Isles confirmed it,' Telsima said. 'This at least the delegation determined.'

Zara's lips twisted. 'To the designated heir. Baba said as much, but who knows where my brother Asrab is, or even if he is alive.' Most likely he and all her siblings, except Jesson, had suffered the fate of their mother. Her whole family wiped out. She scrubbed the tears from her cheeks.

'Daughter.'

She inhaled a long shuddering sigh. 'Yes, Baba.'

'Do you remember the lullaby your matu sang to you youngwuns? She had a beautiful voice. What happened to us ...' tears rolled down his hollow cheeks.

Zara nodded and sang a few words,

'Hush littlewun, don't be a-crying,

Your baba's a prince

Your matu's ... your mat—'

Zara's voice broke and she couldn't go on. Retza's hand gripped her hand.

Baba touched her arm. 'I'm sorry. I ... I started well. Don't Forget the ...' His voiced frayed into silence.

'Take care of your brother, Zuzu,' the words more a suggestion of sound. The bruise-like line branched out and reached the centre of his chest, others following it. He convulsed.

'Baba.'

He took several big shuddering breaths. His blank eyes slid to look past her shoulder and then lay still.

'Baba.' She grabbed his arm and shook him.

Retza took her hands and pulled her into a hug, soothing her.

Her baba looked so thin, so diminished, like an insect husk, shed and abandoned and empty.

'I am sorry child. He's passed beyond the veil,' Barekia said.

Weariness settled on Retza like a broody bird. The last several hours were a nightmare, though much of it was now a confused blur. A dull ache thudded in the back of his head, his ribs protested every time he took a deep breath and his knee was throbbing again, but Barekia had applied new bandages and said he would live. He stole a sideways look at Zara, holding herself together, her face paler than normal, her sky-blue eyes glistening with tears and a half-full beaker of broth cooling on the floor beside her.

He wanted to take her in his arms and smooth away the creases on her forehead. He wanted to hold her tight and comfort her, never mind the others watching.

Instead, he placed his hand over hers. 'You should get some sleep before we leave,' he whispered.

She smiled at him through the tears. 'So should you.'

She wasn't wrong. They had a short time to refresh before the evacuation started. How he would cope with his busted knee and overwhelming desire to sleep, he wasn't sure. He closed his eyes and allowed his mind to drift. He felt her snuggle closer and he slipped his arm around her shoulders, her head warming his chest.

He was drifting into sleep when the door of the Meeting Room slammed and footsteps approached. His eyes slipped open.

'Oh, sorry to wake you, Retza.' Havilah raised an eyebrow. 'If you two needed an extra blanket, you only needed to ask.'

Retza's face warmed, but he refused to drop his arm. He'd almost lost Zara to her father's stupid plans and he wasn't going to let her go now, as long as she would have him.

Zara stirred and stretched her arms. She gave a lazy smile. 'I could get used to this.'

Retza grinned. 'Well I hope you do.' He looked up at Overseer Havilah. 'Do you need us to help?'

Havilah rubbed a hand over her face and stifled a yawn. 'Get some rest. It's going to be a long hike. The ladders up the Cauldron are in position and the weather's holding.'

She didn't say what they were all probably thinking. Even with the guidance of the Forest Folk they were likely to lose people along the way. But they couldn't stay here with no food. If the Tamrin wouldn't come to them, they needed to go to the Tamrin.

Havilah sighed. 'I'm sorry about your baba, Zara. Uzza, Gilarth and I were all friends once, a long time ago, then we grew apart.'

'It still doesn't feel real.' Zara looked up. 'How is ... how is Putarn?'

A shadow passed over Havilah's face. She looked away toward Gilarth and Nebam still on their feet, organising some last-minute crisis with Narval, the Quartermaster. 'I think he's finally realised what he's done and the consequences to that.'

'He's your son.'

'And it breaks my heart. He was always a little brash but the expedition to the lowest level changed him. That and the slither of dark crystal he must have picked up after one of the shadow-taken killed his father, my Ozier. It's been like a poison festering inside him ever since.'

'Maybe that's how Putarn knew where Uzza was?'

'The dark dreams. Yes, that's what Kinleader Telsima thinks.' Overseer Havilah patted Retza's arm and moved across the room to sooth down the Quartermaster.

Retza was just settling back to doze when the door to the Meeting Room opened again, and an excited squeal spiked into Retza's throbbing head like a pick. 'Zara. Retza.' A small figure ran towards them and small arms were wrapped around Retza's neck, almost choking him. 'You're alive.'

'Jesson,' Retza laughed and patted his thin back. 'Where did you come from? Aren't you supposed to be sleeping?'

Zara's eyes lit up and she tussled the boy's bright golden hair. 'Maybe once Korak is rested, he can take you to the food awaiting outside the Gate.'

Jesson loosened his arms and turned to his sister. 'No Zara, I'm old enough to come with you.'

'But the journey will be long and dangerous and your legs are short. We'll meet you there in a couple of days.'

Several days, Retza thought, but he didn't correct Zara.

Jesson's face settled into stubborn lines. 'What about opening the Gate. You found Baba and Baba has the key.'

'I had the seal all along.' Zara touched the crystal at her neck now hung on an old blue ribbon. 'But it only works for Baba and ... his designated heir. Asrab and ...' She closed her eyes, as though unable to finish that thought.

Her older brother was likely dead, like her matu and other sibwuns. She and Jesson were alone, without family. 'Maybe Jesson could try,' she voiced the first idle thought to distract her.

Jesson shook his head, his face solemn. 'Zara should be the heir. Not me. I'm going to go on adventures with Delvina and Zadeki when I'm bigger.'

Zara smiled despite herself. 'I don't think Baba ever thought of me as heir. I'm just a girl after all.'

'So is Overseer Havilah. And Kinleader Telsima.'

'And you're not "just" anything, Zara,' Retza said. 'Maybe you should try it.'

'I'm not sure it's a good idea,' Nebam called across the room. 'We've had our hopes raised so many times only to be shattered.'

'But we've nothing to lose and much to gain,' Havilah said.

It was a good idea. 'It wouldn't take that long either, Overseer.' Retza stood, suddenly excited.

Jesson pulled on his hand. 'Can I come to the Gate this time?'

'Well, why not?' said Retza, then gave a sheepish grin when Zara glared at him. He had a good feeling about this.

Zadeki flew half-a-wing in front of Baba, past the blasted entrance and up the stairwell to the twenty-first level. The elation at rescuing Delvina and the others and the exhilaration of flying at speed just ahead of the explosion had seeped away. He was beyond weary and his resistance to a bird's instinctive panic of being trapped underground was unravelling.

A fat juicy moth fluttered close to the strip of glimmer lights illuminating the lift shaft. Zadeki snapped it up with his hooked beak and gulped it down before he realised what he was doing.

'Time to shapeshift, son of my heart,' Baba's voice sounded from behind him.

'But it will be quicker to fly up the shaft than wait for the lift.' Zadeki snapped back, irritation rising like a cloud of stinging insects. He scanned the tunnel for more tasty titbits, though a rat or rock-rabbit would better sate his growling hunger.

'Jazadek of Great Forest Kin.' Baba's eagle-voice was sharp, urgent. 'Remember who and what you are!'

A shock jolted through him. In his exhaustion and hunger and grief, he was losing his sense of self to the form. He fluffed his feathers and swooped down, his limbs and torso lengthening and changing as he landed in front of the lift.

'Sorry, Baba.' His shoulders and head sagged. Such a youngling's blunder.

Baba landed beside him, shifting into his human

form. He gripped Zadeki's shoulder. 'You've done well. We've both been pushed beyond our limits by pressing need. Eating on the wing is not a bad idea.'

'But not if I lose myself in eagle thoughts.' Zadeki slumped down against the wall.

'Danel and Delvina will be here in a few moments. Let's take the time to rest and eat.'

Despite the moth sitting uneasily in his gizzard ... er ... stomach, at the mention of food, hunger barrelled into him like a devouring crocodile. 'Eat what? Dust and air?'

Baba chuckled. 'Danel left our packs here. We'll raid those, but first ...' He pulled the lever on the control panel. With a judder and a creak, the cables slithered upwards and the sound of the cage descending came from far above them.

Zadeki found the packs stowed in a hidden corner. He rummaged around a bit then tossed a small packet at Baba before pulling one out for himself. He all but inhaled the stale bread roll and a handful of nuts and dried fruit, then chugged down half the water in the bottle. Meagre as it was, the food revived him and life felt a little sunnier.

'Does it worry you, youngest son?'

'What, Baba?' Though Zadeki could sense where this was heading.

'Delvina and Danel?'

Zadeki shifted his back against the rough-hewn wall. Did it bother him? The image of Danel's besotted face and Delvina's tender smile, the two of them walking together side by side, formed in his mind's eye. He leaned his head against the wall and closed his eyes at a sharp sense of loss. Sometimes one didn't fully value a treasure until it was gone.

'You could still win her over, if that is what you want, my son. I'd be proud to welcome her into the family.'

'There is no one else like Delvina. I think, given time ...' Zadeki picked up a pebble and threw it, trying to find some order in his tumbling thoughts. 'I don't think I'd make a good mate just yet, and I don't think it's fair to ask her to wait, especially when she has less time than me. Besides, I think she's decided already, even if she's not aware of it herself.'

'Any regrets?'

'Some,' Zadeki rubbed his face and picked a fluffy down-feather from the floor. 'Danel is a good choice, even if I do feel like pummelling him into the ground.' He rubbed his chest in a vain effort to dislodge the ache. But what he said to Baba was true—the call of the open spaces and wild adventure bubbled in his veins like a heady drink. There are so many places he hadn't explored yet. So many forms he could learn, maybe even the koraktil form. Besides, he wanted so much to get away from all this—Aunt Bikan's death, the pull of the shadow crystals, the smell of death. 'So is it over? Does Zara really have the seal?'

'So Uzza said.'

'And the shadows are gone?'

'They are never truly gone. Not this side of the undying Song. The shadows are liars and twisters of the truth. They grow fat on others' despair.' Baba waved his empty water flask. 'But without the crystals to enhance and focus their influence and with seekers of the light like Havilah to lead the Darane, the shadows become mere whispers in the dark.'

'Stalwarts like Retza and Delvina and Zara too.'

'Of course.'

'So.' Zadeki sat up, suddenly anxious to be off. 'I don't want to miss the opening of the Gate.'

'The impetuosity of youth,' Baba gave a half-frustrated, half-affectionate laugh. He held up a hand. 'Ah, here they are.'

The whine of the descending lift reached a crescendo and the cage came to rest at the bottom of the shaft. Just then, the clatter of boots and soft voices came from the stairwell. Moments later Delvina and Danel emerged and strolled over to them, arms linked and coated from head to toe with grey dust.

'Perfect timing,' Baba said.

Danel raised a teasing eyebrow. 'Nothing to do?'

Zadeki jumped up. 'To the Gate?'

Danel nodded. 'For sure, it makes sense to check the Gate level first on our way up. And I know the way.'

Zadeki grinned back at them. Those two would be good together. He threw the remaining food packs to his friends, then jumped onto the lift platform. They would need to hurry, or risk missing a historic occasion, the opening of the Gate to the Glittering Realms after more than two hundred years.

Delvina stepped off the lift platform and followed Danel onto the concourse running beside the ravine, past the empty entertainment halls and a deserted creche to the once-banned tunnels leading west. Zadeki and Korak traipsed behind them with a weariness in their normally lithe steps. The roar of the river was louder one level down from the Grand Causeway. Commons-rats and crewless were not encouraged to use this area and, with all that had happened since, it wasn't one she'd frequented. Danel seemed to know his way, taking the tunnels towards a large cavern which showed signs of recent use.

'The staging area,' Danel said. 'This way.' He pointed across the space to a huge stone archway flanked by statues of former Overseers. Glimmer-tracks ran down the wide tunnel to one side. Off to the right, another rougher entrance had been gouged out of the rock. Tools and support struts lay broken and abandoned against the raw stone of the wall. A cool damp breeze sighed out of the dark tunnel's mouth, fanning Delvina's fringe and sending a tremor down her spine.

Zadeki hugged his arms and shivered. 'I hope we're taking the bigger brighter tunnel this time.'

'Yes,' Danel's lips quirked up on one side. 'That's Nebam's tunnel. It leads to the cave-in and an underground lake.' He strode over to the bronze control panel and fiddled with the dials. 'Looks like someone took the glimmer trucks just recently.'

'A good sign then,' Korak said.

'Does that mean we have to walk?' Delvina asked.

'Nah, the track is clear. We're good to go.' He pulled a lever. With a series of clanging sounds, a line of glimmer trucks slid from a smaller cavern and came to a gentle stop against a low platform in front of them. 'Load up.'

Highwun Korak climbed into the rear glimmer truck. Zadeki followed and then offered Delvina a hand up. He dropped his hand as soon as she was settled.

'Thanks,' she said, catching his eye.

He returned a wistful smile, and moved to the side as Danel scrambled in behind them. Danel pulled the lever. The trucks gave a jolt and, with a soft whirr, sped down the tunnel toward the Gate.

Highwun Korak covered his mouth in a yawn. 'How long before we get there?'

'Maybe fifteen minutes,' Danel said.

'Might as well get some rest then, and as though he were in a crib room bunk, he settled down and was instantly asleep.

'I'll manage the lever if you two want to rest,' Danel said, eyeing the two of them, a small pleat between his eyebrows.

'Naw, first time I've been in a glimmer truck. Not going to waste the experience.' Zadeki moved toward the front. He perched on the side of the truck, eyes to the front as the walls zipped past with increasing speed.

Delvina looked from one to the other, suddenly conflicted. With a sigh, she brushed the dust off her face.

Zadeki stared into the glow of the tunnel ahead of them, his shoulder stiff. He was wild and glorious and he and his Kin had done so much for her and her people. The failure of the Crystal Heart and the blighting of the farm caves hadn't been their problem, but they'd acted anyway. Given as much as they could and risked danger and death. Highwun Bikan paying the ultimate price.

Danel was a good man. He may not stir the same wild, heady feelings Zadeki did, but Danel was handsome, loyal, courageous and not afraid to face a crisis. She liked that about him. Maybe more than liked it, and they worked well together. Being together felt like a good fit. Not that there was any need to rush into a decision. She needed time to heal and breathe.

The sides of the tunnels slipped past, the air full of old secrets, dashed hopes and fragile promises.

'Almost there,' Danel said, his voice strained.

Catching Danel's troubled look, she smiled and moved to stand closer to him.

Korak opened his eyes, instantly awake. 'Excellent.'

Another archway on an even grander scale loomed ahead then flashed by. The tunnel opened into a high cavern. The trucks came to a stop behind another line of stationary vehicles. A central strip of glimmer lights shone down, throwing into relief the drag marks and bootprints criss-crossing the rough stone and clay floor. Metal sheets, some charred or marked, as well as tools and other paraphernalia were stacked against the tunnel sides. The murmur of voices came from the smaller archway up ahead.

They jumped out onto the low platform.

Danel secured the trucks. 'Go on ahead, but be careful.

Hopefully the seal will have deactivated the traps by now, but ...' Danel shrugged.

'We will heed your words, son of courage,' Highwun Korak said.

'Del?' Zadeki raised his eyebrows.

She shook her head, staying where she was. Korak and Zadeki loped toward the voices.

Delvina waited beside the trucks. Danel jumped down beside her and they stepped through the archway. To the left, scorched and scratched metal sheets shielded a large bronze panel similar to the one in the Heart Room. A newly constructed metal tunnel led to a large polished black gate that reflected back the bluish glare of the glimmer lights like oil on water. The great arched doors hung at bizarre angles, partly broken from their hinges. Had the seal worked and the Gate been opened already?

'The Obsidian Gate, first of seven,' Danel said. 'Nebam really gave it a battering.'

Clustered behind the metal shields around a bronze control panel were a group of familiar people—Gilarth, Havilah, Barekia and then Zara with Jesson, Retza and Nebam. Telsima and Korak were already in deep conversation to one side, Zadeki hovering beside them.

Havilah beckoned them to stand behind a shield. 'You just got here in time. Don't stand in the open. If the crystal fails, the cavern will become a death trap.'

As they hurried over, Delvina realised someone was missing. 'Where is Uzza?'

A shadow passed over Zara's face. 'He ...' her voice broke and she blinked rapidly.

Barekia answered instead. 'The wound from a shadow-wield weapon proved fatal, may the Maker grant him peace.'

'I'm sorry, Zara, Jesson.' Delvina brushed the littlewun's golden hair. 'But he did tell you how to transfer the connection to the seal?'

'No.' Zara's mouth puckered. 'We're hoping it's transferred to me, as Baba's oldest surviving child.'

Delvina looked at Danel. That wasn't what the scrolls had said back in the library at Silantis. Her stomach squirmed. Could it be that simple? What if it didn't work that way. Be still child. Some of the tension eased from her shoulders.

'Come, let's get this done by shift's end,' Nebam said.

'Spectators over here please.' Gilarth herded them back to the archway.

'Can you look after Jesson?' Retza put down the squirming youngwun, who launched himself at Zadeki with a squeal of pleasure. Danel took Delvina's hand and, they moved to the protection of the archway.

Only when Retza, Zara and Nebam were in front of the pedestal, did Zara step forward. She placed her hand in an indentation on the panel's sloping side. A blue light reflected off their intent faces. A small tray whirred open.

Zara took the crystal, now hanging around her neck on a ribbon, and with shaking fingers, inserted the crystal into the slot. The light turned to purple.

Delvina stood on tiptoes to see past Havilah.

The light deepened to blood red and started flashing.

'Blast it! Get down!' Nebam growled.

He, Zara and Retza dropped to the ground, behind the shields. A clunk, clunk, clunk came from the walls and roof, followed by a whirring creak. A few scattered arrows pinged off the makeshift shield.

'Is that what was stopping you? A few paltry arrows?' Zadeki asked with a quizzical look.

'There were swarms of them before. We burnt most of them.' Nebam scowled at everyone. 'Clear as water, the seal's not working. Uzza was playing games with us.'

After several seconds of despondent silence, the arrows petered off.

Danel took a step through the gateway.

Gilarth caught his arm and pulled him back. 'The roof sends down thunder bolts. We need to wait.'

The moments dripped by, until at last Nebam gave the all-clear. Delvina and the others joined Zara at the pedestal, a feeling of shared despondency dampening the atmosphere.

'That's it then,' Nebam said. 'We did everything we could, it just wasn't good enough.'

Zara stood up. 'Perhaps it's the timing ...' Her voice faded.

Delvina shook her head. It couldn't end like this. Why hadn't Uzza transferred the link? Had they run out of time?

Havilah brushed a greying strand of hair out of her tired eyes. 'We'll start the full evacuation in an hour.'

A heavy silence blanketed the cavern, no one quite meeting the other's eyes. With Uzza dead and the link not transferred, the crystal was no more than a pretty bauble. Delvina scuffed the threshold with her boot.

This isn't how it should end. There must be another way. Something niggled at the edge of her thoughts. If Princess Avardin had found a way to transfer the connection from her uncle, the Sea Dragon King, to herself then surely, they could do the same for Zara.

Havilah turned and moved toward the glimmer trucks. 'Come on, we've a lot to do and a long night ahead of us.'

Delvina didn't move. What had she said to Avardin before the drugged drink took effect? Something they'd found in the scrolls from the library in Silantis. The memory of that conversation was hazy—her own sleepy words in Princess' Avardin's aviary and the spark of triumph in the Princess' cruel eyes. She had wanted to know how to bypass a soulstone so she could seize power from Grand Technician Iulien and her cousin, Prince

Selwin. And that's what she'd done. If Avardin could do it, couldn't Zara?

'Zara are you sure your baba or da-baba didn't give you a code?' she asked.

'Baba told me nothing, Delvina. I'm just his eighth child, the second youngest and a girl at that, nowhere close to being his designated heir. He struggled to remember my name.'

'It could be a rhyme or perhaps a saying that had significance to him.'

Retza put an arm around Zara. 'Don't hassle her, Del.'

'Doesn't matter what it is. If she doesn't know it.' Nebam gripped the panel tightly, face grey with defeat. 'Fruitless delay only weakens our chances of survival on the mountain.'

'Yet just a few moments of reflection might save you from a hard journey, son of stone.' Kinleader Telsima held up a slim hand. 'The words may be hidden in plain sight. In his last moments, did not your father ask you to sing a lullaby, daughter of Overseers?'

'Yes, but his mind was wandering—' Zara's mouth gapped. 'Do you think that is the key is?'

Yes! That has to be it.' Delvina turned to the Kinleader. 'Don't you think so?'

Zara grabbed Retza's hands, her eyes like blue fire. Then doubt doused the flame. 'What if it isn't?'

'There's only one way to find out, child,' Telsima said.

Delvina blew out her imprisoned breath. This time, they wouldn't be disappointed.

Zara lifted the shining crystal with trembling hands and swallowed hard. Once again, all eyes were on her, waiting for her to produce a miracle. What if she couldn't? What if ... No! Kinleader Telsima was right. If she didn't try at all, failure was ensured.

She licked her lips, took in a deep breath and sang.

'Hush littlewun, don't be a-crying,

Your baba's a prince'

She felt the crystal warming against her palm. Her heart fluttered. Was it working?

'Your matu's a fine lady

Your cradle is made of ... of

The words thinned and frayed in her mind. It was too long ago. Tears smarted her eyes.

'Relax, let the words come.' Retza whispered and squeezed her hand.

She nodded.

'Your cradle is made of diamonds,

and lined with soft fur.'

A clear sweet voice rose above the thundering of her heart.

Jesson. Zara looked to where Zadeki still held him and beckoned them over. She pulled him into a hug and they sang the next verses in unison.

'Hush littlewun, don't be a-crying

The tunnels are secure

And the farms-caverns a-thriving

The toolwuns are a-mining

The vaults a glittering with gems and ore.'

The crystal quivered beneath her fingers, at first erratically, then in time with her heartbeat.

'The last verse, Zara,' Jesson whispered.

'Hush littlewun, don't be a-crying

You will be a-growing

strong and protected

the gates guarding against harm

And until the day it's time to take what is yours.'

One final tremor of the final note and the crystal stilled in her hand, as though inert.

'This is ridiculous,' Nebam muttered.

Zara looked at him, chest tight.

He scrunched his face and tugged his scrappy beard. 'But go on then, one last try and then that's it.'

Havilah gave her a gentle smile. 'Don't mind the Secondwun. Take your time, Lady Zara.'

'Yes, your Honour.'

She turned back to the control panel, her back straight and her head high. For the hundredth time, she put her hand in the indentation and waited for the tray to slide out. Lifting the crystal, she placed it in the slot.

It fitted perfectly, like the last time. Thud thud thud thud. Her heart beat painfully against her ribs as she waited for the rain of arrows one more time.

Clunk.

That was new.

The light stayed blue and letters flickered and fell into position.

'Welcome, Overseer. Please wait, while the Gate opens.'

Zara caught her breath. Retza mouthed. 'You did it.'

'So, what does it say?' Nebam called out.

Before she could answer, the shattered Obsidian Gates swung open in a drunken arc. She stood stone-still, her knees suddenly weak, hardly able to believe that the simple lullaby had worked.

'Woohoo,' Zadeki whooped. 'Praise the Maker, you did it. How awesome is that?'

'Yay, Zara,' Jesson piped.

Soon everyone was cheering. Delvina scooped her up in a tight hug. Gilarth beamed at her and even Nebam had a huge grin on his narrow face. A torrent of joy bubbled up and up and up, until she thought she would burst with it.

'But, do we need to do this for each Gate?' Danel asked.

Zara deflated a little. It was a lek between each of the

seven Gates. It would take all shift to travel the distance and open one at a time. Yet, if that's what it took to get the food to the people, then so be it.

A strange whooshing sound came from between the broken doors and a fresh breeze laden with an unfamiliar fresh smell rushed through the Obsidian Gate, tickling her nose and ruffling her hair.

'That wind came from somewhere,' Retza said.

Zadeki grinned. 'I can smell the bushes of the ravine in the Valley of Statues. Let's go.'

Nebam rubbed the tear tracks off his cheeks and cleared his throat. 'We should check it's safe. No unexpected booby traps.'

'We can help you with that, son of stone. The sooner we get the food in the better for all,' Kinleader Telsima said.

Zadeki stretched out his arms. 'I'll check the next caverns.'

Korak caught both his shoulders. 'Son of impetuosity, you need to rest. Be still.'

Telsima reached out an arm. 'Yes, you've done enough for now, young pathfinder. No shapeshifting.'

'What? Are you grounding me, Da-Matu?' Then he blinked. 'Pathfinder. Really.' He wrapped his arms around the shorter Kinleader and lifted her off the ground in a ferocious hug. 'Thank you.'

'Put me down, before I'm tempted to change my mind.' Telsima laughed, smoothing down her white tari. 'You have earned your stripes, Jazadek son of Korak and Shema, but don't make me regret it.'

Zara couldn't help smiling at the interaction between the shapeshifters. It smarted to think how distant and self-absorbed her own baba had been. Even if he'd done the right thing in the end, it didn't balance out all the wrong he'd done, not really.

Gilarth caught her eye and strode toward her, his usually serious face softened by celebration.

He bowed. 'Lady Zara, we've rigged up temporary cribs and rooms close by. I can take you and Jesson there now if you'd like to rest?'

She scanned the cavern. Nebam was giving orders, arranging for a team of toolwuns to probe the next cavern. Havilah and the Kinleader were in discussion. Zadeki was slapping Retza on the back, while Delvina gave Danel a teasing smile. Jesson was watching it all with huge eyes and an irrepressible grin.

She had done what they needed from her, and now all of a sudden, she felt bereft, no longer sure where she fitted in. Taking Jesson's hand, she turned to follow Gilarth.

'I want to stay with our friends, Zuzu,' Jesson mumbled, his eyelids beginning to droop.

So did she. She paused. 'One minute, Head Watcher.' She walked up to Havilah and held out the crystal. 'This is yours, Overseer Havilah. And now it's possible, I will leave, if that is your wish.' Her voice hitched on the last words, because Jesson was right, these were her friends, this was her home.

Havilah took her hands. 'You forget that you are still soul-bond both to the seal and the Crystal Heart.'

'And now we know that link can be transferred to the new Overseer, to you. Without you our people would have perished.'

'As much as I appreciate the honour, each of us has played a vital part, not least you, Zara. I think it doesn't hurt having the power shared. And I'd still appreciate your help with the Old Guard survivors.' She took the crystal and closed Zara's fingers over it. 'You and your brother belong here, Lady Zara.' She chuckled. 'Besides, I think there is a young watcher that wouldn't give me any peace if you left.'

Kinleader Telsima took Zara's hands. 'It is not easy to honour your parent, when truth and honour demands you take different paths. You have done well.'

Zara relaxed, feeling at home with these people, her people. She didn't want to leave them.

Bootsteps sounded behind her and a hand brushed her shoulder. She turned. Retza stood before her, his face translucent and washed out with fatigue.

'Lady Zara,' he said, his stance stiff and formal. She could feel the future slipping from her fingers.

'Retza,' she blurted. 'I know it's a bit sudden, but ...' she wet her lips, '... but would you be my partner,' she finished in a rush.

Her chest squeezed tight, suddenly unable to breath as she waited for his answer.

His eyes sparkled like glimmerlight on rushing water. 'Yes. For now and forever.' And he kissed her.

Jesson grinned.

Zadeki laughed. 'Welcome to the family, Zara.'

Delvina rushed over and scooped her into a tight hug.

Zara felt too choked up to speak. Zadeki was right. This was her family. Jesson's family too. Sturdy handsome Retza, brave Delvina, wild Zadeki, stalwart Danel, wise Havilah, enigmatic Gilarth and grouchy Nebam. Or was that taking it too far? She giggled.

The sound of flapping wings came from the direction of the Gate. A white-headed eagle soared through the shattered doors. He swooped down towards them, at the last minute, transforming into a slightly older version of Zadeki.

'Josenif!' Zadeki whooped. 'That means all the Gates have indeed been opened.'

'Yes,' Josenif grinned. 'Umbria is checking the safety at the other end. Once she gives the all clear, the Tamrin will bring the supply yarmas through with their loads of food. More than enough to tide you over until the potato harvest. The younglings and elders too, once they've rested a bit more. Welcome to the dawning of a new day.'

And Zara stood by Havilah and cheered.

A brisk wind ruffled Delvina's fringe, bringing with it the smell of sun on rock, green plants and nervous yarmas from outside the caverns. Long cobweb strands swayed an erratic rhythm on the high cavern roof. Retza walked in silence beside her, his familiar presence comforting. After six lek, they'd walked through six of the seven gates: the Obsidian, Amethyst, Lapis Lazuli, Malachite, Sunstone, and orange Topaz. Only the Ruby Gate remained.

Up ahead, the pad of soft hoofs on stone, the worried humming of the yarmas and the clucking encouragement of their handlers indicated that another batch of beasts had been coaxed into the tunnel carrying their much-needed food packs. The animals were as jittery of the long dark tunnels as her own people were of the open air and sunshine.

Delvina and Retza moved toward the rough stone walls and waited for the group to pass.

Retza squeezed her hand. 'Seems you were right about going on the mission outside, Del, though I'm glad you're back.' He shot a thoughtful look at her. 'That is, at least for now.'

Delvina bit her lip. 'And you were right about joining the Watchers. You look good in watcher bat-leather. Though I doubt I'm going anywhere for a while. There is still much to do to restore the realm.'

'Hey,' Zadeki called out. He peeled off from the group of shambling yarmas, and loped over to them with a wide grin on his expressive face. 'Where've you two been?'

'Both Havilah and Telsima insisted Barekia check us out before assigning us tasks. Zara as well after the ordeal with the shadows in the grotto,' Delvina said.

Zadeki sobered. 'Yes, perhaps you should be resting. You've both done so much already.'

'Can't be resting while there's work to do,' Retza said with a shadow of his old bravado. 'We're to help Danel with the frailwuns.'

Zadeki looked around, his forehead crinkled 'And where is Zara? Is she well?'

'Fine, fine.' Delvina's twin acquired a soppy look. 'Zara plans to transfer the seal-bond to Havilah and Havilah has promised her a place on the council. It's hard to imagine that food will be plentiful again. What about you?'

'The Kinleader has me helping calm the beasts as they first enter the tunnels.'

The last yarma trotted by with a flick of its woolly tail.

'Shouldn't you be going with them?' Retza asked.

'Nah, once they get going, they're fine. I'm heading out again for the next batch. Come on.'

Together they continued walking down the tunnel, avoiding the occasional yarma droppings. Several paces on, the glimmerlights paled in the golden glow flowing and pooling through the open doors, gliding the spinning dust motes and gleaming on the polished stone lintels of the Ruby Gate.

Delvina's skin prickled with excitement. Here, in solid stone and sunlight, was the evidence that the people of the Glittering Realm were no longer cut off from the outside, no longer under the sway of the shadows, no longer shut in with their own fear and paranoia.

Delvina stepped across the threshold of the Ruby Gate and out into the sunshine, Retza and Zadeki flanking her. She blinked at the rosy-orange light suffusing the western sky. Two large statues of toolwuns towered over them on either side of the Gate. A path led down into the ravine, with rolling hills stretching out toward the horizon.

In a makeshift pen, a five-ten of yarmas still milled about with copper-skinned Tamrin securing their loads. Umbria and Josenif stood beside them. On the other side, and closer to them, a small crowd of youngwuns, littlewuns and oldwuns with some carewuns stood or sat under a temporary awning. Cook fires flared brightly in the twilight and brought mouth-watering smells of seared fish, potatoes cakes and warm soup.

One of the littlewuns in the group jumped up and started waving. 'Retza, Retza,' he called out in a reedy voice.

A couple of others joined in, a young girl and a half-grown youngwun.

Delvina frowned, making an effort to identify them.

'Is that Darin?' Zadeki asked, his dark eyes wide with astonishment.

Delvina raised an eyebrow. Darin. Wasn't that one of the young louts that had thrown food at Zadeki. Her stomach tightened. What now?

Retza hooked his thumbs in his belt. 'It looks like him.'

The older of the three ran over to them, the girl and young boy tagging behind. The littlewun gave a final spurt of speed, and ran into Retza and wrapped his arms around him. Darin paused a step away, hands dangling, while the girl stood beside him, staring at the cracked stone path.

'Darin,' Retza said. 'Tosa and Ven.'

'We wanted to thank you,' Darin said.

Retza titled his head. 'What for?'

Tosa looked up, lifted her shoulder and gave a lopsided smile. 'For putting a word in for us with Gilarth, for getting us a space in Greenstone South, for giving us a chance.'

Ven grabbed one of his hands. 'I'm hungry.'

Tosa took Retza's other hand. 'Come with us, Retza. Let's see what they're finished cooking ...'

The brother and sister pulled him away down the slope. After a moment, Darin followed behind with a what-else-can-I-do kind of smile.

Zadeki chuckled. 'Looks like Retza might have more than one youngling to shepherd,' he said, then sobered and looked across the tumbling river in the ravine to the darkening sky.

Delvina caught sight of Danel, laying more wood on the campfire, his face and hair rosy in the firelight. Her pulse quickened and she a bubbly feeling stirred inside her.

She looked back to Zadeki. 'I guess, you'll be leaving soon, now we have the food.'

'Once you're settled, I suppose. You and Retza will always be welcome among my Kin.' His eyes narrowed. 'Avardin still has to be dealt with. The elders will discuss what help, if any, my Kin will send to the rebels on the Lonely Isles. I want to go with them, and then I'm planning on traveling south to learn the koraktil form. Unless ... I mean, you could come with ... ' His voice trailed off.

She moved closer. 'Zadeki, I'll think about it, but ...' She chewed her lip, not sure how to tell him.

He looked back. 'He's a good man, Danel,' he said, a hint of sadness tinging his voice.

Delvina blinked. That wasn't what she thought he was going to say. 'So are you.'

The shapeshifter shrugged. 'Maybe.' He tilted his head. 'Just saying is all. I think he likes you.'

It was as though a door had swung shut, closing off some possibilities but opening others.

He turned to stare at the bright beacon of the horizon star in the turquoise sky, a droop to his wide shoulders.

Zadeki and his Kin had done so much for her and her people. The failure of the Crystal Heart and the blighting of the farm caves hadn't been their problem, but they'd acted anyway despite the risks. Highwun Bikan paying the ultimate price.

She brushed her hand against his. 'Friends?'

His whole face lit up with a wide grin. 'Family?'

'Oh yeah, just like a brother.' And she laughed and play-punched his arm.

'Ow, watch it.' He chuckled. He turned his head, eyes narrowed. 'Oh, I better go, Umbria is signalling for me to join her. Another batch of yarmas to calm. See you around.' He sprinted away.

Delvina pulled her Tamrin cloak tighter against the growing night chill and walked down the slope towards Danel. He looked up, his one good eye narrowed.

'I thought you would be helping Zadeki, Messenger Delvina,' he said, his voice gruff.

'He has his own path to follow. I doubt it will be in these caverns.'

He placed a branch on the fire, straightened, and brushed his hands. Firelight danced in his ash-grey eyes. 'Yet you love adventures on the outside, the flying, the exploring, the thrill.'

'Maybe not the sea-sickness.' She moved closer. 'Yes, I do. But this is our home. I would find it hard to give up on the Caverns.'

He gave her a one-sided grin. 'Even after the Gate is open, we'll have much work to restore the realm. After that, who knows. I'm not adverse to a few adventures myself.'

She laced her fingers through his and squeezed his hand. 'I'd like that.'

He turned and pulled her into his arms and kissed the tip of her nose. 'With you beside me I could face a whole flock of fire-breathing koraktil.'

She smiled, remembering the first time she and Retza had crept out of the caverns into the double moonlight. All they'd wanted was to be prentices in the Greenstone South Crew. So much had happened since then—too many good people lost, others found and good friends gained. And now, they'd come full circle, not least due to precious Danel.

Delvina snuggled closer and pressed her lips to his. By the Maker's favour, her adventures with this man of the caverns were just beginning.

The End

Author Note

Reviews: If you've enjoyed this foray into the world of Nardva, please leave a review on Amazon, Goodreads and/or your favourite reviewing site.

Newsletter: If you would like to keep up to date with new releases, giveaways and events, sign up for Jeanette O'Hagan Writes email newsletter http://eepurl.com/bbLJKT and receive the short story set in the world of Nardva.

You might also like

Akrad's Children–the first in the Akrad's Legacy series
Shadows of the Deep – a more harrowing prequel of the Under the Mountain series, published in the Tales From the Underground (Inklings Press; 2017)
Ruhanna's Flight and Other Stories— a collection of short stories, mostly set in Nardva

Coming Soon

Rasel's Song–the book 2 in the Akrad's Legacy series
The Chameleon Protocols trilogy

Acknowledgements

With Caverns of the Deep, the fifth and final novella in the Under the Mountain series, a journey comes to an end, as this book completes the series. When I first started writing a short story based on the theme 'glimpses of light', I had no idea how far it would carry me. From delving deep into the dark corners of a mining realm, to the edges of the Great Forest of the Forest Folk, and even across the ocean to the Lonely Isles. These places were already a reality from plotting and daydreaming the Akrad's Legacy series (of which only Akrad's Children has so far been published), but it has been exhilarating to explore them in greater detail and in a previous time period. And, in the process, Delvina, Retza and Zadeki have burrowed their way into my heart. It may not be the last we see of our intrepid young heroes, in fact astute readers might identify Zadeki in another of my books. But that, as they say, is another story.

Writing isn't a solitary pastime. I am especially grateful to my critique-partners, beta-readers, editors and proof readers who have helped me polish and refine my work. So many people and places have been an inspiration for my world building, from the mines of Mt Isa to a couple of voyages across the Indian Ocean, to rainforests of my homeland, among books and movies and research, and even places I've never been, but would love to one day.

Special thanks to Kathleen Hillenberg who is such an

enthusiastic and untiring supporter and has given great feedback on practically every story I've written. Also, Suzanne Hay-Bartlem, Nola Passmore, Lynne Stringer, Raelene Purtill, Adam Collings, Cate McKeown, Linsey Painter, Ben Dixon and to the Intricate Worlds and the Sparkly Badgers groups for feedback and encouragement. Nola Passmore of The Write Flourish is a fantastic editor and I love her work.

I'm grateful for my family—my loving husband Tony, my precious children Kathleen and David, my parents Tom and Jean Curtis—who instilled in me a love of faith and fantasy—and siblings, Tom Curtis, Frank Curtis, Chris Curtis and Kathleen Hillenberg, with whom I've shared many wonderful adventures. And thankful to my 'elder sister', Elsie Bonning Milrea for the adventures we shared when she lived with our family in Mt Isa and Zambia, Africa. It's been wonderful to reconnect after losing touch for many years.

Most of all, I'm grateful to my Maker in whose creative footsteps I can only hope to follow.

Jeanette O'Hagan June 2019

About the Author

Jeanette spun tales in the world of Nardva since the age of eight or nine. She enjoys writing secondary world fiction, poetry, blogging and editing. Her Nardvan stories span continents, time and cultures. Many involve courtly intrigue, adventure, romance and/or shapeshifters and magic. Others, are set in Nardva's future and include space stations, plasma rifles, bio-tech, and/or cyborgs.

The last four years have been a whirlwind, with the publication of the Under the Mountain series, a debut novel, Akrad's Children (in the Akrad's Legacy series), a collection of shorts, Ruhanna's Flight and other Stories, as well as short stories and poems in twenty anthologies, more recently Maroon's Sanctuary in God's of Clay (Sci-Fi Roundtable), Space Triage in Challenge Accepted and Wolf Scout in Tales of Magic and Destiny (Inklings Press).

Jeanette has practised medicine, studied communication, history, theology and, a Master of Arts (Writing). She loves reading, painting, travel, catching up for coffee with friends and pondering the meaning of life. Jeanette lives in Brisbane with her husband and children.

You can find her on social media at:
Facebook | Twitter | Instagram | GoodReads | BookBub
And at Jeanette O'Hagan Writes http://jeanetteohagan. com
Email newsletter http://eepurl.com/bbLJKT Akrad's Children

Akrad's Children

Caught between two cultures, a pawn in a deadly power struggle, Dinnis longs for the day his father will rescue him and his sister from the sorcerer Akrad's clutches. But things don't turn out how Dinnis imagines and his father betrays him. Will he seek revenge for wrongs like his sister or forge a different destiny?

Akrad's Children is the first book in the Akrad's Legacy series

Available on Amazon and other retailers:
http://books2read.com/u/31xWMM

Ruhanna's Flight
and other Stories

Ruhanna's Flight and other stories includes previously pubished and brand new stories set in the world of Nardva. A delightful introduction to Jeanette O'Hagan's fantasy world of engaging characters and stirring adventures.

"This author has the gift of immersing a reader in a different world and caring about the people in the world." Amazon Review.

Available on Amazon and other retailers:
http://books2read.com/u/mKKeJE